BLOOD CRIME

BLOOD CRIME

SEBASTIÀ ALZAMORA

Translated from the Catalan by
Maruxa Relaño and Martha Tennent

First published in Catalan by Raval Edicions, SLU, Proa, 2012

Published by arrangement with Cristina Mora Literary & Film Agency SL (Barcelona, Spain)

English translation copyright © 2016 by Maruxa Relaño and Martha Tennent

This book was translated with the help of a grant from the
Institut Ramon Llull

LLLL institut
ramon llull
Catalan Language and Culture

Published by Soho Press, Inc.
853 Broadway
New York, NY 10003

Library of Congress Cataloging-in-Publication Data

Alzamora, Sebastià, 1972–
Tennent, Martha translator.
Blood crime / Sebastià Alzamora
translated from the Catalan by
Maruxa Relaño and Martha Tennent.
Crim de sang. English

ISBN 978-1-61695-628-8
eISBN 978-1-61695-629-5

1. Vampires—Fiction. 2. Murder—Investigation—Fiction.
3. Spain—History—Civil War, 1936–1939—Fiction. I. Title
PC3942.1.L83 C7513 2016   849'.9354—dc23   2016010982

Interior design by Janine Agro, Soho Press, Inc.

Printed in the United States of America

10 9 8 7 6 5 4 3 2 1

To María José Lagos

From man's deepest recesses emerged the monster.
—JOSEP LLUÍS AGUILÓ

BLOOD CRIME

HE WROTE:

Often, when I am overcome by thirst, I put myself in mind of the Holy Spirit. Contrary to what superstition holds, vampires do not experience disgust when we find ourselves in a church. The sight of the symbol of the cross has never bothered me, except on one occasion, in a tract along the Hungarian border, when a pastor seized the opportunity while I lay sleeping on my litter and drove a cross into my chest. I yanked it from my body with one hand, and with the other I ripped out the pastor's heart, squeezed the blood from it, and drank greedily. Then I impaled his body on a stake that marked the separation between two fields. Buffeted by frigid gusts of wind, he quivered like a tattered scarecrow lost in a night without reprieve or hope. I left the cross plunged in the ground at the pastor's feet.

No—neither the cross nor Christian temples trouble me; as a matter of fact, in another life, deep in my past, I was very devout. And now, in my present-day life, I find the thought of the Holy Spirit soothing. For finally, it too is a devil—a *daemon*—both of us classed among those beings whose existence is inconceivable to men. I admire the qualities ascribed to the Holy Spirit, for they are the traits best suited to the governing of one's own nature: wisdom, understanding, counsel, fortitude, science, compassion, the fear of God. Mercy is the manifestation of a killer's compassion; the fear of God, a euphemism for the victim's anguish when faced with imminent death. Science to refine the method of slaughter, fortitude so as not to falter in the hunt, understanding in order to reach one's final goal, counsel to accept the void of an existence beyond the confines of time, and wisdom to bear it. The word most frequently employed to label what I am is *monster*, and it does not trouble me to put it down in black and white. The Holy Spirit is also a monster. God is a monster. And it is a well-known fact that He infused monstrosity into all of creation.

From where I stand I can hear the sound of bombs exploding, resounding in the night like a threat, like an approaching thunderstorm. Men killing men, for gain or for the pleasure of it. I have seen it again and again, and I never tire of it. Places where violence reigns suit me, for there I can hunt most easily. Countries at war, ravaged cities, blood-filled streets: in all of them I have been moved by man's perseverance in the exercise of cruelty. There is a mathematical figure that quantifies evil— unknown even to monsters, demons and most vampires—and a war always expresses at least a decimal fraction of this figure. Perhaps even more than that here in Barcelona, where an evil of uncommon brutality thrives and has taken possession of men in the most absolute of terms. I roam with complete freedom, unnoticed by brothers who sacrifice brothers, fathers who inform on sons and sons who kill fathers or have them killed; among merchants of misery and whoremasters of death, among gossipmongers of crime and peddlers of depravation. Vile, ravaged city that takes pleasure in toying with the idea of its own extinction.

I am sated as I write this, fully satisfied after drinking the blood of the priest I slaughtered only moments ago, though I must admit it entailed more of an effort than I had anticipated. To satisfy one's thirst is a vampire's only duty, and in order to fulfill it, one of the first things every vampire must learn is to single out and favor the easy prey. Men and women of faith are often precisely that, all the more so in this city, pulverized by a war that has turned them into cannon fodder. And besides, even if no one were pursuing them, a life of prayer slows one's reflexes and weakens the muscles; devotion supposedly prepares one to accept death serenely, or at least with resignation. Supposedly, I say, because this one today made things as difficult for me as he could: he fought, struggled, scratched, and screamed as if he had gone mad; on two occasions he even uttered the most terrible blasphemies against God, whose minister he boastfully purported to be. I should mention the slight trace of incense on his clothes, for it enhanced the sweetness that filled my mouth as I greedily swallowed the blood that gushed from the ruptured vein in his neck.

Before killing him, I paused for a moment to observe him. He was in his alcove, hunched over a desk reading the Gospel According to Saint John. He was reading in the manner of the elderly, his finger following the lines, mumbling through the text in a low voice. I was able to catch a few words. He had chosen the story of the resurrection of Lazarus, which is also the story of a monster. I have frequently asked myself: Was Jesus truly moved to see Mary Magdalene weeping? After all, she had anointed his feet and shown such veneration when she wiped them with her hair. Is it not possible, then, that by resurrecting her brother he was simply trying to please her so that she would show her gratitude by lavishing more ointments and caresses on him? Be that as it may, the evangelist recounts that, upon hearing Mary of Bethany's weeping, Jesus asked to be led to the tomb of Lazarus, where he addressed God with solemn words and immediately thereafter ordered the sepulcher to be opened. The dead man stumbled out, his arms and legs bandaged, his face wrapped in a shroud. Jesus then instructed that he be unbound and allowed to walk. And that is what the dead man did, his intact face showing no sign of decay, not a trace of stench, his skin rosy, his limbs flexible and agile—his condition much the same as that of a vampire emerging from the tomb.

This was most assuredly not the reading that my priest made: for him, the resurrection of Lazarus could only be seen as God's commitment to man—set down in the Sacred Texts—granting the true life promised by His Church after earthly existence. At this very moment the priest must be ascertaining the authenticity of this commitment. If he was correct, his soul must now be tumbling down through the circles of hell, because he died offending God in thought, word, and deed, as well as by omission. An entire life of renunciation and prayer only to fail at that final moment in such a pitiful and irreversible manner. As my priest writhed and I quenched my thirst, I could sense the Holy Spirt among us: *Ruach HaKodesh,* as the Jews say. The voice from heaven.

The futility of the human being reaches its maximum expression in the chill of the tomb and the putrefaction of the flesh. The ludicrous dream of great human endeavors—whether of empires, ideas, cities, or fortunes—finds resolution in the grey, repulsive color that dead things acquire. For not only men are mortal; the things they construct, clash over, and covet are similarly transient. Only monsters are exempt from death, for the simple reason that we are not alive. I have known men and women who have willingly surrendered their blood to me in exchange for a false promise of immortality to which they clung as an infant clutches at its mother's breast. The transit from human form to that of a monster is arbitrary. No will can guide it, no incantation can arouse it, no peculium can procure it. No one can save anyone from death, least of all God, who has little interest in the matter.

These, then, are the terms of the farce, and one's reaction depends solely on the expectation each has formed for himself. If there is, however, one thing I can affirm with certainty, it is that, of all the usual errors that plague the human adventure, expectation is without a doubt the most ridiculous. Not because everything can be attributed to chance, as is commonly believed, but because chance does not exist. There is no order, or pattern, or hierarchy. The human species is an isolated accident that occurs in the midst of chaos. There is nothing more.

Faced with such inconsistency, I find it surprising that men have not been more inclined to supplant God and assume His functions and powers, thus committing the great sin of imposture with the loftiest, most blasphemous intention of all: to infuse life into inanimate objects. I was in Prague when an angry, deranged rabbi known as Judah Loew created the gargantuan and clumsy Golem—a vaguely anthropomorphic doll modeled from clay. The rabbi would place in Golem's mouth a piece of papyrus with a written command, and the doll would begin to move its arms and legs and execute its master's directive; at a later moment, Judah Loew would retrieve the papyrus from the creature's mouth and it would fall inert, like the simple, ordinary mass of clay that it was (the rabbi liked to spread the rumor that the command written on the piece of paper was one of the secret names for God, and curiously enough, in many people's opinion this lent veracity to the whole charade).

I also happened to find myself in Paris when one Vaucanson gained notoriety with his Duck, an automaton that became the talk of the town. It was a copper figure that was a perfect rendering of a duck in every way, allegedly able to eat and drink, splash about, preen, and, finally, defecate into a silver basin. "Duck with digestive tract," it was called. Of course, eventually it was revealed that the whole thing was a hoax: the grain that was supposedly fed to the duck ended up in a compartment hidden among the gears, and the animal's defecation was nothing more than a paste stored in the lower part of the automaton, a device far more limited and naïve than Golem. As was the mechanical chess player that another visionary—Maelzel, he called himself—paraded around Europe to the enthusiastic acclaim of the crowds. No one wished to believe that the purportedly invincible dummy housed a master player inside it, a man who indeed was never defeated by any of the incautious men who challenged him, including Emperor Napoleon himself.

All were frauds, crude attempts to imitate life, or to appear to. But the truth is that, with the same dedication expended on destroying life, men have often endeavored to understand and marshal the mechanism that makes it possible. For finally, what exactly is life? What separates it from death? Life is an enigmatic and often repulsive phenomenon: the flesh of men and animals pulsates after death, and peristaltic contractions persist in the intestines for quite a while. Even after being ripped from the body to which they belonged, muscles contract when stimulated. There is the well-known story of an English officer sentenced to death for high treason: he was slit open while still alive, his heart ripped out and tossed into the fire; the organ started bounding up and down, reaching almost a meter into the air, and continued to do so for seven or eight minutes. A similar phenomenon can also be observed in polyps, which do not simply continue to move after they have been cut into pieces—they regenerate in a matter of days and form as many new polyps as slices have been cut. And worms, caterpillars, flies, and eels all have one thing in common: their mutilated parts preserve the ability to move; and this ability is augmented when the parts are submerged in hot water. Frog hearts can beat for more than an hour after being removed from the body, especially when exposed to the sun or placed on a surface at the proper temperature. Living bodies, like those of automatons, are merely machines. Is it a certain temperature, then, that activates their spring mechanisms? Or is the temperature the effect, rather than the cause of the process? Is the breath of the Holy Spirit the original cause of life?

I often find it difficult to distinguish men from beasts

because I feed on them both and because they react with similar terror when faced with their own demise. While I was enjoying myself my priest was still writhing on the mosaic floor, spasmodic like the heart of a frog or a decapitated hen, fury and hatred in his eyes. If it is true that eternal life awaits them (not this monstrosity of a life that we vampires share with God and the Holy Spirit, but the golden, luminous redemption that people promise one another) then we can only assume that they would be capable of conducting themselves in a less disappointing fashion.

Men abhor the idea of being murdered, yet enthusiastically embrace the possibility of becoming murderers. All of them, without exception: the human race is nothing more than a long lineage—ancient and extraordinarily populous—of assassins. This is the problem of human freedom: as soon as an individual believes he has attained it, the first thing he does is concentrate on eliminating his congeners. Order is reestablished when another person takes his life; almost without exception, order entails repressing the appetite for crime by committing another crime. That is why, more than anything else, war is the simultaneous fulfillment of the desire to kill accrued to all the individuals of a generation. A moment of collective deliverance, an enormous, devastating sigh exhaled from the depths of the souls of victims and executioners alike.

For this reason, in the presence of a boy, I do not see a child but a potential murderer, and in some instances this potential has already been fulfilled. Once I had finished with my priest, I searched for an exit that would allow me to flee without being seen, and I slipped through a small side door and found myself in a narrow, unpaved alleyway. That is where I found him: he was playing with a spinning top on the dusty ground. He couldn't have been more than six or seven years old. He was wearing trousers of coarse cloth and a tattered sweater, and had snot all over his cheeks. There he stood in the soft light of morning with the toy in his hand, his wide-open, almond-shaped eyes fixed on the blood smeared across my face. I found myself again filled with that thirst that is never fully quenched.

PART 1
Memento Mori

"***Ego te absolvo*** *a peccatis tuis in nomine Patris, et Filii, et Spiritus Sancti.* Go in peace, Brother Plana."

Kneeling on the floor, Brother Plana raised his head, grasped the stole Brother Darder was wearing around his neck, and tried to kiss it but only managed to cover it with saliva. Brother Darder gestured impatiently with his hand.

"Please, Brother Plana, rise and take your leave now," he grumbled.

The priest obeyed and slowly moved away, dragging his feet as he went and murmuring words of gratitude. Gaunt and slovenly, with a small head, a hunched back and protruding belly, four straggly hairs on his scalp, and a mostly toothless mouth, Brother Plana strongly resembled a rat, a large rat, and in his presence Brother Darder was unable to control his revulsion, especially when asked to hear his confession. The litany of Brother Plana's sins always repeated itself, and from hearing it so often Brother Darder was capable of stating them in advance.

It began with a series of sins of thought or omission against the Mother of God or some saint, which Brother Plana recited quickly, grumbling almost incomprehensibly, and then it proceeded to his sinful actions, which almost always consisted in raiding the pantry to steal a bit of sugar or a head of garlic, which later, when no one could see him, he would wolf down in solitude. The mental image of Brother Plana snooping around the pantry of the pension, or hiding away gnawing on some garlic in the dark, was fused in Brother Darder's mind with that of the plump, repulsive rats he had seen as a child in the storage room where his father kept the grain, a memory that only increased his repulsion toward the priest and made him want to terminate the confession as quickly as possible. For Brother Plana's insignificant sins he assigned a routine penance, and he refrained from removing his stole before the little man could take it and wipe his snout on it with an excessive show of devotion that could almost be taken for gluttony.

On the other hand—wondered Brother Darder as the wormholed, moisture-logged door closed behind Brother Plana and he rose from his chair and could finally remove the stole and fold it carefully—who was he to administer forgiveness to anyone? In the two months since the war had begun, it had contaminated everything: the streets of Barcelona, the air one breathed, men's words and children's looks, the sunlight on the façades of buildings, the gleam of the moon and the stars on summer nights . . .

Everything was pervaded by that putrid smell, as if the world had turned into a bloated cadaver and men and women were but parasites swirling around it. That breath of air that sweeps through human communities where people live in peace, ventilating the cities where they reside, allowing people to prosper, had been extinguished in Barcelona; the city now appeared rigid, shackled, resembling an enormous wooden stage that only vibrated with the wailing of sirens and the trembling of falling bombs. For some time now a patina of filth seemed to cling to everything, and Brother Darder's soul was no exception.

He stretched, sighed, and let his eyes again take in the sadness of the room where he lodged: the chipped tiles, the cracked, whitewashed walls, the ubiquitous damp patches that were like a rash on sickly skin. After contemplating it for a few moments, the sadness descended from his eyes to his mouth; he could almost taste it, as if it were a sweet potato. That was what he ate most days: boiled sweet potatoes, which he sometimes enlivened with a dusting of that same sugar Brother Plana occasionally pinched from the pantry. Sweet potatoes for lunch and for dinner. And even for that they were grateful to the landlady who secretly lodged them in Pension Capell, her boarding house on Carrer Ferran. Ever since the anarchists had driven them from the seminary (which had been seized, like the rest of the order's property, including the Luis Vives Publishing House), the Marist Brothers had been forced to appeal to the clandestine charity of those who were brave enough to take them in. That is, the brothers like him who were fortunate to have avoided arrest or execution. Religious killings, both of priests and laymen, had commenced the first day of the war, and until then, 20 September 1936, they had shown no signs of abating. No matter what Brothers Gendrau and Lacunza might say—and even in the midst of calamity they strove to keep morale as high as possible—the anarchists' plan was perfectly clear in the eyes of Brother Darder: their intention was to annihilate the entire order. The only thing the brothers could do was hide like frightened animals and attempt to pull whatever strings they could to obtain permission to leave Barcelona, the city that held the stench of stagnant death.

In the last few weeks one question had stuck in Brother Darder's mind, and every day he could feel it lodged deeper in his head, and closer to his heart: Where was God? Where was He hiding while all of this was unfolding? Why did He not respond? Brother Darder sought relief by filling his nights with tears and prayer, but neither weeping nor praying brought a response: the silence merely swirled around like a cold wind in Brother Pau Darder's brain, which was constantly lacerated by the same question. Where was God? Why had He abandoned them, as He had abandoned His Son, nailed to the Cross? Love and compassion, where were they? Yes, it was true, like the entire city of Barcelona, Brother Darder's soul had been poisoned, transformed into a piece of boiled sweet potato in Brother Plana's drooling mouth.

"Bon dia, Brother Darder. Have you seen Brother Gendrau?"

Brother Darder was always slightly embarrassed by his dark thoughts when he was in the presence of the indefatigable Brother Lacunza. The parsimonious, unassuming Navarra native, who was the director of a Marist seminary in Burgos, had had the misfortune of accepting the invitation of the Provincial Superior of the Marist Order in Catalunya to teach a summer course for novices at the Casa de les Avellanes, in Balaguer. And that is how Brother Lacunza happened to find himself in one of the worse possible places in Spain on the day the war broke out. After that he was forced to go into hiding, as they all were, and he had not been able to return to Burgos, or even to Navarra, where he would no doubt have enjoyed very different accommodations.

But he never complained or showed any displeasure at this misfortune. Quite the opposite: he and Brother Pere Gendrau had immediately placed themselves at the service of the provincial superior, their mission being to move heaven and earth in search of a solution. There had to be some way to leave that crazed city, and they had to find it. Through some remaining contact at City Hall, the superior had procured a few safe-conducts, signed by the president of the Supply Committee, allowing free circulation in the city, and Brothers Lacunza and Gendrau,

on behalf of the superior, had been using them to meet
with authorities in an attempt to secure permission for
members of the order to leave Barcelona. So far, all of the
negotiations had failed. It had been impossible to obtain
passports or safe-conducts to go abroad. But what had
seemed like an opportunity presented itself toward the
end of July: an Italian ship had arrived at the port of Barcelona to collect the first group of refugees. With a
recommendation from an Italian acquaintance of his
known as Mageroni, Brother Lacunza had managed to
extract from the Consulate the promise to embark the
Marists together with the other refugees, provided they
had the pertinent approval from Senyor Josep Maria
España, the minister of the interior of the Generalitat, the
Catalan government. But the honorable personage had
refused to sign the authorization, fearing that the anarchists—who controlled ports and borders—would kill
him if he did. This first failed attempt was followed by
others before the French and German consulates, and also
the minister of culture of the Generalitat, Senyor Ventura
Gassol. All of them had listened with serious demeanor
and understanding nods, and all had gently rebuffed the
religious with a repertoire of stale excuses. In the meantime, the news reached them that surveillance patrols
had killed more than fifty Marist Brothers in Catalunya
after they were caught trying to flee or hiding in some
pension or private home. Like the brothers in Pension
Capell, who any day could be discovered or betrayed or

God knows what, and then trampled like a nest of ants. Yet despite this, Brother Lacunza and Brother Gendrau (who had assumed in the eyes of Brother Darder the role of the father he had lost) had maintained a sort of impenitent optimism that allowed them to continue searching for a means of escape, their zeal growing with each new door that closed. Yes, Brother Darder admired their spirit and was embarrassed by the blandness that guided his own. But he also detected, and this troubled him, a rather pathetic touch of unswayable determination in Brothers Lacunza and Gendrau. After all, if it was God's decision to turn a deaf ear on their plight, they would not be the ones to force Him to listen.

"No, Brother Lacunza, I'm sorry. As a matter of fact, I haven't seen Brother Gendrau all morning."

"I checked his room, but he wasn't there . . ." Brother Lacunza was holding an envelope in his right hand and paced nervously. "Well, I'll try to find him. If you see him, please tell him I need to speak with him. It's urgent."

"More bad news?" Brother Darder assumed, with a grimace of compunction.

"I don't know yet, I don't know . . ." murmured Brother Lacunza anxiously. "I received this and need to discuss it with Brother Gendrau. It's a letter from the *Federación Anárquica Ibérica* . . ."

"From the FAI?" exclaimed Brother Darder. He was unnerved, thinking someone at Pension Capell had informed on them to the anarchists, perhaps even Doña

Gertrudis, the woman in charge, no doubt fed up with their presence.

"It seems so," huffed Brother Lacunza. "It's signed by two of the top members of the Department of Investigations." He pulled the paper out of the envelope and read: "Aureli Fernández and Antoni . . . Ordaz. Yes, that's it."

"But what do they want? How is it they have contacted you?" inquired an increasingly frightened Brother Darder.

Brother Lacunza shook his head and opened wide his hands and eyes.

"Some young men handed it to me in the middle of the street, on Passeig de Gràcia. Three men, one of them a Marist." Ignoring the sweat pearling on Brother Darder's brow, he added: "It's an appointment. They are requesting a meeting with representatives of the Marist order on the twenty-fifth. Not far from here, in Plaça Universitat."

"BUT . . ."

The door opened and Brother Plana stuck his rat-like head into the room.

"Brother Darder . . ." he stammered.

"What do you want now?" Brother Darder asked impatiently. "I've already heard your confession, remember? And besides, I'm speaking to Brother Lacunza."

"Yes, yes, I can see that . . ." He stuttered again. "Forgive me. It's about Brother Gendrau."

"*CONFITEOR DEO OMNIPOTENTI vobis fratres, quia peccavi nimis cogitatione, verbo, opere et omissione, mea culpa, mea culpa, mea maxima culpa. Ideo precor beatam Mariam semper Virginem, omnes Angelos et Sanctos, et vos, fratres, ores pro me ad Dominum Deum nostrum . . .*"

Muffled by the sound of the rain against the glass windowpanes, Bishop Gabriel Perugorría's strained voice flowed gently through the Santa Agata Chapel in the Capuchin Convent in Sarrià.

"Amen," twenty-seven cheerful voices responded in unison.

They were celebrating a special liturgy to mark Sister Adoració's one-hundredth birthday; despite having reached such a ripe old age, she was not the oldest in the community. Sister Ascensió, with her one hundred and four years and robust health, had an indisputable edge over the most recent centenarian, who was gnarled like an old branch and clung to her cane. So hunched was Sister Adoració that it was sometimes difficult to distinguish whether she was standing or sitting. Sister Ascensió, on the other hand, stood tall, stout, in one piece, so to speak, her only visible symptoms of deterioration a few liver spots the size of a two-*ral* coin, which spread over her skin, darkening her face as if it had been forged from old copper no one had bothered to clean. If Sister Adoració appeared more and more stooped, like the tilted columns of the cloister, Sister Ascenció brought to mind a chest-of-drawers made of cherry wood. However that may be, the health and lucidity of one and the other were regarded in the community as an auspicious sign for all the sisters, and even the mother abbess sometimes referred to it with a pious joke: between the adoration of the Magi and the Assumption of the Mother of God lies an eternity of health, she would say. And they would all laugh.

They had to do something to cheer themselves in that half-deserted convent. All twenty-seven religious were aware that, if the new revolutionary order had allowed the Capuchins of Sarrià to remain within the venerable walls of the monastery instead of expelling them and seizing the building, it was only thanks to the mother abbess, whose brother was an FAI bigwig—a sinister man, a cripple by the name of Manuel Escorza. In the first days of the war, he had raided the convent and made bogus arrests: the mother abbess herself, a novice named Sister Concepció, and six or seven young nuns, all of whom had been duly alerted to the plan, were made to get into a van while the other religious, unaware of the ploy, wept and prayed as they huddled together in the Santa Agata Chapel. There was a moment of horror when the squad of militiamen tasked with breaking into the Capuchin premises, carried away by an excess of enthusiasm and zeal, had desecrated the tombs of five previous mother abbesses, exhumed their mummified bodies, and hauled them to the main entrance to the convent, where the bodies remained in plain sight for more than a few hours. This caused swooning and fainting spells among the sisters, as well as a laywoman who had the misfortune to be passing by the monastery that day and found herself face to face with the mummies. The gimmick, however, had the intended effect of convincing the entire neighborhood that the Capuchin Sisters of Sarrià had been arrested and dispersed, their residence—and all other religious buildings in the city—seized in the name of the revolution. As for the members of the squad—who only began to suspect they were pawns in some twisted ruse when they were instructed to return the arrested nuns to the convent and remove the mummies in front of the building—Manuel Escorza had little trouble charging them with high treason and having them executed by firing squad to ensure there would be no indiscretion on their part.

It is easy to imagine the joy of the religious of Sarrià at the return of their beloved Mother Abbess and the young sisters, and the ensuing fervor with which they resolved to satisfy Manuel Escorza's two conditions for not forcing them to abandon their home and subject themselves to ignominious treatment. As they were cloistered nuns, the first condition was easy to comply with: they were forbidden to have any communication with the outside world. Officially, the Capuchin convent of Sarrià had been evacuated and no one lived within the perimeter bordered by a five-meter-high wall that protected them from prying eyes. It was a building that ostensibly had been reclaimed for the people—to use the turn of phrase generally employed in these cases—until its new function could be decided. Escorza had instructed one of his deputies to see that the convent was supplied with food, firewood, clothes, and everything necessary to keep the community afloat, an easy enough task, as the warehouses were full of confiscated goods.

The second condition came a few weeks later and was accepted without questioning: the Capuchins were to welcome among them no less than the bishop of Barcelona, His Excellency Monsignor Gabriel Perugorría. After a long, tortuous persecution that had begun in the early hours of the day, the bishop had managed to escape a revolutionary assault on the episcopal palace by fleeing through a back door; Escorza had finally caught the big fish and was under strict orders to hold him in the most suitable fishbowl until he could be made use of. A surveillance patrol had arrested the bishop without knowing who he was after raiding the house of a silversmith suspected of harboring priests and nuns. At the Sant Elies detention center, someone had recognized Don Gabriel Perugorría as the poor soul ordered to strip before being interrogated and subjected to all manner of vexations, and Manuel Escorza was immediately notified. After that a number of people had to be wiped out and a false report was filed informing of the bishop's execution, thus ensuring the necessary caution and silence. When Escorza believed there was no longer any danger of a leak, he personally escorted His Excellency to the Capuchins and delivered him to that perfect confinement he himself had devised with the connivance of his sister. The community accepted the presence of Don Gabriel Perugorría—believed in the city to have died some days before—as an auspicious manifestation of divine providence. And this was precisely the subject of the bishop's homily during the Mass in celebration of Sister Adoració's one hundredth birthday.

"Divine providence, sisters," he said as his voice rose, "is the presence of Our Lord in all of creation, and it is unceasingly expressed by the eternal will to create and to preserve that which has already been created: a sovereign will through which God continues to speak according to the nature of the goodness that is uniquely His own, in the service of *being* and against *nothingness*, in the service of light and against shadows, in the service of life and against death."

When the bishop completed a sentence he believed especially well-wrought he would raise his hands slightly and the nuns would exclaim, "Amen." A group of six young sisters standing to the left of the altar would then open their mouths in unison and, with fine-tuned voices, intone a brief invocation:

Pie Jesu Domine.

The novice directing that small, precise chorus was Sister Concepció, who had secured the mother abbess's affection by accompanying her in the episode of the false arrest. The song was the beginning of the *"Pie Jesu"* from Gabriel Fauré's *Requiem*, a beautiful accompaniment to the pastor's words on that exceptional day. Pleased and moved by the choir's singing, Bishop Perugorría continued.

"Let men of honor and property strip me, let illness despoil me of my strength, let me be parted from grace by sinning: not for that will I lose hope; nay, I will sustain it until my final breath, and vain shall be the efforts of all the devils in hell to wrench it from me, for with Your aid I will rise above guilt. All of my trust rests on the certainty with which I await Your assistance, for You, Lord, have singularly confirmed me in my hope."

And the attentive nuns:

"Amen."

And the crystalline chorus:

"Pie Jesu Domine."

And the quick bishop:

"I have learned full well that, alone, I am fragile and inconstant; I know that temptation overpowers the most robust of virtues, yet I am undaunted by this. As long as my faith is sincere, I will be safe from misfortune, and my faith in Your coming shall remain strong, as will my faith that You will fulfill this unwavering hope."

"Amen."

"Pie Jesu Domine."

"I am certain that what I expect from You will never exceed Your ability to give and I shall never have less than

I hoped for. That is why I hope that You will sustain me in the face of impending risk, that You will guard me from vicious attacks so that my frailty might triumph over the most ruthless of enemies. It is my hope that You shall love me always, and that I shall never falter in my love for You. I hasten to reach the farthest confines of my hope, where I shall await You, my Maker, for all my days on this earth and for all of eternity. Amen."

"Amen," repeated the nuns with the same exultation that had seized the pastor.

And at that moment Sister Concepció signaled to the singers to tackle in earnest the piece whose melody they had until then merely insinuated. The chorus burst forth:

Pie Jesu Domine
Dona eis requiem
Dona eis requiem.

It was wondrous. In the vocal section, the soprano voice for which the composition had originally been conceived had been divided into two parts, a powerful canon in two voices that started in unison and unfurled in counterpoint: it was an elementary exercise, but very effective. Logically enough, the orchestral instrumentation had been eliminated, but the new vocal arrangement had faithfully respected Fauré's achievement of harmony and melody.

Sister Concepció often devoted herself to exercises of this sort. She was the youngest of the prosperous Bachs Pinté family (PAPER, CARTONS AND DERIVATIVES, read the sign above the spacious Barcelona shop on Carrer Tallers that was the public face of a family business generally ranked among the most important paper companies in Spain). In her secular life, she had benefitted from an impeccable education, with special attention devoted to music, as befitted a senyoreta of her station in life. While in the children's section of the Orfeó Català, the storied Barcelona choral society, she had received quite a few lessons in piano playing, singing, and sol-fa, some taught by Master Lluis Millet himself. This had conferred on the vivacious girl sufficient knowledge and courage to compose her first pieces, reinterpretations—she called them *rereadings*—of pieces and authors she admired. In addition to Fauré, who was one of her favorites (there was a time when she had added a guitar arpeggio to his *Pavane* and the beginnings of a lyric that started with the phrase "Jesus, guardian of my heart"), she had attempted, with mixed results, rereadings of Saint-Saëns's *Claire de Lune*, Toldrà's *Matinal*, and Garreta's *Amor de Mare*. If anyone ever asked Sister Concepció about her curious fondness for these reinterpretations, she usually blushed and responded that her efforts were of no artistic merit, but they were important to her as a form of prayer.

However that may be, her rereading of "Pie Jesu," intercalated into Bishop Perugorría's sermon, had made quite an impression on the sisters of the community. When the chorus finished its performance, a contemplative, reverent silence filled the Santa Agata Chapel, which contrasted with the droning of the increasingly heavy rain that buffeted the church windows. An almost palpable sentiment of gratitude and admiration had settled among the Capuchins of Sarrià. Sister Concepció remained standing, arms at her sides and head bowed, as if she had exhausted all the strength in her young body. Sister Anunciació, one of the members of the choir, wiped tears from her eyes. The rotund sisters Benedicció, Dormició and Visitació—exempted from kneeling during the service because they had to be helped back to their feet (on one occasion, this had caused the mother abbess to sprain her wrist)—could scarcely suppress shrieks of awe. And the bishop himself appeared like a flame—lit from within—as he exchanged an odd look with the mother abbess, one that could be read either as amazement or as complicity.

No one dared utter a word. For several moments a prolonged silence filled the chapel, until Sister Adoració, stooped over her walking cane, murmured with a toothless voice: "Thank you, child."

Sister Concepció emerged from her reverie and gave the one-hundred-year-old sister a frank smile; she appeared to be on the point of responding appreciatively to the old woman's show of courtesy when a loud, thunder-like clap made everyone whirl around toward the back of the chapel. For a fraction of a second the same fear ran down everyone's spine, but then calm quickly reasserted itself: it was only the wind that had thrown open the two leaves of the door, banging them loudly against the massive walls. A gust of cool air swirled into the chapel, and the rain streamed in through the portal, bringing with it a handful of hail like tiny glass balls.

"It was only a scare," said the mother abbess in an attempt to calm everyone. "Anything has the ability to frighten us these days, isn't that so? Let us congratulate our beloved Sister Adoració on her one hundred years, a true privilege that Our Lord has granted her and all of our community, and we thank His Excellency the bishop, humbly and in the fear of God, for his magnificent, enlightening sermon."

"Amen," responded all the voices.

The mother abbess added, a gentle glow in her eyes: "We would also like to thank our sisters in the choir, and especially young Sister Concepció for the beauty of her piece."

"Amen," chimed the voices.

Sister Concepció folded her hands at chest level and bowed her head, embarrassed by the laudatory remarks. Inopportune and faraway, the strident sound of a squawking seagull drifted in through the open doors of the chapel.

"MAY GOD HAVE mercy on us," mumbled a worried Brother Plana, folding his arms as if seeking refuge in prayer.

"God? I can assure you God has nothing to do with this.

And if you want my opinion, that suits me just fine. That would just be adding insult to injury . . ."

It was Superintendent Gregori Muñoz speaking, and his gruff manner matched his appearance, which recalled a peddler or a Gypsy—or both.

"Dammit . . ." said the police officer who had arrived with Superintendent Muñoz, purely for the sake of saying something. He was a red-haired youth with a pockmarked face whom his boss called Sirga. Or idiot, depending on his mood.

"Don't speak unless spoken to, idiot," Superintendent Muñoz snapped, cutting him off.

"Yes, sir," Sirga replied dutifully.

A fourth man, the towering, rather forbidding Judge Miquel Carbonissa, joined his arms behind his back and clicked his tongue.

The men had gathered around Doctor Humbert Pellicer, who nodded in agreement and cleared his throat as he squatted to examine the body of the murdered child. The corpse was lying on a stretcher that the Red Cross nurses would load into the ambulance as soon as the doctor had finished the preliminary examination before the autopsy. Inside the vehicle was the boy's mother, a wasted, consumptive-looking woman, who had had to be treated for a nervous attack. The father—a squat automobile mechanic still in his work smock—was aimlessly pacing the alley by the entrance to Pension Capell, an expression of infinite stupidity on his face, as if someone had slugged him with a sledgehammer. Every now and then he spotted a coagulated mass of blood on the ground, and using the tip of his shoe, he broke up a clod of earth and covered the blood with it.

The nurses also had to tend to Doña Gertrudis, the woman who had found the two bodies. That of Brother Gendrau, splayed in the middle of the kitchen with his mouth open and a his throat gashed, and the child, whose body she had stumbled upon in the alleyway as she raced from Pension Capell, so horrified she had not even cried for help. The boy was curled up on the ground with his eyes closed and, had it not been for the ugly, complicated laceration on his neck, he might have been sleeping peacefully. Beneath his head was a pool of blood that had curdled into lumps as it came into contact with the dirt and gravel; there were splotches all around him, as if the blood had gushed from a sprinkler. Doña Gertrudis had been so stunned that it was all she could do to let out a terror-stricken howl that attracted the attention of some passersby before she collapsed beside the little corpse. She was now seated in a wicker chair by the open door to Pension Capell, her eyes fixed on a section of floor tile with traces of Brother Gendrau's blood. Following Judge Carbonissa's orders, the medics were removing the body as Doña Gertrudis stared at the palms of her hands, mumbling and ruminating like an alfalfa-chewing goat.

Doctor Pellicer rose from the child's side with all the

ease his age and excess weight permitted and signaled to the nurses, who immediately loaded the stretcher into the ambulance, sending the mother again into hysterics. The blasphemies that spewed from her mouth would have rattled even the most dispassionate of agnostics, and Brothers Plana, Darder, and Lacunza pretended not to understand her as she clipped her words, offering her death in place of her son's, swearing to kill a multitude of people, and then regurgitated them in the form of drawn-out, disturbing bellows. In the end she had to be removed in a straightjacket, trussed up with leather straps. Her husband, completely oblivious to the state she was in, refused to get in the ambulance and chose to remain in the alley where the boy's body had been discovered, as if intent on standing guard. He plodded up and down the lane, absorbed, hands deep in his smock, eaten up by the absurdity of it all.

Doctor Pellicer covered his face with his hands and gently massaged the spot above his eyebrows, as he let out a disgruntled sigh. He exchanged a fleeting glance with Judge Carbonissa; the two men nodded to each other in resignation or, perhaps, agreement. The ambulance—a Ford model delivered a few weeks earlier together with three others, a gift from the American Friends of Spanish Democracy—cranked up amid a cloud of smoke that left a taste of burning gasoline in everyone's mouths. It was shortly after noon and a drizzle was starting to fall; no one could think of anything to say. It was Sirga, wringing his police cap with both hands, who finally spoke.

"It's like there's an epidemic of priest-killings," he said with an ugly smile that showed at least two rotten teeth.

"Shut up, you idiot," Superintendent Muñoz barked, not bothering to look at him.

"Yes sir, superintendent," Sirga replied, lowering his head.

Silence again elongated itself, even more uncomfortable than before. The three religious exchanged brief, anxious looks. Oblivious to everything, the father of the murdered boy sat in a corner by the weedy strip that ran along the side of the alley, his elbows on his knees, his head in his hands. Suddenly the wailing of a factory siren sounded from afar. A comforting sound, thought Brother Darder, unlike the strident affront of the air-raid warnings. Factory sirens heralded decency and announced fair wages for work well done. It occurred to him that that far-away siren was like a lament or an apology for the horror that his eyes were seeing. But whose apology? Finally, with an almost trembling voice, he posed the question he hardly dared to formulate.

"If I may ask, why did you make that comment about . . . about priests?"

He had addressed Sirga, but it was Superintendent Muñoz who responded: "He made the comment because the dead man is obviously a religious. Like the three of you," he said, pointing to each of the Marists. "You may dress in plainclothes, but it's written all over your faces, brothers. You *are* brothers, aren't you?"

Brother Darder turned scarlet, and Brother Plana gulped with such vehemence that everyone heard him swallowing. Brother Lacunza stared at the ground as if he had lost something valuable. Under the ongoing drizzle they were beginning to be soaked through, making them appear even more helpless.

Superintendent Muñoz gave a little laugh. "Relax, I'm not here to arrest you. In my report I won't even mention that you are . . . how should I put it—friars away on leave?" He waved his hand in a gesture of disdain. "In any case, there's no need to worry."

The three religious studied the police officer in silent distrust.

"Don't give me that look!" exclaimed the superintendent. "I mean it. To report you—and everything that would entail—would be too much trouble. Not worth it. And as for Sirga," he said, turning to the redheaded officer and slapping him on the back, "he's not seen a thing either, right?"

"Whatever you say, Chief."

Judge Carbonissa observed the exchange with a look of satisfaction, and Doctor Pellicer started rolling a cigarette.

"Very well then," concluded Superintendent Muñoz. "I'm much more interested in what's taken place here. Not only do we have a dead priest, but also a dead boy. I don't know what you think," he said addressing the doctor and the judge, "but this doesn't look like the work of anarchists to me."

Doctor Pellicer lit his cigarette, took two heavy drags and exhaled a thick, coiled shaft of smoke. Then he said: "I am of the same opinion, superintendent. Besides, the manner in which these deaths occurred has nothing in common with the execution of religious that we've seen these last weeks. Clearly no firearms were used in this case. The victim's throats were slashed. The priest's with a kitchen knife; as for the child, the gash on his neck suggests a bite wound from some animal that also chewed on the boy's face. This does not appear to be the work of a squad, but of one man, accompanied perhaps by a large dog."

"Good Lord!" Judge Carbonissa muttered, overwhelmed.

"We have checked the gravel for footprints," Superintendent Muñoz said. "Nothing. Every track has been erased. There's also no trace of a dog or any other animal."

"Are you quite sure?" Doctor Pellicer said, blowing smoke out of his nose.

"Is it absolutely necessary that you smoke?" the police officer spat at him. "Of course I'm sure, you think I'm not able to recognize dog tracks when I see them?"

"No need to get worked up," the doctor said in a conciliatory tone as he took another drag on his cigarette.

"What else did you uncover when you canvassed the scene? Anything worth mentioning?"

Superintendent Muñoz fixed his eyes on Sirga, signaling his turn to speak.

"A t-top . . . a spinning top," Sirga stammered nervously. "It was . . . right there on the ground, by the boy's body."

At that moment there was a guttural sound that recalled a cat in heat. The child's father, whom they had completely forgotten about, apparently emerging from his stupor at the mention of the toy. He stood, spread his arms and legs wide, and with his head tilted back let out a half-smothered groan. Seemingly unaware of the group of men observing him, he headed out of the alley into the drizzle and tottered away toward La Rambla along some imaginary route. He wobbled with each step, as though carrying a tremendous weight on his back. His work smock billowed from a gust of air, as if no one inhabited it.

"Poor devil."

"I'll need to examine the spinning top," said Doctor Pellicer, thinking aloud. "We might find a hair stuck to it, or a drop of the dog's saliva . . ."

"Why this insistence on the dog, all this damn dog malarkey?" Superintendent Muñoz snapped.

Brother Darder—unlike Brothers Lacunza and Plana—finally dared to open his mouth. "In any event, it strikes me as premature to discard the war-crime hypothesis straightaway. Since the beginning of the conflict we have suffered the terrible loss of dozens of brothers, and that is only within the Marist institution . . ."

Superintendent Muñoz cut him off. "Pardon me, Father," he said, "but you're not from around here, are you? I mean you aren't from Barcelona."

"No," replied the disconcerted religious with some hesitation. "I was born in Palma and lived there until the family sent me to Barcelona to finish my studies at the Conciliar Seminary."

"Palma de Mallorca, huh?" The officer's tone was sarcastic. "I hear people there are really easy going, no? So I would ask you to kindly simmer down and stop getting ahead of yourself."

Like a scalded cat, Sirga surreptitiously inched away from his increasingly hostile superior. Judge Carbonissa raised his eyebrows and Doctor Pellicer blew a puff of smoke directly in the superintendent's face.

"Goddammit!" roared the officer, fanning his face with his hands. "What are you trying to do, asphyxiate me?"

The superintendent's cursing didn't seem to have reached the ears of Brothers Plana and Lacunza, who were staring at the ground, dejected. Brother Darder, however, intervened again, annoyed by the comment.

"Listen, superintendent, what exactly did you mean by . . ."

"No, you listen to me, brother. I represent the Law here, and you can rest assured that I will track down the man who murdered this poor boy and your . . . associate—or

whatever I'm supposed to call him—and I will apprehend
him and give him the works. I've already told you, and I
will repeat it: I am not going to report you. But I warn you,
if I hear one more word with that friarly petulance of
yours as to how to conduct this investigation, I *will* use
whatever cooked-up excuse comes to mind to report you,
and I will personally see to it that you piss yourself with
more holy water than you have seen in your whole miserable life. Are we clear?! We already have a forensic
pathologist, a judge, and two police officers here—as for
you, aren't we led to believe that your kingdom lies
beyond this world? So go hear the pious confess and let
people get on with their jobs, dammit!"

Everyone froze, except Sirga, who was biting his lip to
keep from laughing; he had always had a taste for bom-
bastic invectives directed at the clergy, but he wanted to
avoid being called an idiot again. Suddenly the rain thick-
ened, its sound the only counterpoint to the silence that
had settled among the circle of men.

"Come on, Sirga, let's get moving. We don't have all
day," Superintendent Muñoz finally said. "Bible thumpers," he muttered.

Brother Darder had a look of sour grapes, but he
accepted the officer's invective meekly. A drop of rain
trembled at the tip of his nose and fell to his shoe. Doctor
Pellicer marveled at the priest's self-control, for Brother
Darder was still a young man, no more than thirty, tall
and heavy-set, with the appearance of a farmer, and black,

penetrating eyes. Superintendent Muñoz, on the other hand, was short and scrawny, probably around forty, though his sunken cheeks made him appear older. Were it not for the vaguely distinguished look his uniform gave him he could have easily passed for a kitchen helper with the haughty airs of a gamecock—habits born of ill-breeding, thought the doctor, the lap dog barking at the big dog.

He tossed the cigarette butt on the ground and decided to head to the morgue, where work awaited: the autopsies on the child and Brother Gendrau. But at that moment Judge Carbonissa approached him and took him by the shoulder; Doctor Pellicer glanced at the judge and nodded by way of response.

The judge then turned to the two policemen, who were moving away. "Superintendent! Excuse me, superintendent!"

Superintendent Muñoz reluctantly turned around. "What is it, Judge Carbonissa? Tell me fast or we'll be drenched like two farm chickens."

"Right. It's just that something just occurred to me . . ." He hesitated. "Regarding what the doctor was suggesting, about a dog's involvement in the death of the boy . . ."

"Not that again!"

"No, no!" Judge Carbonissa barreled on. "What I wanted to say is that . . . well, it's appalling to even think about . . . but could the wounds on the child's neck have been caused not by an animal but by a man?"

The superintendent studied the judge with the

curiosity of an entomologist. He would have liked to come up with a lapidary response, but at that moment the rain turned into a downpour and a few seconds later it began to hail. Everyone scattered, scurrying down Carrer Ferran as fast as they could.

"IT WAS ESCORZA. He says he's on his way here," said Antoni Ordaz, replacing the telephone earpiece.

"Shit," grunted Aureli Fernández.

One of the heads of the Defense Committee of the Barcelona neighborhood of Sant Martí de Provençals, a clandestine military group with anarcho-syndicalism ties, Ordaz was also a founding member of the Central Committee of Antifascist Militias of the CNT-FAI, the anarchist labor union. He was a slight man, short and chubby and grim-faced, but when he thought it could play in his benefit he tried to put on a show of cordiality and frankness. Sadly, he never succeeded.

"I spoke with Gil Portela from Safe-Conducts this morning," Ordaz said. "It's all under control."

"Excellent," murmured Aureli Fernández. "*Collonut.*"

Ordaz, who always tried to ingratiate himself with his superior, was dismayed by the fact that Fernández's replies inevitably included something to do with *collons*—balls. It was also true that Fernández had quite a lot on his plate: he was as involved as Ordaz in the Committee of Antifascist Militias and had been put in charge of the Department of Investigations, whose mission was to revamp the group's security policy and create a secret police that would collaborate with surveillance patrols. The aim of the department was to persecute the enemies of the new revolutionary order, clamp down on fascist activities in Catalunya, and control the flow of merchandise, goods, and people across land and maritime borders. It was a herculean task that Fernández had to coordinate without a single slipup if he wanted to avoid falling victim to the brutality of Escorza, the Cripple of Sant Elies—a brutality which, if it were up to FAI kingpin Escorza, would be swiftly and diligently meted out. This was the reason Aureli Fernández went about with a downcast, worried air.

Seated in Fernández's small office in the headquarters of the surveillance patrols unit on Gran Via, between Calàbria and Entença, Ordaz was rummaging through papers and going over matters when suddenly Fernández remembered something and raised his nose like a gladiola reviving: "So, have we heard from those blasted Marist brothers we sent the letter to the other day?"

Ordaz smiled. It was the trump card he had up his sleeve.

"It's all going swimmingly, according to plan, Aureli. We met with them yesterday afternoon." He slipped a handwritten note in Liliputian script across the table. "It's their answer, signed by that Marist from Navarra by the name of Lacunza—says they agree to the meeting on the twenty-fifth."

Aureli Fernández raised his eyebrows. "Well, that's just *collonut*," and his face complicated into an expression that was probably meant as a smile but seemed more like a grimace of pain. "Truth is I didn't expect much from this group of friars."

"They aren't just friars, but a teaching order," Ordaz corrected him.

"Imbibers of sacramental wine, strokers of little boys' willies . . . whatever you want to call them," said Fernández. "Where did you dig up these birds?"

Ordaz puffed up, reveling in his little triumph. "Well, they haven't exactly been discreet. Apparently they came by a couple of safe-conducts from Supplies, and with them in hand, they've been running all over town knocking on doors, begging to be allowed to leave Barcelona. Seems the Marist Institution, as they call it, originated in France, and they want to head up there . . ."

"Running all over town, huh?"

"Every door they could find, I'm telling you. They even talked to some ministers in the Catalan government: José María España, Ventura Gassols . . ."

"What about Tarradellas?"

"No, not with him. They must not have been able to get through to him; if they had, you can bet they would've rushed there. But we'll need to bring Tarradellas up to speed . . ."

"Sure. I'll take care of it," Aureli Fernández volunteered. "But first we should discuss matters with Escorza." He ran his hand over his face. "So the meeting's set for the twenty-fifth then . . ."

"Right."

"Where will it be?"

"At Tostadero, in Plaça Universitat, a joint that has private rooms, good for closing business deals . . . In their letter they say two brothers will come: Plana, who's our man, and Lacunza, the guy from Navarra who's been handling the negotiations. Funny they don't even mention the fellow who is always with them, Gendrau, a brother from Barcelona. But the important thing is that some bigwig will be there, coming down from France expressly, man by the name of . . ." Ordaz searched for a moment. "Adjuntant Émile Aragou. In any event he's the guy who holds the purse strings."

"*Collonut.* You'll be there of course."

Antoni Ordaz smiled again.

"Tell Gil Portela that I said he should accompany you. And take along someone else you can trust."

"Excellent. Thank you so much, Aureli," said Ordaz.

"But only to shake 'em up. No violence," warned Fernández. "We want to avoid any snags. We get all we can out of them, allow them to leave—and that's it. We can't spend our time filling the streets of Barcelona with dead friars, nuns, and pietists."

"Why not, Fernández?"

It was Escorza speaking from the door to the office. Antoni Ordaz felt a chill run down his spine. Aureli Fernández swiveled his chair around to face the newcomer and tried to appear nonchalant.

"*Collons*, Escorza. *Because*. We need to be careful that things don't get out of hand, no? And stop eavesdropping on other people's conversation, will you? You're going to give someone a heart attack one of these days."

He immediately regretted his words, but it was too late. Manuel Escorza del Val didn't need to burst into a meeting in order to frighten someone. His appearance alone was enough to, at the very least, elicit a feeling between compassion and disgust. A bout of polio as a child had left Escorza a cripple and something of a dwarf, with a body folded over itself, a ball of ravaged flesh from which emerged his head, a neckless protuberance with bulging eyes and a disproportionate, bulbous mouth. He used crutches and wore shoe lifts to compensate for his stature, but it only made him appear even more deplorable. At first glance people tended to think he was retarded, but he possessed a keen, pragmatic, methodical intelligence that had served to make him the head of the Department of Investigations. As such, he was Aureli Fernández's immediate superior, and his subordinate always tried—unsuccessfully—to appear deferential to the authority of the Cripple of Sant Elies. The sobriquet by which he was known was derived from the old convent on Carrer Sant Elies that now housed the FAI's headquarters and detention center. Under Escorza's command, systematic assassinations and tortures were carried out there, the tales of which made even the most hardened of revolutionaries go white. The coldness, ruthlessness and, above all, murderous rage of Manuel Escorza—a cripple in body and spirit—had no parallel.

"We were speaking about a . . . how shall I put it? . . . a certain transaction with the Marist order. Comrade Ordaz has located them and made contact." Aureli Fernández was attempting to sweep his inappropriate comment under the carpet. "They intend to cross the border into France and apparently they are ready to offer us money in exchange, but we don't know how much yet . . ."

"Please, Comrade Escorza." Antoni Ordaz rose from his chair and offered it to the cripple.

Escorza shot Ordaz such a withering look that he sat back down. Escorza remained standing in the doorway propped on his crutches, looking as bedraggled as a puppet with a couple of broken strings. But the fragility became ice-cold ferocity when he opened his mouth: "And our Comrade Aureli Fernández believes that these solicitous Marist brothers deserve to be spared a rendezvous with the firing party."

"I simply find it unnecessary," Fernández responded nervously. "If they leave the country, it seems to me that we needn't trouble ourselves about them anymore. Especially if they pay up . . ."

"Aureli Fernández appears to be suffering from a problem of perception," Escorza said in a hissing tone, separating his words into syllables in an odd system of scansion. "We are the keepers of the revolution, not of some convenience store. If they want to pay, let them pay,

but every enemy of the revolution will meet his destiny—
that is non-negotiable. We haven't got seven hundred of
our men combing the streets of Barcelona night and day,
interrogating and arresting people, so that we can set up
shop and start peddling favors and dishing out preferen-
tial treatment to the highest bidder. The voice of the
people is clear, firm, uncompromising. If we don't act from
this conviction, failure can be our only aspiration."

Aureli Fernández noticed the white froth forming at
the corner of Escorza's mouth. When his superior ended
his diatribe, Fernández said, "A meeting with representatives of the Marists has been arranged for the twenty-fifth
in a café in Plaça Universitat. Ordaz and Gil Portela will
be there to try to establish what we can get out of this. No
matter what emerges, we will be following your orders,
Comrade Escorza."

"If that is all you have for me . . ." Escorza grumbled.
The Cripple of Sant Elies adjusted himself on his crutches
and disappeared down the corridor. The squeaking sound
of the thick shoe lifts being dragged along the tiled floor
slowly faded. Aureli Fernández and Antoni Ordaz
exchanged a meek, pestilential look, the former lacking
even the energy to mutter, "*Collons.*"

THE DAY AFTER Brother Gendrau's death was decid-
edly bleak for Brother Pau Darder: cold, full of anguish
and dismay, like the news of an unfavorable diagnosis.
Don Pere Gendrau—as many referred to him—had not

only been Darder's teacher and confessor but also his friend and, to the extent that one could say as much, one-half of the father he had not had. The other half lived in Palma de Mallorca and was the mayor of the city.

The assassination of Brother Gendrau had prompted Brother Pau Darder to review the last years of his own life, and after a night of bad dreams and a day of grief, the only thing he managed to discover was a radical lack of consistency. The young Marist had been born into one of the most prominent families of Palma, and as such he had always slept—as they said back home—on seven mattresses. In exchange for such coddling, he had never made a decision for himself: as a young boy he had studied, with an acceptable level of achievement, in schools chosen by his father, Master Gabriel Darder, who determined that an ecclesiastical career would be fitting for his second son, having settled on the law for his oldest son. Don Gabriel's wife—the very wealthy Senyora Joana Serra d'Orfila—never dared to oppose (even in thought!) the decisions made by her husband, and reconciled herself unconditionally to them in the name of an impeccable communion of interests. When faced with events outside her control—which in her mind were those that extended beyond the domestic realm—Doña Joana Serra resorted to an all-purpose maxim that was her trump card, and, perhaps, her talisman:

If God so deems it . . .

Coasting on that open-ended phrase that his mother

was so partial to, the young Pau Darder was admitted to the Minor Seminary in Palma, where his studious, dutiful character soon distinguished him as a diligent disciple who earned his teachers' praise. More than that: rumors circulated of a possible transfer to Rome, where the budding theologian would be better able to develop his potential.

In the end, the city chosen for Pau Darder's higher education was not Rome but Barcelona. This decision was of course not his own. His Uncle Emili had taken charge of the boy's education after Don Gabriel died of a stroke. A medical doctor specializing in clinical analyses, a progressive, Catalan nationalist and republican, Don Emili was the counterpoint to his older brother Gabriel, who had never missed the opportunity to declare that Emili would bring shame on the family. Don Gabriel didn't live long enough to see his shameful brother become the mayor of Palma, running on the ticket of the Balearic Island Republican Left, or to see his son Pau sent off to the Conciliar Seminary of Barcelona, where the flamboyant politician—who, though a Republican, had never abandoned his Catholic faith—had many connections. Between sobs, the respectable widow, Doña Joana Serra d'Orfila, had acquiesced to Pau's departure: "If God so deems it . . ."

And God must have deemed it thus, for the novice Pau Darder i Serra was admitted to the Conciliar Seminary. Not only were his academic results exceptional, but his intellectual acuity and exalted faith in God—which led him to proselytize to his classmates—soon caught the attention of one his professors, the Marist brother Don Pere Gendrau, who had little trouble convincing him to join the pedagogical ministry. The day he was ordained, Don Pere Gendrau wiped away tears as he stood beside Mayor Emili Darder and Doña Joana Serra d'Orfila, the three of them sharing in the joy of that momentous occasion.

The rest was history—until the appalling death of Brother Gendrau. How was it possible to have come to this? Don Pere Gendrau had been a pedagogue of advanced ideas, a good friend of Pere Vergés, whom he had helped to found the Escola del Mar—the School by the Sea—with little regard for the controversy surrounding the militantly secularist nature of the project. Indeed, Brother Gendrau had always been far more preoccupied with cultivating active, conscientious citizens than with indoctrinating new soldiers of the faith. He trusted that a solid civic education would sooner or later awaken in students an interest in the divine mystery. At the same time, he worked to prevent the more exalted juvenile vocations from calcifying into the bellicose attitude of the priests who populated many parishes that deserved better.

As Darder paced his tiny room at Pension Capell, his eyes on the rosary in his right hand, he thought about Don Pere Gendrau, an educator who had devoted all of his learning to preaching the need for compromise and compassion in that period of fanaticism. Did he deserve the miserable, heartrending death he had suffered, together with the child who had also been so vilely murdered? How had it come to this? Like so many others in the past months, Don Pere Gendrau had paid with his life for his faith in the hereafter. But did the afterlife truly exist? Did infinite mercy exist?

It pained Brother Darder to pose such questions. The fervor he had experienced for many years was gone, and for some time now he had been unable to find a clear, conclusive answer to his questions. How was it possible that, confronted with an act of horror such as the murder of Don Pere, God had not intervened to prevent it? This had occurred, he told himself, precisely because God had bestowed on humanity the gift of free will, so that each of us could freely decide whether to choose good or evil; scores would be settled later, when the moment of reckoning arrived.

But the answers found in catechism no longer satisfied Pau Darder. Theology could not supplant life and life could not find answers in theology: theology could be quite absurd, but life was even more so. Fear superseded life. Brother Darder had observed that, subject to the rule of fear, human life was often revealed as ridiculous and futile, and any intellectual effort to imbue it with meaning almost always seemed grotesque. The claim that a Creator existed—filled with grace and mercy, the keeper of the human kin—became a mockery in light of recent events:

the murder of a child, the end of Don Pere Gendrau's life as a mere statistic in an ongoing massacre. God's ways might be inscrutable, thought Brother Darder, but he found it more and more difficult to condone God's indifference toward creation.

A crisis of faith. He had often encountered the term in the biographies of some of the great men of the Church and in the stories of the lives of certain saints. But precisely because exemplary men—models of conduct, guiding lights for all true believers—had stood the test, he had never imagined a day when he, who was nothing and no one, would be similarly tested. This thought soothed him; at least he had identified the evil that was gnawing at him, even as it was disheartening to find he did not know how to combat it. Sometimes he sought refuge in the memory of his mother, who was so proud of her son the priest, but then he would recall the woman's stolid refrain:

If God so deems it . . .

Just thinking about this filled him with a burning need to rebel against everything that would be pleasing to the foolish, mean-spirited God embedded in the mind of Doña Joana Serra d'Orfila. To counter this feeling, he tried to summon the figure of his Uncle Emili, the respected, charismatic mayor, his other father figure. But instead of the effigy, voice or mannerisms of his uncle, his mind conjured up a strange figure that seemed to be modeled in ice, opaque and ever-changing, indifferent and silent.

He then sought solace in his awareness of the Marist institution and the community that upheld it, devoted to educating young people and celebrating the mystery of the Mother of God in accordance with the motto of the order: *Ad Iesum per Mariam.* And yet, when he looked around him and discovered in the daily lives of his fellow religious defects identical to those that predominated in the lives of laymen, he realized his sense of belonging to the Marist order would not be the source of the repose he needed. Only praying offered him a certain consolation, and that was what he was preparing to do: he would remove the crucifix that he kept hidden in the bedside table and stand it up, and kneeling before the little table as if it were an altar, he would recite once more the Lord's Prayer, perhaps with tears in his eyes, in the hope that he would again experience the plenitude he had known in happier times but that now appeared lost to his soul, melted away like snow on the cobblestone streets.

"Brother Darder . . . Pardon me . . ."

Brother Darder turned his head to the door, to the voice that had just interrupted his prayer. There he discovered the waxen figure of Brother Plana, a man who, when the sunlight fell on him, seemed on the point of melting. Scheming and obsequious, Brother Plana was a roving calamity, in himself sufficient motive to exacerbate any crisis of faith. Brother Darder braced himself.

"Yes, Brother Plana." He cleared his throat. "You must

forgive me, I wasn't expecting anyone. Can I help you with something?"

"You are too kind, Brother Darder," the intruder said with a rat-like smile. "It's not about me. You have a visitor."

Before Brother Darder had the chance to ask who it was, Brother Plana had shifted his glance toward the dark corridor and gestured to someone to draw nearer. Judge Miquel Carbonissa appeared on the threshold, looking rather stiff.

"Good afternoon, Your Honor," Brother Darder greeted him with surprise. And addressing his fellow religious: "If you wouldn't mind leaving us alone, Brother Plana . . ."

The sallow-faced Marist slipped away down the hall and was engulfed by the dark, his aquiline nose pointing straight ahead as if tracking something.

"Take a seat, please." The priest pointed to a small round table with a chair on each side. With an appreciative gesture, the judge pulled out one of the chairs and sat; Brother Darder seated himself opposite him. "How may I be of service?"

The judge rubbed his wrists, nodded as if in agreement, and then spoke: "First of all, brother, forgive me for showing up in this untimely fashion—it is not something I would normally do . . ."

Brother Pau Darder waved off the strangeness of the situation. But he was intrigued to know the reason for the unexpected visit.

"Well . . ." said the judge in a halting tone, "I just wanted to let you know that . . . your exemplary deportment notwithstanding, I realize that yesterday's crimes must have affected you deeply. I wanted to offer my condolences."

"Thank you, most sincerely," Brother Pau Darder responded in a priestly manner.

Judge Miquel Carbonissa stared at the crucifix on the bedside table, exhaled, tapped his foot on the tile floor, scratched his chin. He was clearly nervous, as if he didn't know how to begin. Finally he blurted out, "Brother, do you . . ." He exhaled again before finishing the question. "Do you believe that *upirs* exist?"

Brother Pau Darder raised his eyebrows. "Do I believe in *what*?" he asked, fearing the judge had been able to guess his religious doubts.

"In *upirs*," the judge whispered excitedly, wide-eyed, his face close to the priest's. "I'm asking if you believe in the existence of the *Dip*—the black dog emissary of the devil—of revenants, of the undead? Do you believe in the existence of vampires, Brother Darder?"

"YOU WERE RIGHT, superintendent. There's no trace of a dog here."

Superintendent Muñoz was about to respond that he usually kept his mouth shut when he had no idea what he was talking about, but decided to be diplomatic: "Dammit. I'll never get used to this lousy place." Superintendent Muñoz let out a sigh and opened his arms wide, as if embracing the entire morgue. There were few windows, and those were high up, which meant that the huge venue—an old textile warehouse in a corner of the Gothic quarter that had been put to new use after it was seized and ransacked—had to be lit by means of a generator which, in addition to producing a thick, dull light, reeked of gasoline, and that odor was mixed with the vaguely sweet smell of formaldehyde and the stench of ammonia from the bloated, decomposing bodies. Expert evidence was essential, but obtaining it was always excruciating. As for forensic evidence—it was always nauseating. He covered his nose and mouth with a handkerchief and observed Doctor Humber Pellicer going about his job with the thoroughness of a professional.

The body of the boy found in the alleyway near Pension Capell lay on the dissection table; the cadaver of Don Pere Gendrau was on the next table, hacked into pieces. Superintendent Muñoz tried to spare himself his sterile reflections on how we are all united in death, but the truth is he couldn't avoid the thought, not even to distract himself from the view that surrounded him: row upon row of wheeled cots, covered with sheets that had once been white, atop which rested the human remains that had found their way to the morgue. Rarely were the bodies intact: here the trunk and head (but not the arms or legs) of a middle-aged woman; farther along, half of a trunk, one leg and the crushed skull of a young boy, giving the impression that he had been run over by a train; still farther, the disfigured face and mutilated body of another woman killed by God knows who. To the catastrophe that was war one had to add humanity's perennial willingness to inflict upon itself the vilest of degradations: another stupid thought, but it was the kind of thing that popped into Superintendent Muñoz's head. He could not avoid feeling sick when faced with the present panorama. Doctor Pellicer's sense of humor and taxonomical zeal unnerved Muñoz. No matter how mutilated the human remains placed on the trays, one way or another the doctor tagged them all. "One way or another" was the proper expression, as it wasn't always easy to find a suitable place to which to affix a tag. The doctor's most recent acquisition was a headless, limbless male torso, which he had christened "Alfonso" in honor of the King of Spain, tagging the name to the man's penis, which was of considerable size.

Doctor Pellicer finished his examination and raised his head. "You were right, as I mentioned. There are no fang marks on the wound that would be indicative of any animal, only bite marks from perfectly human canines, molars, and incisors. The priest and child were obviously killed by the same person. Neither shows any apparent sign of sexual aggression."

"There are times when I would prefer not to be right," the policeman mumbled to himself.

"That's hard to believe coming from you, given the . . . how shall I put it? . . . the firmness with which you express your point of view." The doctor scrubbed his hands with a disinfectant in a metal basin.

Superintendent Muñoz raised his eyebrows. "Excuse me, but I'm not sure what you're referring to."

"Well." Doctor Pellicer smiled. "You came down pretty hard on that poor young Marist brother yesterday."

"Ah, that," Superintendent Muñoz said with indifference. "I can't stand for people to stick their noses where they don't belong."

"That much is clear. If I can be honest with you for a moment, someone who didn't know you might have thought it was the clergy you couldn't stand."

The policeman tensed. "What are you insinuating, doctor? I specifically—"

"You specifically," interrupted the doctor, "promised not to mention the religious brothers in your report or the fact that one of the victims was himself a member of the clergy. It was a gesture that pleasantly surprised all of us there, and it could cause you serious problems if word reached your superiors, but it was tinged with contradiction after the dressing down you gave the religious. I think I can safely say that you managed to sow considerable confusion."

Doctor Pellicer exercised a curious authority over Superintendent Muñoz, who nodded and tried to stem any possible misunderstanding. "I admit I have my own motives for disliking the Church, but it doesn't answer to any particular stratagem: I said I wouldn't report that we were dealing with a troop of Bible thumpers, and I didn't. I wholeheartedly disapprove of this nonsense of religious killings, if that's what you want to know."

"That's exactly what I wanted to know, superintendent," said the doctor with a nod, causing his double chin to contract and expand. "And if you want to know the truth, I'm relieved to hear you say so."

A conciliatory silence formed between the two men, softening the grotesque scene before them. The superintendent was reminded of the times in his childhood when a sudden silence came over the dinner table and his mother would say that an angel had passed by. The notion that an angel stopped by his house from time to time to pay him a visit had brought him happiness all through his childhood, and it struck him as reasonable that one should observe a moment of respectful silence on the occasion of such an important visit. He hadn't given any thought to the angels or his mother for a long time, and now they had come into his mind together; it comforted him to imagine that even an abhorrent place like a morgue might be visited by angels.

Don Humbert Pellicer lit a cigarette he had rolled in a matter of seconds. The unpleasant smell of the tinned tobacco roused Superintendent Muñoz from his abstraction. "You mean you smoke in here too?" he exclaimed.

"It doesn't seem to bother them much." The doctor smiled, making a wide sweep of his arm.

The superintendent waved the smoke away from his

face. "I don't know how you can tolerate the odor of your tobacco, especially in this horrid place. If you have no other information you wish to share with me, doctor, I'll leave now. It's late and work is piling up down at the station."

"You're free to go when you wish, superintendent, but there is in fact something I think will interest you." Doctor Pellicer continued to smile, exhaling smoke through his nose.

"I was afraid of that. Could we get straight to the point, please?"

"What kind of criminal could you imagine committing these two killings?"

Superintendent Muñoz shrugged. "Some kind of sadist, I suppose. The judge suggested as much, I suspected the same, and now you corroborate it: the bites on the boy's neck were done by a man. This virtually precludes any involvement on the part of the anarchists. It's more like some sort of macabre ritual. We'll need to take a look at the crackpots we have on file."

"Have you considered the possibility of a vampire?" asked Doctor Pellicer. The question was accompanied by a small cloud of smoke which hit Muñoz directly in the face.

"What in thunder are you saying, doctor? A vampire!" he wheezed. "Don't you think things are complicated enough of late?"

The doctor adopted a serious expression. "The autopsy

has yielded some very relevant information, superintendent: both the priest and the boy were drained of blood. Conscientiously, meticulously. The amount of blood missing from the two cadavers is most unusual and cannot be explained by the blood we saw at the crime scene. Some of it had to have been let directly from the bodies. It's as if it had liquefied or evaporated. Or as if someone had drunk it."

The superintendent clicked his tongue. "Please don't take this the wrong way, doctor, but I've been in this field for a few years already and I have yet to encounter a vampire. On the other hand, I've seen plenty of bad guys and more than a few loonies. Know what I mean?"

The doctor took another drag on his cigarette. His large body stirred as though it was flea-infested. "I'm not speaking of any paranormal phenomenon, but of clinical vampirism," he said. "I mentioned a moment ago that there is nothing here that would indicate sexual assault. By that I mean that neither the genitals nor any other part of the victims' bodies show signs of violation. But that doesn't mean we can rule out the fact that the motive, the primary cause behind the two killings, might have been a specific sexual deviance."

"How about you clarify this a bit for me." The superintendent was feeling increasingly nauseated and confused.

"Vampirism," the doctor waxed didactic, "is a disorder in which an individual's sexual response is aroused by the sight or ingestion of blood, either from an animal or a person. This is what psychiatry labels a paraphilia, meaning a sexual behavior where the source of pleasure in not derived from intercourse but from some activity that replaces it. Specifically, those affected by vampirism tend to climax when biting their victim, usually on the neck, in order to sever the carotid and ingest their blood ... What is it, superintendent?"

Muñoz had turned pale. "For the love of God, would you put out that blasted cigarette of yours?"

"But of course." The doctor squashed the cigarette butt on a copper tray. "And going back to what we were saying, as an illness, vampirism doesn't have a clear-cut classification or diagnosis. Some authors include patients suffering from vampirism in the group of psychotics or schizophrenics, but others claim it is a specific, clearly differentiated pathology related to other paraphilia such as fetishism, necrophilia or, as you yourself suggested, sadism. Proponents of this second view named the disorder Renfield syndrome, after one of the characters in *Dracula*, the famous vampire novel. Did you get a chance to see the film, superintendent? With that Hungarian actor? What was his name . . . Bela Lugosi, I believe. Splendid characterization. Of course that's a very romanticized rendering. Real vampires, now—"

"What about the top?" Superintendent Muñoz cut him off.

"Sorry?"

"The spinning top, the toy." The officer spoke slowly, making an effort to ignore the chill and nausea running from his brain to the pit of his stomach. "There was a spinning top at the crime scene and you said you would examine it as evidence. So?"

Doctor Pellicer didn't flinch. "I haven't inspected it yet. Frankly, the autopsy seemed much more urgent." He scrunched up his nose, relenting. "But I'm pretty sure you already have an opinion about the top. Am I right, superintendent?"

Surmounting his revulsion with difficulty, superintendent Muñoz managed to smile. "You are, no doubt, familiar with the expression *memento mori,* doctor."

SISTER CONCEPCIÓ WAS in the laundry when she got word that the mother abbess was waiting to see her in the chapterhouse. The novice enjoyed every laundry-related chore and implement: the stones used for pleating, the metal and wood irons for pressing garments, the different techniques for sewing and spinning. She especially enjoyed making lye, and frequently offered to switch shifts with other sisters in the community, as the majority found the task disgusting. She, however, relished the process, which began by collecting the ashes from the oven or the kitchen stove, the heater in the refectory, or the hearth in the chapterhouse—for thanks to the efforts of Manuel Escorza, the Capuchin convent never lacked for firewood. Sister Concepció collected the ashes with a shovel and sifted them to remove the remainder of the coal. Once the ashes were silvery and fine, she put them in a bucket and added a pot of hot water—four parts water, one part ash—stirred the mixture with a stick, covered it with a cloth and allowed it to settle for a day or so. Then it was time to pour the liquid into a wooden basin through a strainer that fit around the rim, collecting the leftover ashes and keeping the lye from spilling. Sister Concepció always marveled at the greasy texture and delicate scent of a final product that was destined to bring a modicum of cleanliness to the world.

The novice crossed the courtyard, where the nuns bent over stone sinks, armed with washboards and homemade soap bars, and then the vegetable garden, where the smell of damp earth enlivened her senses. The end of summer had been exceptionally rainy that year; the cold gave no sign of arriving any time soon, and the beds lined with vegetable seedlings had been kept so moist by the rain they hardly needed watering. The well too was practically brimming, and the coolness of the water was felt everywhere. The convent was kept so well stocked by Manuel Escorza's man that even the animal pen held two happily-grunting pigs, a flock of hens fluffing their feathers in the fenced-off section, and a palm tree, a myrtle and bougainvillea that were a glorious sight. A lap dog—adopted by the community the same day that the war broke out—was scratching its fleas by the door to the wood shed, and a bit farther along, in the middle of the Gothic cloister, four cats lay dozing, unperturbed by Sister Concepció's hurried steps. What could the mother abbess want with her?

Her fingers trembled as she knocked on the massive door to the chapterhouse. On the other side, distant and authoritarian, the voice of the mother abbess answered: "Come in."

"Ave Maria Purísima," Sister Concepció greeted her, pushing the heavy door open.

"Conceived without sin," Mother Abbess and a male voice responded in unison, something Sister Concepció was not expecting.

Bishop Perugorría was seated in a large, plush armchair, beaming. The mother abbess was standing beside him, also smiling, though more subdued. Dressed in religious habit, they stood motionless before the glass cabinet that contained the famous black clay urns—the convent's most emblematic treasures. The whole scene looked like an altarpiece.

"Mother Abbess. Your Excellency," the novice whispered, head bowed, hands folded.

"Come closer, my daughter," said the mother abbess, her voice cloying, as if addressing a pet.

Struggling to overcome her apprehension and embarrassment, Sister Concepció approached her interlocutors with four hesitant steps. She didn't dare raise her eyes. Some twenty seconds of leaden silence followed. Finally, the mother abbess addressed her in a vexed tone: "We have sent for you, my child, because His Excellency the bishop and I are keen to express our appreciation."

The novice's eyes opened eagerly. "To me, Mother Abbess? But why?"

Mother Abbess shook her head. "It is not for you to pose questions, my child."

"Forgive me, Mother Abbess. Forgive me, Your Excellency."

"His Excellency and I," continued the nun condescendingly, "were very impressed by your musical contribution during yesterday's celebration."

"Truly marvelous, my dear," added Bishop Perrugorría. "There is no doubt but that Our Lord has bestowed on you the gift of talent."

Sister Concepció began to wring her hands so it wouldn't be obvious that they were sweating. She murmured, "What ... what I do is ... of no importance. I—"

"Nor is it for you to decide what is or is not important," the mother abbess interrupted.

"Forgive me, forgive me! I didn't mean ..." She realized her thread of a voice was barely audible. In an effort not to weep, she bowed her head lower until it almost touched her chest.

The mother abbess gave the girl an ambivalent look, a mixture of severity and pity. The girl did not yet know that her parents—a prosperous magnate in the paper industry married to the daughter of a venerable line of silversmiths—had been killed during the first days of the war, and if she had joined the convent it was not through the express wishes of her parents (whom she believed had been forced to leave the country and would return as soon as the war ended) but through the intervention of the girl's aunt, her father's older sister, who could find no better solution for her. The mother abbess, mindful of the many favors the community of Capuchins of Sarrià owed the devout family, had accepted the custody of the young girl, who had entered the community as a novice with the name of Concepció. The episode of the sham arrest, during which the girl had shown surprising fortitude and presence of mind, her readiness to adapt to the rigors of convent life, and the power of her innate musical talent had earned Sister Concepció the admiration—and commiseration—of the mother abbess. The mixed feelings the novice evoked in her troubled the mother abbess, and precisely because of this she thought it best to treat the gifted girl in an especially distant, rigid manner, until the moment arrived when Sister Concepció could be apprised of the hopelessness of her situation.

Seeing that the interview was not progressing, the bishop rose from his chair and approached Sister Concepció; the proximity of His Excellency only made her trembling more noticeable. The bishop waited a few seconds to infuse solemnity into what he was about to say, and finally asked, "Do you know why I am here, my child? By that I mean, here among you in this convent?"

The novice shook her head without daring to raise it. She felt the bishop place a hand on her shoulder. The gesture was meant to transmit trust, but it only terrified the girl even more.

"Do not be frightened, my child," murmured the prelate, his voice low and cavernous. "Look me in the eye, please."

She slowly raised her head and looked at Bishop Perugorría. She couldn't have said why, but she was surprised that his eyes were the color of a pale sky, with aqueous pupils that seemed as if they too were on the point of weeping.

"I am here because outside the convent there are men who want to kill me." The bishop paused again after these words, then added: "Not only me, but also all those who serve Our Lord. Including Mother Abbess. And yourself. People think that I am dead, and as long as they believe that to be the case, the best possible shelter for me is within the walls of this convent." He gave a long, deep sigh. "It has always been this way, my child. Since the beginning, since the apostles. Already in those distant times God's beloved were despised by others who worshiped idols. Persecution and torture. Derision and death. In many ways, one could say that our devotion has often been our downfall. But we will never abandon our beliefs, will we, my child? We will never renounce our love of God, never turn our backs on Him or abjure the light He shines on us even in the darkest of nights . . . Tell me, my child:

Will you remain steady in your faith in God Almighty, his son Jesus Christ, and the Holy Spirit?"

Without opening her mouth, Sister Concepció nodded, an almost imperceptible movement of her head, but it sufficed.

"But of course you will, my child, as it must be," said Bishop Perugorría with pride, his claw squeezing the top of her shoulder. "It could not be otherwise, because our faith is strong, and inasmuch as He grants us the strength of our faith, no wind shall bend us, nor will the fury of the tempests diminish its strength. Faith is the weapon by which we are transformed into the most indestructible of armies; Satan's name is Legion, and he may surpass us in number but never in steadfastness or temperance . . . How old are you, my child?"

Sister Concepció stole a glance at the hand grasping her shoulder. It was hurting her, but most especially she felt disgust at the sight of it: it was a languid, pale hand, covered with bristly hairs all the way down to the knuckles, its long fingers hooked, gnarled. It was all she could do to control her revulsion.

"Aren't you going to answer His Excellency, child?" inquired the mother abbess with a touch of irritation.

The novice took a moment to breathe. "Thirteen, Your Excellency," she responded in one sudden exhalation, the air coming out as though through a pump.

"Thirteen," repeated the bishop, finally withdrawing his hand. The girl's breathing steadied with relief. "The age of Saint Eulàlia, of course. Do you know who Saint Eulàlia was, my dear?"

Sister Concepció was silent again.

"Do not be rude. Answer when you are spoken to," the mother abbess ordered.

The novice recited, "Saint Eulàlia is the patron saint of Barcelona, Your Excellency, and she should not be confused with Mare de Déu de la Mercè, the Virgin of Mercy, patron of the Diocese."

"Very good, my dear," the bishop said approvingly, with a cankerous smile. "What else can you tell me about her?"

"Nothing more, Your Excellency," the novice admitted, lowering her head.

"Nothing more, Your Excellency," Bishop Perugorría mimicked. "What do you think of that, Mother Abbess? Nothing more, Your Excellency!" He broke out in a thunderous laugh. "Santa Eulàlia gloriosa! Santa Eulàlia gloriosa!"

The outburst of hilarity was quite improper given His Excellency's dignified position. The mother abbess observed silently; Sister Concepció looked on with trepidation.

"Enough!" the bishop shouted abruptly, as if addressing himself. Reassuming his serious bearing, he bellowed: "You should know that when Saint Eulàlia was a young girl like you she lived in a house right here where we are now, in Sarrià. As a matter of fact, we cannot rule out that this very convent was built over the ruins of Saint Eulàlia's house. What do you say to that, child?"

"Nothing, Your Excellency."

"Have you ever visited the cloister of the Cathedral, my dear?"

"No, Your Excellency."

"I wonder what parents teach their children these days!" said the bishop disapprovingly. "It is no surprise that we find ourselves at war and that God's children are being harmed, reviled and murdered." Feigning serenity, he continued: "If you had visited the cloister of the Cathedral, you would have seen the charming flock of geese. Do you know what a goose is, my child?"

"I think so, Your Excellency."

"You think so! God help us! And what exactly do you think a goose is, pray tell?"

"It's a kind of duck . . ."

A protracted, uncomfortable silence followed. Then the prelate gasped and again began to vociferate: "A duck?! A duck and a goose have nothing in common! Have some respect for God's creation, child! Don't you know that man named all the animals at the dawn of time? And if a goose was named goose and not duck, it must be for a reason, don't you think?"

"Of course, Your Excellency."

The novice had surrendered to the absurdity of the moment and no longer felt like crying.

"But let us not get off track, child," said the bishop. "You probably do not know the name of the estate where Saint Eulàlia grew up. Am I right?"

"You are, Your Excellency. I do not know."

"Just as I thought. How about you, Mother Abbess?"

"The Desert of Sarrià," she answered, with the air of a diligent student.

"Precisely!" exclaimed the bishop. "And why, in such a remote time, at the end of the third century, might a villa on the outskirts of Barcelona receive such a curious name?"

"Because of the palm trees on the land," replied the mother abbess at once, to spare Sister Concepció from having to reveal her ignorance again.

"That is correct, Mother Abbess. Palm trees." He turned to the novice. "But the most interesting part of the story, my sweet child, is that those trees had not always been palm trees. No, previously there had been a small forest of cypress trees. One day, as Saint Eulàlia was strolling in the forest, an angel appeared to her and announced that she was to become a saint, the patron of Barcelona. And so the revelation might be duly recorded, the angel turned the cypress trees into palm trees. And this, my dear, is the point I was leading to: Why do you think the angel appeared to the child, a girl such as yourself, and worked such wonders before her bewildered eyes?"

"I don't know that either, Your Excellency," responded a weary Sister Concepció.

"Because she was a Christian, my child. As simple as that. The angels protect those of us who love God and place our faith in Him, and they show us the path to His

Glory. This is the supreme benefit that we, Our Lord's servants, receive from our faith." As he spoke these words, the bishop's face seemed to light up from within, but then it darkened. "Alas, that is but one side of the story. What would be the other, my dear?"

The novice again looked Bishop Perugorría in the eyes. She was suddenly certain of the answer. She opened her mouth to speak, and she had the feeling it wasn't her own voice but someone else's, deep within her stomach that answered firmly: "Torment, Your Excellency."

The bishop spread his arms wide. "That, now, is a clear-sighted response, my dear." And he pinched her chin with two of his offensive fingers. "It is through torment that Christians give testimony of our will to abide in the Lord and of the firmness of the commitment that binds us to Him. And this torment is also a source of joy, the greatest, most trying joy of all." The bishop lit up again, like a blinking light. "Blessed are those who endure derision, violence, or death for their faith, for they will be favored by the Lord. Saint Eulàlia lived in the time of Diocletian, a cruel, bloodthirsty emperor. She was arrested, and though still a child, she paid dearly for her devotion. Are you familiar, child, with the torments inflicted upon Saint Eulàlia?"

Sister Concepció shook her head timidly.

"Thirteen torments, one for each of her years," explained the bishop. "First she received one hundred lashes, then hooks were driven into her body, ripping the skin and flesh from her back and belly. She was forced to walk across a bed of red-hot embers and then her breasts were cut off."

The bishop interrupted his account to steal a quick, unctuous glance at the novice's budding breasts.

"Saint Eulàlia's entire body was an open wound; in order to inflict still more pain, her captors rubbed the sores with pumice stones, poured boiling oil on them, doused her in molten lead and left her an entire night in a well of quicklime. Then they placed her in a wine barrel filled with shards of glass and broken pieces of tile and rolled her down a slope. They made her sleep one night in a flea- and bedbug-infested animal pen so that her sores would become infected, then they placed her briefly over a bonfire, but not long enough to kill her because the death reserved for Christians was crucifixion at dawn. Saint Eulàlia, reduced to a stump of flesh and crushed bones, remained alive on the cross for fourteen more hours before expiring and giving up her soul to God. Thirteen torments," noted the bishop, holding up the five fingers of each hand, then the thumb, index and ring finger of his right hand.

A faint, disagreeable nausea settled in Sister Concepció's stomach. His Excellency continued his enthusiastic speech under the mother abbess's watchful eye.

"Christians worthy of the name must rejoice, my child, for we are again living through a period of torment, and this affords us the opportunity to test the purity of our faith. These are times that demand fortitude of spirit, even of young girls of thirteen like Saint Eulàlia who, without a shadow of a doubt, received her guidance from the Holy Spirit." The bishop took the novice by the chin again. "Tell me, my dear: If the time came, would you have the strength to endure such torment for the grace and love of God?"

"Yes, Your Excellency," lied the girl, doing her best to appear poised and keep from retching.

The bishop raised her face, and with a blank look, panted, "Excellent! Excellent!"

He withdrew his fingers from Sister Concepció's face, turned his back to her, trudged over to the armchair and laboriously lowered himself into it. He seemed exhausted, as if he had just performed a herculean feat. His cheeks and double chin quivered, and he gasped for air like a fish out of water.

The mother abbess spoke: "Nevertheless, it is not necessary that we all follow the path of martyrdom, is it, my child?" She had dropped her authoritarian tone and tried to seem cordial, maternal even, but she only managed to appear hesitant. "Someone must live to sing praise to the martyrs and saints. And you, as His Excellency noted, have the gift, the great privilege granted by Our Lord, of expressing yourself through music."

Sister Concepció responded with a nod intended to show gratitude but which brought with it a mouthful of bile that she had trouble holding back.

"His Excellency," continued the mother abbess, some-what deflated, "believes—and it is also my humble opinion—that there are many ways of facing the vicissitudes of these difficult times when Our Lord, as our bishop explained, subjects us to such harsh trials. One of these is to contribute, each according to our ability, some measure of beauty to this world."

The mother abbess paused again, searching for words she could not find. Finally, she blurted out: "In short, my child, His Excellency would like for you to begin working on a musical composition. Not a variation on a preexisting piece, but your own composition. After the pleasure derived from what we heard yesterday, we feel it is reasonable to believe that you are in a position to . . ."

Sister Concepció understood that the ludicrous request was a whim of Bishop Perugorría's, and the mother abbess, against her will, had had no choice but to support it. She also realized there was nothing she could do to put a stop to the nonsense, and so she simply gave the mother abbess a stale, resigned smile. She glanced at His Excellency, who had sunk down into himself.

The mother abbess opened the glass door to the cupboard, selected one of the black clay urns and set it on the long, dark, rough-hewn table of the chapterhouse. She then reached into her habit and withdrew two little trinkets that she held out in the palm of her hand to show Sister Concepció.

"Do you see this bean and this almond, dear child?"

The novice nodded without understanding. "We will put them both in the vase, and then, without looking, you will reach in and take one of them."

It was some sort of raffle, then, probably something to do with the task being assigned to her. She watched as the mother abbess dropped the bean and the almond into the urn and shook it energetically. When she tired, the nun stretched out her arms, and holding the vase with both hands before the girl, said, "Go ahead, my child."

Sister Concepció raised one hand, but stopped midway. It suddenly occurred to her there might be a scorpion or poisonous spider in the vase that would sting her, and she would have a terrible death, with tertian fevers and delirium. It was torment, or the idea of torment, that had seized her imagination and filled her head with unspeakable images in which she saw herself being whipped, tortured, mutilated, burned alive for the glory of Our Lord. And these images produced an oppressive, clammy nausea that was not just physical but something that bled through the walls of her heart and into her spirit.

"Child . . ." the mother abbess insisted, softening her stance.

The girl plucked up her courage; she closed her eyes and, stretching out her arm, she grasped the first seed she found and swiftly extracted it from the vase.

"A bean," the mother abbess announced in a serious tone.

"Magnificent!" exclaimed the bishop, suddenly reviving. "So then, we shall have a Stabat Mater."

What foolish endeavor the almond represented Sister Concepció would never know, nor did she have any desire to.

Bishop Perugorría now seemed unexpectedly cheerful, elated even. "I am especially partial to the Stabat Mater," he declared, beaming. "It is a genre that has produced some of the most valuable expressions in the history of music. The Mother of God's lament for her son's suffering ... The height of the torment and the purification derived from it."

"When Mary weeps," added the mother abbess, "it is the sum of all the tears shed by every mother who has ever seen her child in the grip of pain and misery and has nevertheless kept her faith in the infinite mercy of Our Lord."

The bishop inhaled deeply through his nose and said, "You will compose your Stabat Mater in honor of Senyora María Maeztu, my poor dear mother. She must now be in what used to be my home in Navarra, mourning the death of her son, the news of which she of course believes to be true." His Excellency's eyes moistened even more than usual, and he raised a hand to wipe away a tear. "My mother and I will be amply rewarded for this suffering when we are reunited and can embrace, whether in this world or in the higher life that divine providence offers us beyond death. But for the moment," he said, addressing the girl, "your music can serve as a salve to cauterize the wounds of the souls debased by this war, the mothers subjugated by this scourge . . ." His voice broke and he began to weep, lost in his own frenzy.

Sister Concepció found the courage to object. "I don't believe I am capable . . ." she said, almost in a whisper.

Bishop Perugorría came to and grasped her again, this time with a hand on each shoulder. It hurt. The faint light of the chapterhouse contrasted with the icy glow in the prelate's still teary eyes.

"My sweet child," he hissed, "if you can state that you are strong enough to endure Saint Eulàlia's ordeal, then the Holy Spirit will surely grant you the courage to comply with what is asked of you."

The mother abbess was no longer able to conceal her sadness. "The exceptional nature of this request means that you will be relieved of your usual chores in our community. But we would appreciate your effort not to neglect them completely . . ." She realized she was contradicting herself and stopped herself before she contributed more to the novice's confusion. "You may go in peace, my child," the mother abbess concluded.

The sound of the closing door to the chapterhouse echoed behind Sister Concepció as she departed. In a daze, the novice took a few hesitant steps; then she had to stop to vomit in a corner of the cloister as the cats looked on, intrigued.

BROTHER PAU DARDER was disconcerted after the conversation with Don Miquel Carbonissa. The judge proved to be a repository of knowledge when it came to accounts of the deceased who had somehow returned to life, either as vampires or in some other form. Those tales did nothing to help Brother Darder find the spiritual comfort he needed, but he had had little choice but to beg for the patience of Job and feign interest.

The topic, according to Judge Carbonissa, could be traced back to ancient times. In *The Histories*, Herodotus tells the story of a revenant of antiquity by the name of Aristeas. The son of a long line of distinguished nobles from the city of Proconnesus, Aristeas composed narrative poems, explaining in one of them that Apollo had inspired him to travel to the land of the Issedones, high above which lived the one-eyed Arimaspi, and a bit farther away, the gold-guarding griffins, and farther still, by the sea, the Hyperboreans.

The young Aristeas entered a fuller's shop one day to request that a few cotton bales be spun so he could weave some cloth from them; but Aristeas suddenly dropped dead in the middle of the shop. The fuller was beside himself; he locked his shop and ran as fast as he could to inform the dead man's family. The news quickly spread, but a man from Cyzicus who had just arrived in Proconnesus announced that Aristeas could not possibly have died in the fuller's shop, for he had had just had seen him and spoken to him at the city gates. The Cyzicenian defended his story before the people who gathered in the agora. Indeed, when Aristeas's tearful family arrived at the fuller's shop with the funeral carriage and shroud, there was no sign of their son, either dead or alive. Nothing more was known of Aristeas until seven years later, when he returned to Proconnesus as mysteriously as he had vanished and apparently in perfect health. He remained in the city for a short period, during which time he devoted himself to writing poetry, and then he disappeared again as if the earth had swallowed him up.

Judge Carbonissa also knew of several extraordinary cases of dead persons who had momentarily revived when saintly men had called upon them to return to life. He gave the example of a story, recorded by Saint Augustine, of a young man who was pursued by the law for an unsettled debt which the young man's father had in fact repaid, though the paper that proved it could not be found. The father's soul, wrote Saint Augustine, appeared piously before the son and told him where he could find the receipt for the troubling debt.

In Egypt, there was the remarkable case of Saint Spyridon, who found himself in a difficult situation after his daughter Irene died, for a certain man professed that she had agreed to safeguard some money for him, a fact she had not disclosed to her father. As the money could not be found anywhere in the house, Saint Spyridon finally went to his daughter's tomb, called to her by name and questioned her about the contentious sum; she responded from her grave, revealed the location of the money, and Saint Spyridon was able to return it.

The judge also told the story of Saint Macarius of Egypt, who revived a dead man so that he might testify as to the innocence of the person accused of having killed him: the dead man exonerated the accused but refused to divulge the name of the perpetrator. In another one of his feats, Saint Macarius implored the help of a dead person in a dispute with a heretic of the Amonoean sect—or the Hieracitae, depending on the author. As the heretic would not listen to reason, Macarius proposed: "Let us go to the tomb of a dead man and ask him to reveal to us the truth which you do not wish to accept." The heretic did not dare to make an appearance, but Saint Macarius, accompanied by a multitude, went to the sepulcher and questioned the departed man, who responded from the depths of the tomb that if the heretic had attended the assembly he would have risen from his grave to convince him and give testimony of the truth. Saint Macarius then ordered the dead man to resume his slumber, in the peace of the Lord, until the end of time.

The majority of the stories of revenants were not, however, saintly tales, but macabre or morbid ones, and once Judge Carbonissa had begun to retell them it seemed he would never finish. Brother Darder was particularly struck by the story of Count Estruch—or Estruga—a vampire who, according to legend, had inhabited the castle of Llers, in the Alt Empordà region of Catalunya; it was believed that a group of witches also lived in that area, and, according to the judge, they had recently been sung by the local poet Carles Fages de Climent. This Count Estruch, a Catalan noble, had died at the beginning of the thirteenth century (coinciding, as some authors noted, with the birth of the Catalan King Jaume I), and he came back to life in the form of a vampire. He would sink his teeth into animals and people and drink their blood, but his most appalling deed was seducing young girls and impregnating them: at the end of nine months they gave birth to tiny, deformed, aberrant monsters that died shortly after being born. The horror lasted until the day Estruch's sleeping body was discovered by a hermit—a half-Jew—who drew on an ancestral cabalistic spell to force the count to rest in peace.

These lurid fantasies originated, in the judge's well-founded opinion, in matters of faith. Such as the controversy that arose between the philosophers Celsus and Origen when the former made public his writings attacking Christians, in which he maintained that the appearances of Jesus Christ before his disciples were not real, but simply the result of dancing shadows that some wished to interpret as something they were not. But Origen turned the argument against Celsus by reminding him that pagans had also left written accounts of appearances by Apollo and Aesculapius: If they accepted these accounts as factual, as Celsus did, how could they not accept as true the ones referring to Jesus, which had eye witnesses and were acknowledged the world over? After all, a long list of enlightened minds—including Saint Augustine and Saint Thomas—had demonstrated that what Christian narratives tell us about Jesus Christ helps to confirm one of the saving doctrines of humankind.

Origen had recorded it thus, and it had been accepted as such by the uneasy judge. The magistrate then brought up the remarkable figure of the Benedictine monk Antoine Augustin Calmet, author of the admirable *Commentary on the Old and New Testament,* which garnered him the well-deserved distinction of being one of the most scholarly and pious men of eighteenth-century France. But this same excellent author also penned—and at the height of the Enlightenment, no less—a rather obscure, troubling volume titled *Treaty on the Apparitions of Spirits and Vampires; Or, Ghosts of Hungary, Moravia, &c.,* a collection of all the accounts he could find about the dead and undead who had returned from the other world to feed on the blood of the living. Naturally, Calmet's conclusion was that there was no place for this type of story in Christian moral and thought. So why, then, would a man of such faith and reasoning have invested so much effort in collecting, classifying, transcribing, and publishing these accounts? Why had he devoted as much zeal and attention to this treatise of obscene fancies as to his prestigious works of Biblical erudition?

With a lump in his throat, Judge Carbonissa recalled some of the traits and attitudes Father Calmet ascribed to revenants or *vrykolakas*, as he sometimes referred to them. For example, it was believed that revenants used to masticate inside their tomb, devouring everything they encountered, including their own flesh; there were reports that claimed that the sound of chewing—similar to that of a pig—could be heard coming from inside certain tombs. The stories of the vampires of Moravia were no less horrifying, such as the one concerning a locksmith from a Bohemian village; after his death, he would appear on the streets and with an unearthly voice he called out the names of certain villagers, who inevitably met their death a few days later. This situation persisted until the villagers agreed to dig up the locksmith's body and hand it over to the executioner, who placed the corpse in a wagon, transported it to the outskirts of the village, and threw it into a bonfire. As it burned, the body wailed furiously, its feet and hands flailing as if he were still alive. When the executioner drove a stake into the chest and abdomen, the corpse let out a spine-chilling scream and a large amount of bright-red blood gushed forth. The corpse was finally reduced to ashes, and the ghostly infestations ceased. This cemented the belief that the only effective remedy against these apparitions was to behead the revenant, pierce its body with a sharp stake, and incinerate it.

Just as Brother Pau Darder was tiring of Judge Carbonissa's long-winded account, the magistrate returned to the question that seemed to obsess him: Why would a man of the Church as prominent as Father Calmet concern himself with this drivel about vampires? The judge could only find one answer: for the simple reason that Calmet must have believed it worthwhile. And if the illustrious Benedictine had drawn this conclusion it meant he did not believe these stories to be nonsensical, idle tales passed down from fathers to sons during long winter nights by the hearth, but saw them as depositories of valuable information. Something most men disregarded, but the wise Father Antoine Augustin Calmet had not overlooked.

For finally, the judge reasoned, tales of vampires speak to us of horror, a reality over which we generally prefer to draw a veil of incomprehension and scorn. And yet, this capacity for horror is inherent to all human beings. The wonder of creation—which had been capable of fecundating nothingness and spawning the Universe from it—was so immense that it inevitably contained imperfections, like a perfect musical score bespattered by miniscule ink spots: insignificant, but sufficiently noticeable to cause the reader of the score to make mistakes. Applied to the full scale of creation, the sum of these errors in reading produced what is conventionally known as evil, which finds in monstrosity one of its preferred forms of expression.

However—the judge continued—the awareness of evil is precisely the instrument God gives us to defend ourselves from it. Because we are possessed of reasoning, we are able to understand the existence of evil and the meaning of horror, and to take measures to correct these defects—to become, in a way, collaborators in God's work and to make ourselves useful in the task of restoring balance to creation. As the good Antoine Augustin Calmet noted, it was possible that persons buried alive either by mistake or out of wickedness might become so crazed on waking inside the tomb that they would begin chewing on their own flesh or on the bodies of the dead buried alongside them, and it was terrible to imagine such baseness. But the notion that the truly dead would move their jaws and occupy their time chomping on whatever was at hand would have to be regarded as the figment of a childish imagination, perhaps on par with the Manducus of Ancient Rome. The Manducus was an anthropomorphic, articulated doll with a large mouth and teeth. The game that amused children and adults alike consisted in activating the jaws by means of a special mechanism; the Manducus would then grind its teeth with a crunching sound, giving the impression that the grotesque figure was starving and begging for something to eat.

Brother Darder, at this point even more confused than when the conversation began, asked Judge Carbonissa to kindly explain where all this was leading. "Machines," the judge murmured. It wasn't clear to the Marist if he was responding or simply thinking aloud. But then the judge added that the Manducus was obviously a machine, that

is to say, an artifact devised by human intelligence: specifically, an automaton which, as such, emulated human
behavior. In addition to providing entertainment during
the Roman Empire, centuries later the Manducus had
helped Father Calmet to situate the legend of the masti-
cating dead in its proper realm—that of monsters. The
ability to reason that has been bestowed on us over all
other creatures in this world allows us to compose
texts and construct machines that can not only describe
evil—and in so doing help us to comprehend it—but also
combat it. "Automatons," Judge Carbonissa murmured
again, seemingly overwhelmed, his forehead in his hands.
Tired of not comprehending, Brother Pau Darder again
pressed the judge—more vehemently this time—to clarify the meaning of his senseless rambling. But the judge
consulted his pocket watch and, exclaiming that it was
late, thanked Brother Darder for his attention and apolo-
gized for his sudden departure. Before Brother Darder
could reply that there was nothing to thank him for, the
judge had disappeared down the corridor of Pension
Capell and headed out of the building, slipping away as
abruptly as he had appeared.

Brother Darder was left stunned and listless, sitting in
a chair in his sad room. Enveloped by the benevolent
summer light that streamed through the tiny window, he
considered the visit from Judge Carbonissa. The man was
clearly an eccentric, but was there anything in all of the
hodgepodge he had spewed that was worthy of attention?

What could that nonsense about vampires and automatons have to do with the death of Don Pere Gendrau? And with the child found in the nearby alleyway? The vulnerability and terror conveyed by the two horribly desecrated bodies tormented Brother Darder, and he could not help but return again and again to the same question: What kind of God would contemplate, unmoved and unresponsive, as his creation sank into sordidness and barbarity? Was this the infinite, divine mercy he had so often extoled in heated conversations at the seminary?

"Brother Pau? Are you there?" a ridiculous voice called from behind the door.

Brother Darder sighed. It could only be one person.

"I'm here, Brother Plana." He rose from his chair to open the door. "Are you needing to confess, perhaps?"

Brother Plana squirmed about with a reptilian movement. "No, no. Thank you, Brother Darder, it's about a different matter." He cleared his throat. "Brother Lacunza sent me to inform you that Don Émile Aragou, the adjutant dispatched by our esteemed order, is now in Barcelona. Brother Lacunza and I will meet with him this afternoon to welcome him and prepare tomorrow's appointment with the negotiators from the FAI. Brother Lacunza asked me to keep you abreast of the news and wishes to know if you would like to accompany us tomorrow . . ."

The indefatigable Brother Lacunza and his mediations that never led anywhere. Only a couple of days ago he

would have expressed his reservation rather unceremoni-
ously. But now the memory of Don Pere obliged him.

"What time is the meeting?" he asked.

SPRAWLED IN A chair in his office on Via Laietana,
enveloped by the grainy light of a carbide lamp, superintendent Gregori Muñoz breathed deeply as he struggled
to dispel his queasiness and cleanse his senses of the
memory of the stench at the morgue. He always left with
the feeling of being soaked in that smell, as if he too had
been submerged in formaldehyde in the company of the
cadavers—whole or dismembered—that Doctor Pellicer
enjoyed naming and labelling. Blood, lymph, bodily fluids.
Death, Superintendent Muñoz reflected, was a sticky matter, and once you had seen it up close it was difficult to
rid yourself of it.

The superintendent was absentmindedly twirling an
object in his hands; then he suddenly stopped and studied
it with close attention, as though transfixed. It was the
spinning top—a *memento mori*, according to his own
conjectures. The criminal might have been an absolute
beast, but he was certainly not inept—the superintendent
was forced to admit that he had never seen a crime scene
so scrupulously neat and clean, so maddeningly devoid
of information. No fingerprints, no hairs, no textile fibers,
none of the tiny bits of filth you would usually find on the
ground or on walls. Nothing that could offer the slightest
clue as to the assassin's provenance or motivation, much

less his identity. The footprints in the gravel of the alleyway had been carefully erased, and only the blood-stained
top was left as a token of the crime. *Memento mori.*
Remember that death awaits you. Awaits us all. A macabre and unscrupulous redundancy in a time when death
marauded through the streets taking lives at every turn.
Women, children, the elderly. Young lovers preparing to
marry and start a family. Mothers who cared for their
children and children who tended to their elderly parents.
Robust, strong men who for fifteen or sixteen hours a day
worked without faltering in metal foundries, in heavy
equipment factories. Distinguished businessmen and
prosperous merchants who had enjoyed exemplary
careers and whose children were preparing to take over
the family business, or men who worked as doctors, engi-
neers or attorneys. It didn't matter: they would all be
wiped out, disemboweled by a bomb, ripped apart by a
murdering sniper, riddled with bullets by a hired gun, or
shot by members of the FAI who expressed their revolutionary orthodoxy through executions carried out on the
Arrabassada road. The superintendent gave a resigned
smile as he recalled Doctor Pellicer's questions: no, no he
did not care for priests or nuns or any of those sacristy
rats, but they did not evoke in him one tenth of the disgust
he felt for the beasts from the FAI—that band of preten-
tious pricks who were running the show now, real macho
men when they got their hands on a loaded revolver. They
made him sick. Especially Aureli Fernández from the

Department of Investigations and his toady, a real bastard by the name of Ordaz, who were sucking the life out of him. All day long bugging him for reports, citations, more reports. They didn't trust him, and truth be told, they were right not to: Superintendent Muñoz would have been especially pleased if someone had stuck a gun up Fernández's ass—after all, he loved guns—and emptied the clip. The same went for that blasted Ordaz, but he wouldn't be that fortunate. And besides, there wasn't much he could do about it; he was only a functionary of the Generalitat, at the service of whoever was at the top. And those were times of unquestioning obedience. Fortunately, he didn't have to deal with the big guy in the Service, a man named Escorza, of whom it was said that his body was maimed, though not nearly as much as his brain.

Doctor Pellicer was right: if the Department of Investigations got wind that he had let a flock of pious turtledoves fly the coop, he would be pissing blood. Fernández and Ordaz would be thrilled. But he had decided not to partake of the madness that had been unleashed in Barcelona against people of the church; he could do nothing to stop it, but he hoped at least to come out of it with his hands unbloodied. He set the tip of the spinning top on the table, grasped the crown between his thumb and index finger and gave a quick twist with his right wrist. The top spun around, fast, weightless, its red and green decorative pattern immediately blurring, then blending into a single smudge of an indefinite color. Never mind that the toy was forensic evidence—acting on impulse, the superintendent had appropriated it for himself. It wouldn't make any difference, he thought. Give or take a top, it's not going to determine whether we catch our killer. On the other hand, he had no use for the spinning top: he had no children, no nieces or nephews, no child close to him to whom he could give it. The fact was, Superintendent Muñoz's solitary, austere habits applied to all aspects of his life. But when nothing seems to mean much anymore, he mused, the purpose of things is also lost. One such example: for many years he had defended the notion that the function of the police was to guarantee that no crime went unpunished. But reality—at least the reality taking shape in the folds of Superintendent Muñoz's brain—showed that in an age of assassins, the presence of yet another killer was a trivial matter. The motive? That was beside the point. He smiled, recalling the petulant young Marist brother who spun theories as to the reasons for murder. He must not have been taught at the seminary that in a large percentage of cases there is no motive, or it is so slight as to be irrelevant. A murderer needs no real motive for killing; a favorable environment is all he requires. And there must have been few cities in the world now where killing came as easily as in Barcelona.

When the spinning top lost momentum and finally fell on its side on the desk, the superintendent clicked his tongue against his teeth, as if expressing a sense of fatality. He picked up the toy, slipped it in his pocket and sighed again. He had to admit that Doctor Pellicer's explanations about vampirism had surprised him, but then again, there was no need to overemphasize their significance. Lunatics had always existed, in all shapes and sizes, and since the war began they were even more common. About a month ago they had arrested a drunk who got turned on by exposing himself to young girls, no doubt an example of the paraphilias Doctor Pellicer had referred to. Regardless, psychiatric theories were of no use to the fellow when they dragged him off to the basement and gave him the usual treatment in these cases. When they were through with him, neither the guy nor anyone else would ever have to worry again about anything happening below his belt.

He swallowed: the aftertaste of formaldehyde and decay were still there. But now there was an added ingredient.

"Goddammit, Sirga!" roared the superintendent without turning around. "You smell like whorehouse soap!"

"What's that, sir?" asked the red-haired policeman standing at the threshold to the superintendent's office.

The superintendent wheeled his chair around brusquely and faced his visitor. "You whoring bastard, that's what I said." He rose from his chair, strode toward the officer and gave the visor on the man's cap a thump, flipping it backward. The superintendent was acting on instinct; he liked to heed his intuition.

"Ha, ha," laughed Sirga, in appreciation of the gesture of camaraderie.

"Don't laugh, you idiot," the superintendent snapped at him. Sirga's laugh instantly froze. "I don't like whoremongers. Reminds me of my father. You know what my father used to say, Sirga?"

The young man was silent; he was so stiff it looked as if he'd been starched. He didn't even dare to blink.

"He used to say: sometimes a man's gotta empty his sack of *cojones*! And then he would smack Mother around a couple of times and head to the whorehouse. Downtown they all knew him as the Moor. The Moor who liked to go slumming. What do you say to that, Sirga?"

The man being questioned swallowed. "Disgraceful, sir."

"Disgraceful—good word. And you know why they called my father the Moor, Sirga?"

"No, sir."

"Because he had a big one, very big, that's why!" he thundered, holding his hands far apart. "Haven't you heard that Moors are well endowed? And my father's was long, hairy, thick, and veiny, and he had black balls that were glued to his ass, like a tiger! You know what tiger's balls are like, Sirga?"

The officer couldn't smother his smile, and for once Superintendent Muñoz didn't call him an idiot, but gave a roguish smile in return. "When my father strutted into the slum, the whores ran for the hills so they wouldn't have to take that huge gift of God between their legs!

Can you imagine? They said it almost ruptured them, and after being with my father they were out of commission for a solid week. But the man always managed to find a girl willing to take it for a few more coins. It's like he said, from time to time a man needs to have his pouch emptied . . . But not his coin pouch!" And Muñoz roared with laughter, his hands cupped in an evocatively vulgar gesture. "You follow me, Sirga? The pouch, the pouch!"

Sirga couldn't hold back either, and he burst into a, guttural, rubbery laugh. After laughing together for a long while, Superintendent Muñoz placed his hand on the officer's shoulder. "So, Sirga, since we're here chewing the fat, I can tell you aren't one to settle for just anything . . . You're not like my animal of a father, who would go for any old street hooker. No, sir, you're a fellow with a fine palate who prefers a first-class bawdy house with pretty girls with soft asses who wash your cock with expensive soap. Right? So, here's my question: With your miserable salary, where do you find the dough to pay for such select merchandise, if you pardon my curiosity?"

Sirga stopped laughing; he stood there, his mouth half open, unable to say a word, which made him appear as stupid as the superintendent believed him to be. Following his intuition, Muñoz tried to unblock him.

"Got a seat on some gravy train, Sirga?" He placed his hand flat on the desk and stared at Sirga. "You got a job outside the police department?"

Sirga ran two fingers through his red hair and scratched his scalp. The shadows that the carbide light cast on the whitewashed walls seemed on the point of engulfing him, and it was possible that Sirga himself thought that would actually be a good idea. After a long moment, he mumbled: "I . . . I do a few hours at a warehouse, sir."

"Well, I'll be damned!" the superintendent exclaimed with disdain. "And where exactly is this warehouse, Sirga?"

Another thick silence ensued, so Muñoz asked again.

"Is this warehouse perhaps in the neighborhood of Poblenou?"

"Yes . . . yes, sir," Sirga managed to stammer out, discomfort written all over his pockmarked face. "Yes, it's in Poblenou."

"A warehouse for grain storage, Sirga?"

"And . . . and flour. Flour and grains, sir."

"And your job there is to load and unload sacks?"

"My job there is to load and unload sacks, yes . . . yes, sir."

Superintendent Muñoz nodded a few times as if pondering a difficult question.

"Well done, Sirga. A man has to work to earn a living," he said, smiling again. "So, you'll give me the address of this splendid bordello?"

"DID YOU HAVE a word with Superintendent Muñoz, as I suggested?" Judge Miquel Carbonissa asked.

"Yes, of course," replied Doctor Pellicer. "But, as I warned you, I only said what I thought was most appropriate. Even so, I didn't get the impression he was paying much attention." He sighed. "What about you, judge? Did you frighten that poor young Marist brother with your stories of revenants who suck the blood of the living?"

A faint ironic smile flickered across the judge's face. "Your dismissive tone is remarkable, considering the issue that has brought us here."

The doctor nodded in agreement. "You are right. The truth is, I am quite anxious to see it," he said with a nervous laugh, excitement in his eyes.

"Well, let's get on with it then!" exclaimed Judge Carbonissa, as he placed a hand on either side of the gutta-percha armchair, preparing to rise.

The two men had arranged to meet at the judge's home, the ground floor of an elegant building at the bottom of Carrer Aribau, almost at the corner of Gran Via. They were in the library. Judge Carbonissa had drawn the heavy velvet curtains across the large windows to keep out the intense light of that September afternoon. On the small ebony table between the two winged armchairs, he placed a bottle of Armagnac and two tiny glasses of etched crystal and quickly filled them. The room was large. Three bookcases filled with volumes of every size and width reached all the way to the ceiling, occupying three full walls. A rolling ladder set between two of the bookcases—so as not to be in the way—ensured access to the uppermost shelves. Altogether it created a welcoming atmosphere, orderly, clean. The two men raised their tiny glasses, and Doctor Pellicer made a toast: "To Hadaly," he said with gusto.

"To Hadaly," repeated the judge, then downed his glass in one gulp.

At that moment the wailing of a siren was heard outside, announcing an imminent air raid. It was a muffled sound that reached Judge Carbonissa's library, as if it were coming from afar. But soon they heard the roar of explosions in the streets and buildings, and a slight tremor shook the room. The judge filled his glass again, after serving his guest; this time both men sipped the brandy, savoring it as they listened to the rumbling of the air strike. Doctor Pellicer rolled a cigarette and busied himself blowing smoke rings that hung in the air for a few seconds before dissolving without a trace. They sat like that for quite a while. Then, exchanging looks of complicity, they rose from their armchairs as one, their movements practically synchronized.

They left the library, crossed the rather formal dining room and a more diaphanous foyer and came to a door that led to a courtyard the size of a watermelon patch (that was the comparison that came to Doctor Pellicer's mind). From there they could distinctly hear the air raid, the deafening wail of the sirens, the sinister whistle of the bombs that rained from the sky. But this was not what captured the interest of the two scholars, enticing them to rashly appear in the open at that terrible hour. Without wasting a second, Judge Carbonissa strode to one side of the courtyard and approached a sort of rectangular cinder-block storeroom that measured about two meters in length by no more than one in height. The judge removed a key from his trouser pocket and inserted it in the lock of the cover across the top of the rectangle and opened the double doors, exposing an empty space. An entranceway.

"If you would be so kind," the judge said, pointing to the open doors.

Doctor Pellicer peeped inside and saw a metal ladder attached to a wall, by which he surmised he was to climb down it. Which is what he did, but once again, his age, and especially his considerable heft, made the maneuver more difficult than expected. Finally, with the judge's help, he managed to get a firm grip on the rungs of the ladder and began to descend like a slow, fat spider. As he moved down, he heard the judge's footsteps as he closed the doors behind him—forcing them to descend in darkness—and then the magistrate's feet on the ladder. The echoes of the air strike, as it ran its course, were farther and farther away.

Suddenly Doctor Pellicer remembered an expression from his rural childhood near a village in the Ponent region, one they used when the wagon-man passed by the farmhouse where he grew up. The man's job was peculiar and specific—to collect the carcasses of dead animals: a lamb, a dog, a pig, a goat, occasionally a cow or horse that had died from accident or disease. *Flesh of misfortune*, they called it. The wagon-man—who in the doctor's memory always seemed so jovial and industrious—passed by the various farmhouses in the district, loading the wagon everybody recognized; then he carted the animals away and tossed them in a lime pit, where putrefaction transformed them into fertilizer. Flesh of misfortune, they called it, although that cheerful, agreeable man subjected the dead animals he collected to a process by which they nourished new life. And in this fashion nature demonstrated that life always asserts itself, that from death and putrefaction emerges life and that which supports it. There is no beginning and no end, reasoned the doctor, only a loop, a cycle that recommences over and over again throughout time.

As the two men climbed farther down, the air grew colder and more humid, making their skin feel cool, as if they were near a water tank. After a long while, Doctor Humbert Pellicer's foot finally touched the ground.

"I've reached the bottom!" he exclaimed, looking up into the darkness, his hands cupped around his mouth to amplify his voice.

"Don't move, I'll be right down," came the reply, attenuated by the echo.

LYING ON A cot in her cell, Sister Concepció tried to settle her breathing in an effort to overcome the anguish that had been gnawing at her stomach like a pack of mice since she had the fit of retching in the courtyard that morning.

It had frightened her, she had never vomited so much or with such virulence, to the point that only greenish spittle issued from her mouth: evil thoughts escaping, she told herself. It was dark now and Sister Encarnació—who made it clear that she had been sent by the mother abbess—had finally departed after convincing her to drink a glass of almond milk, leaving the novice alone in her cell. A lone candle lit the bleached nudity of the room: a case for her change of clothes and the habits she wore on Sundays and feast days, a bedpan in the event of bodily needs during the night, a narrow cot with a straw mattress to sleep on and, above the bare cot without a headboard, affixed to the wall, a crucifix. Nothing else. Sometimes Sister Concepció entertained herself by observing the Christ figure, carved in something resembling ivory that reminded her (she always confessed thoughts like these) of a doll she used to play with when she was a child, a little sailor.

Had she been thinking about mice? She had seen some the other day in the woodshed when she was fetching kindling for the kitchen stove. Being the youngest, she was always dispatched on the most tedious errands. She didn't mind, of course, but gracious, how everyone had settled into the ease of having *the girl* (as the majority of the sisters called her) handle the heavy chores. Well, at the woodshed she had surprised two mice, and when they noticed her presence they had scurried to hide behind a stack of the largest trunks, where they must have had their nest. The cats that haunted the cloister were too lazy, too well fed by the nuns, especially Sister Encarnació, who always saved the table scraps for them. Naturally, they were fat and their shiny fur was lovely to look at (particularly the tabby she liked and petted every time she encountered it); but they didn't so much as glance at the mice, which roamed the convent at their leisure.

She thought she heard a little sound at the door, and she half-raised herself to see what it was: Could a mouse have gotten into her room? She hoped not; she was afraid of them and if there was one she'd have to leave her cell and go ask one of the sisters for help. Perhaps Sister Anunciació, who was a bundle of nerves—that's why she was so thin—and went about killing spiders and beetles, and now that it was hot and it was the season for them, also the bedbugs that got into the vegetable garden, as well as the grasshoppers, and every now and then a mantis—those curious insects that were so cute and looked as if they were praying with their legs, though she'd been warned they were poisonous and couldn't be trusted. Well then, if there were mice in her cell she'd go fetch Sister Anunciació and have her take charge and kill them, because she didn't want them near her while she was sleeping. But, straining her eyes a bit, she confirmed there were no mice, only the glimmer of the flickering candle flame on the floor.

She let her head fall back on the thin pillow on her cot and started weeping. Softly, simply. She was just a frightened girl who imagined she was seeing mice all around her.

How was she to compose a Stabat Mater? How could His Excellency the bishop have charged her with such an impossible mission? And why had the mother abbess appeared so severe and downcast, and why had Bishop Perugorría—God in heaven—caused her such repulsion? Still more thoughts for which she would have to confess, thoughts that seemed viscous and green like the saliva drooling from her mouth a few hours before. How could she possibly set about composing an entire Stabat Mater? Her modest reinterpretations of famous songs weren't up to a challenge of such magnitude. She hadn't the slightest idea where to begin. Vague intuitions of arrangements, as feeble as herself, came to her from time to time, presentiments that were not yet notes, not even ideas, but mere sensations—of scope, of distance—that the novice was eager to transfer to the pentagram, even though she did not feel herself capable of it. She rejected those intuitions, but they still plagued her thoughts. She needed a long, uninterrupted sleep to restore her from the chill, the aching bones, and the stomach cramps that governed her body. But she could not fall asleep.

Almost mechanically she leaned over the hymnal that

Sister Encarnació had brought at her request, together
with the almond milk, and began to read:

> *Stabat mater dolorosa*
> *iuxta Crucem lacrimosa,*
> *dum pendebat Filius.*
> *Cuius animam gementem,*
> *contristatam et dolentem*
> *pertransivit gladius.*
> *O quam tristis et afflicta*
> *fuit illa benedicta,*
> *Mater Unigeniti!*
> *Quae mœrebat et dolebat,*
> *pia Mater, dum videbat*
> *nati pœnas inclyti.*
> *Quis est homo qui non fleret,*
> *Matri Christi si videret*
> *in tanto supplicio?*
> *Quis non posset contristari*
> *Christi Matrem contemplari*
> *dolentem cum Filio?*

The Stabat Mater poem was the work of Jacopone da
Todi, who wrote it in trochaic tetrameter, and over the
centuries it had been set to music by countless compos-
ers, among them some of the most exalted. According to
her book, at least five hundred musical versions of the
Stabat Mater were known, for soloists or for choir, or even

for choir and soloists. Reinterpretations, then: calling the word to mind relieved some of the weight of the task that had been pressed upon her. She had listened to some of these versions with enormous pleasure: the one by Rossini, majestic; the one by Pergolesi that sent chills down her spine and made the hair on her arms stand on end; Dvořák's, so precise. And hers? What sort of rereading of the Stabat Mater could Sister Concepció offer, she who was but a child and the most humble servant of Our Lord, the beloved daughter of a mother whose foremost concern had been to bring her up in the joy of her faith?

One didn't need much Latin to grasp that the poem spoke of the excruciating pain of the Mother of God upon the death of her son on the cross. Sister Concepció also understood that she could not fully comprehend that supreme pain, for she was still a child, and furthermore, she would never be a mother. But she strived to, her head dizzy as it struggled to find a way to convey the feelings of a mother confronted by the sight of her immolated son: Jesus of Nazareth, God become man, who took upon himself the cruelty, contempt and infamy of the men of his time in order to free—and shield against the insult of original sin—the men of future times and the souls of the living and of the faithful deceased.

It was this imaginative leap that led her to recall Saint Eulàlia's torments, which had made such an impression on her and quite possibly had caused her stomach cramps. She envisioned Saint Eulàlia in her starched white dress, grazing her thirteen geese that were also white, not thirteen ugly, sad, savage geese like the thirteen torments, but thirteen merry, pretty geese, like Saint Eulàlia's thirteen years. In her mind, Saint Eulàlia resembled a beautiful girl named Emília who had taken singing and sol-fa lessons with her in the children's section of the Orfeó Català choral group. What could have become of her? Sister Concepció had missed her friend since entering the convent, and she prayed that the war had not destroyed Emília's house or her life or those of her brothers and sisters and parents. And now, as she read the Stabat Mater poem and tried to imagine the lacerated soul of the Mother of God kneeling before the cross, the name, face and voice of her own mother came to her. She missed her and wished with all her heart that she were there, protecting her now when she was feeling so poorly, tending to her, caressing her with those hands that were strong and soft and always smelled of jasmine. She started reciting the Lord's Prayer to implore that no harm would befall her mother or father and that one fine day the three of them would find themselves at home again, reunited, she hand-in-hand with her beloved mother, far from the convent, far from her cell and the Stabat Mater and the verses of Jacopone da Todi. She realized again that she would have to confess and ask for forgiveness for these thoughts that went against everything His Excellency the bishop and the mother abbess expected of her—if they indeed expected the same of her. Could there perhaps be in the bishop's absurd request a trial that she must endure in order to gain the salvation of her soul? If that was the case, what sin was she guilty of that she now had to face such an extreme task?

Of all the torments that Diocletian had ordered to be inflicted upon Saint Eulàlia, the mutilation of her breasts had upset Sister Concepció the most. Hers had just begun to grow, and this too caused her myriad doubts, for on the one hand she was pleased and on the other ashamed of being pleased, and she supposed she was committing a sin when she sometimes stopped to observe herself as she was undressing for bed. If they cut off her breasts to prove her love and trust in God, would she be able to bear it, as His Excellency had asked her? She wasn't at all sure, and this made her feel doubly guilty: both for having lied to His Excellency the bishop in order to please him and because all those stories of affliction and pain—like Saint Eulàlia's or those sung in the Stabat Mater—didn't spark in her the wish to become a martyr if that moment ever presented itself. It only produced in her an uncontrollable urge to weep and an upset stomach that couldn't be alleviated.

Again she thought she heard a noise at her door, and again she raised her head and rubbed her eyes. But it was to no avail because the flame from the candle was starting to die and gave off a flickering light that only lit up the candlestick itself and part of her; a step beyond her cot nothing could be distinguished in the darkness. She felt a growing chill, similar to what she felt when she descended the steps to the cellar to fetch butter or bits of lard that the nuns stored there, a chill that intensified with each step so she had to tuck her hands in her armpits so they wouldn't be stiffen cold. The novice couldn't rid herself of the presentiment that near her, in her cell, perhaps right beside her, lurked an intrusive presence that was not the mice that had been troubling her earlier.

All at once she felt a dampness oozing between her thighs, warm and slippery like bad thoughts, or like the bile someone spits up after vomiting too much. Frightened, she reached down and touched something wet; she held her hand to the light of the dying candle to see what it was. The sticky liquid that stained her fingertips was not the green color of bile, but the dense, dark red of blood. The jabbing pain in her stomach grew stronger, and a sudden, uncomfortable warmth ran up her back and chest, all the way to her face, and she could feel that it was flushed.

She covered her head with the pillow and wept even louder, with a new sadness.

PART 2
Surge et Ambula

HE WROTE:

The extravagant notion that sunlight is lethal to a vampire is not accurate. Nevertheless, it is a belief that is worth promoting as it allows me to move about in broad daylight without arousing suspicion, not even among those who give the possibility of my existence the benefit of the doubt. But, much like the superstition regarding the cross and other Christian icons, this too is without any basis or connection to reality.

As far as I know, the origin of this error can be traced to ancient China. The writings of Chi Wu-Li state that the bodies of the dead should not be buried until after they begin to decompose. In this way, the demon known as Chiang-shih is prevented from entering the body and taking possession of the *po*, which is how Li refers to the human soul. Putrefaction as a salve against infestation. In addition to being foolish, this is a rather crude belief, but it prevailed for many centuries in a large number of countries across different continents.

The practice consisted of exposing the corpses to the sun to accelerate decomposition. But sometimes the body became mummified, and then it had to be burned, which is what should have been done in the first place. Recent authors such as Faivre maintain that both the body and the coffin should be destroyed in the fire, at the same time and on the same day. Others, such as Willoughby-Meade, warn that no cat should be allowed in the same room as a corpse because if it were to jump on the body it might transmit the essence of the tiger to the *po* that is still inside the body, transforming it into a Hyperborean. Of course, this too is pure childish ideation with no rhyme or reason.

On the other hand, old Chi Wu-Li was right when he stressed the importance of absolutely preventing any natural light, whether from the sun or the moon, from falling directly on a body once it has been possessed by the Chiang-shih, as this might revitalize the demon and infuse the body with enough vigor to make the dead rise from the tomb. That is why coffins were sealed and all manner of precautions were taken to prevent even a single ray of sun or moonlight from filtering through. And I must stress again how right they were to take these measures, because, contrary to what superstition holds, light not only does not destroy the Hyperborean, but it imparts to it a surplus of strength, energy and appetite. Ancient Chinese chronicles also tell of known cases of a single Hyperborean drinking the blood of more than two dozen people in the course of one day—and I believe them.

Some poets have approached the subject of vampires'
exposure to the sunlight in a veiled fashion. Among them
I have always had a special predilection for William Blake
and his splendid poem about chimney sweepers:

> When my mother died I was very young,
> And my father sold me while yet my tongue
> Could scarcely cry " 'weep! 'weep! 'weep! 'weep!"
> So your chimneys I sweep, and in soot I sleep.
>
> There's little Tom Dacre, who cried when his head,
> That curled like a lamb's back, was shaved: so I said,
> "Hush, Tom! never mind it, for when your head's bare,
> You know that the soot cannot spoil your white hair."
>
> And so he was quiet; and that very night,
> As Tom was a-sleeping, he had such a sight!
> That thousands of sweepers, Dick, Joe, Ned, and Jack,
> Were all of them locked up in coffins of black.
>
> And by came an angel who had a bright key,
> And he opened the coffins and set them all free;
> Then down a green plain leaping, laughing, they run,
> And wash in a river, and shine in the sun.

They wash in the river and shine in the sun. Magnificent! At the end, the need to dissimulate forced Blake to
add another stanza with a bit of clumsy moralizing about

doing one's duty. But anyone so inclined will understand the story of this poor Tom who, like his fellow chimney sweepers, rests locked in a coffin until an angel comes and frees them all. The angel, naturally, is a monster who takes pity on other monsters. And God, the gigantic monster burrowed in the folds of the universe, watches with pleasure as the children leave their coffins and disperse among mankind. And smiles.

God's smile before the impending atrocity is phosphorescent, and that strange glow is the same that courses through the streets of Barcelona at sunset. Some still stubbornly confuse this glimmer with the light of hope, and they will approach it only to meet their own death. The resemblance between men and moths never ceases to amaze me: fascinated, blinded, moths cannot resist the temptation to approach a light, not realizing that behind it lurks the lizard waiting to devour them. I am the lizard: I search out places where moths congregate and I become that which they fail to see or pretend not to see—until it is too late.

Confusion and disorder facilitate the passage from life to death, and for that reason bomb shelters are the ideal hunting ground. It is exhilarating to set out, roaming the streets, driven by one's thirst, and suddenly to hear the ominous whistle of the sirens permeating the air. Amid the hordes, I too run to the nearest shelter, which can easily be identified from the street by the multitude of people elbowing each other to gain entrance, like fear-stricken rats fighting to be the first into the nest.

The entire underbelly of this city is festering with people's fear. Fear is an oxide that spreads like briny sea spray and clings to the cobblestone of city squares, the walls of buildings, people's skin, transforming everything it touches into an amorphous, undifferentiated mass, a poison-impregnated ball rolling down the slope toward extinction. Fear gouges out eyes, cuts off tongues, peels the flesh from skeletons, boils the bones until they are shiny and clean. Fear is the acid of the soul, it corrodes without distinction children's dreams and men's desires.

"I WANT YOU to remove him from here, Manuel."

The mother abbess lowered her eyes as she spoke. It was a gesture she made frequently in the presence of her brother, especially when they argued. They had argued since childhood, though she was forbidden to do so. The ravages of Manuel's polio had made their mother overly protective of the little boy, who was five years younger than his sister Isabel. That was the Christian name Sister Micaela of the Holy Sacrament was known by before entering orders and becoming the mother abbess of the Capuchins of Sarrià. She had always been instructed not to disturb her brother, for he was sickly, and a good little girl who loved baby Jesus should never take advantage of the situation: that would only anger baby Jesus. She obeyed, or tried to, but her brother was shrewd as the devil and always managed to make her look bad with lies or tricks that placed her in equivocal situations; he would even hurt himself on purpose in order to blame his sister, who accepted the scolding and spankings without protest. But afterward, she would argue with Manuelet, as their mother called him, even if the argument almost always ended in her being punished yet again. It was a vicious circle that Manuelet knew how to manage with unusual cunning for a boy of five or six.

And now, Manuel Escorza, head of the Department of Investigations of the FAI, sat opposite his sister the mother abbess at the dark, unpolished table of the chapterhouse in the convent in Sarrià. Seated and in profile, Manuel Escorza resembled an ox: large head, domed forehead, slack snout.

He made a sound that verged on sniggering.

"So now you want me to remove him?" he said, clasping his hands together and resting them on the table. "I thought it was an honor for you to have him as a guest, little sister."

The mother abbess glanced up briefly.

"The community is happy to have him here. They believe, because I have told them so, that it is a privilege and a sign of hope. I am the one who wants him gone. I am asking as a favor, Manuel."

"A favor?" huffed Manuel Escorza. "How many favors are you prepared to owe me, little sister? Do you by chance think it a small favor to have you hidden away within these walls, fed and protected—you and the circle of fanatics you have at your orders? What more do you want of me?"

"I never asked you to hide us," the mother abbess responded. "You did so because you wanted to. Or because it was convenient, in order to have a place where His Excellency the bishop could be kept out of sight and looked after. You have never done anything without expecting something in return."

Manuel Escorza banged his fist on the table so hard that his crutches, which had been resting against the edge of the table, slipped and fell to the floor with a crash. The mother abbess was startled by the noise, which reverberated in the echo chamber of the chapterhouse; she stared at the fallen crutches as if they were a pair of dead birds.

"How can you be so ungrateful?" Manuel Escorza's thunderous voice did not seem to match the maimed body from which it issued. "Do you know what they are doing out there," he pointed to the door, "to people like you? Do you know what they are doing?"

"I know they are being killed, Manuel. By people like you."

His sister's serenity did not calm him. "Do you know who I am, little sister?"

"Better than anyone, Manuel." She raised her eyes and this time she did not look down.

"And even so, you come to me with demands," he said with scorn. "I have to admit that it takes guts to do that."

"I am not demanding anything," she corrected him. "I've told you. It's a favor. A favor I'm asking of you."

A moment of disagreeable silence followed. The mother abbess glanced at the portrait of the founder of the order, Saint Eduvigis Ponce de León, which hung on the white wall behind her brother. Manuel had leaned down to pick up his crutches, assuming a ridiculous posture, the lifts on his shoes pointing up. The mother abbess recalled that, according to the Book of Saints, Eduvigis Ponce de León received several visits from the devil, but she was always able to reject the temptations. The book also noted that on more than one occasion, swept aloft in a mystical rapture, she had even levitated.

Muttering expletives, Manuel Escorza managed to get back on his feet. He again leaned the crutches against the table and asked, "And why should I remove the bishop?"

It took the mother abbess a few seconds to emerge from her pensiveness. "I don't like him," she said simply.

"You don't like him."

"Yes, that's right."

Manuel Escorza let out a sigh of impatience, his mouth filling with little bubbles of saliva. "Could you be a little more specific?"

The mother abbess knew she had no choice but to explain. "I don't know what happened to that man during his days as a fugitive," she began, "or what they did to him after he was arrested . . ."

The comment annoyed Manuel Escorza.

"That is not what I asked."

". . . but his behavior isn't normal. We have a young girl

in the convent, thirteen years old, a refugee we took in as a novice. She has a truly special gift for music. His Excellency the bishop has commissioned her to compose a musical piece, a Stabat Mater."

"A what?"

"A genre of sacred music," the mother abbess explained. "No matter. What I wish to say is that the girl is not ready for that, but it's obviously not for me to oppose His Excellency's plans. But apart from that—and may God forgive me—there's something strange about the interest His Excellency has taken in this novice."

"Strange?" repeated Manuel Escorza impishly.

The mother abbess crossed herself, first on the forehead to exorcise evil thoughts, then on the mouth to cleanse her words.

"As a result of the anguish caused by the assignment, she's taken ill and is now confined to her cell. A couple of nights ago I heard footsteps and peered down the corridor to see who it was. His Excellency was standing guard by the girl's cell. May God forgive me, but I think the war has unbalanced the man and he could be dangerous for a community like ours." She crossed herself again and looked her brother in the eyes, tense. "This is why I ask you to kindly take him from the convent."

Manuel Escorza broke out in a greasy laugh. "Now that's a good one! His Excellency the bishop of Barcelona has succumbed to the charms of a gifted little girl! What do your sacred texts say about that, sister?"

The mother abbess did not budge from her chair. She glanced at the portrait of Eduvigis Ponce de León and prayed that the saint would help her show restraint. "I knew you would make fun of this, Manuel. But will you do as I ask? Once more, I implore you." She swallowed. "I'm prepared to beg, if that's what you want."

But he was choking with laughter and wouldn't have been able to answer even if he had wanted to. He alternated between hilarity and a coughing fit, laughing in that peculiar way of his that Isabel Escorza—the mother abbess—detested. Obtuse and hurtful, it was the same laugh that Manuelet spit out every time he succeeded in getting his sister slapped, her cheeks scarlet, or when she was punished and not allowed out to play for a week because she had hurt her poor, sick little brother. And the little brother laughed and laughed, obscenely, after crying crocodile tears. She found his laugh repugnant, hated it to the point that it evoked thoughts as bitter and violent as the laugh itself—thoughts so dark that she would have to repent and ask the forgiveness of baby Jesus and the Mother of God and all the saints. And there sat Manuelet, misshapen like the devil himself, bent over with laughter, his face covered with snot and saliva, relishing his superiority in the game that pitted the two against each other, a game of life or death.

There was a knock at the door to the chapterhouse.

"May I come in, Comrade Escorza?" asked a man's voice from the other side.

The cripple stopped laughing and adopted an authoritarian pose. "Enter, Sirga," he ordered.

The heavy walnut door opened slowly and Sirga appeared on the threshold, his red hair covered by a calico cap, which he removed at once when he realized he was in the presence of the mother abbess.

"Comrade Escorza, Mother Abbess," he greeted them with a nod.

"You can call her Isabel, which is her name. And put on your cap. Have you finished unloading?"

"Yes, Comrade Escorza."

"Did you remember the oil?"

"Six bottles of oil that I left in the larder, Comrade Escorza."

"And the preserves?"

"A barrel of herring and two dozen salted cod, Comrade Escorza."

"And the flour?"

"One sack of barley and three of wheat, Comrade Escorza."

Manuel Escorza turned to his sister, who looked stiff, still awaiting an answer to her request.

"There you are, sister: everything you and your fanatics need for your own upkeep. Sirga procured it all on the black market, on my orders. You know what that means, don't you, sister?"

The Mother Abbess shook her head. "No, I don't know, Manuel. You tell me."

He leaned across the table until his large face was next to the nun's. "That means it's war booty, sister. Obtained by robbing and pillaging. Men have died so that you nuns and that girl-crazed bishop could cheerfully feast on all of this. It's the multiplication of the loaves and fishes, sister. How does that strike you? Your little brother also performs miracles. Think you could reserve a chapter for me in the sacred scriptures?"

He erupted into particularly offensive laughter; and even though the mother abbess had promised herself that she would not give him the satisfaction of seeing her cry, she couldn't keep two tears, thick as the veins on one's wrist, from rolling down her cheek. Manuel Escorza stopped laughing, as if he had a sudden cramp, and addressed Sirga: "So, have you finished your job?"

"I've finished, Comrade Escorza," the redhead said, his cap still in his hands.

"Well, let's go then." He glanced at his pocket watch. "We still have to put in an appearance at the meeting at the Tostadero, and time is short."

"Yes, Comrade Escorza."

Sirga grasped Manuel Escorza under the armpits to ease him out of the chair and get him onto his crutches, then moved ahead to hold the door for him. Manuel Escorza left the chapterhouse to the sound of his older sister's sobs and the screeching of his shoe lifts dragging along the floor.

———

"Ouch!" exclaimed Doctor Pellicer.

"Mind your head, doctor," warned Judge Carbonissa. "The ceiling is quite low."

"Thanks. If you hadn't mentioned it I would never have noticed," the doctor said sarcastically, rubbing his head with his left hand.

His right hand gripped the torch he was carrying even tighter as his vision tried to adjust to the quivering, unreliable light. The judge led the way, three steps in front of him, and Doctor Pellicer struggled to keep up. At the bottom of the ladder they had reached a sort of crypt—vaulted ceiling, unhewn-stone walls, half-paved ground—where the judge had some torches ready, which he lit with a match and a gasoline-dipped wick. Then, without wasting a moment, they had crouched down and started along the passageway that began on one side of the crypt. A few seconds later they could no longer hear the distant sound of exploding bombs.

The passageway was wide enough for a large man like Doctor Pellicer to move without any problem, but the ceiling was very low, to the extent that in some places the two men were obliged to kneel and crawl. The ground was full of weeds and scree, and it was easy to twist an ankle if one did not tread carefully. Though the entire crossing took less than three minutes, it seemed interminable to Doctor Pellicer; he was about to ask if they had much farther to go when he heard Judge Carbonissa's reassuring voice: "We've arrived. Wait right there and come when I call you."

The doctor did as he was told and watched Judge Carbonissa disappear behind a bend. He waited, crouching in the strangest of positions beneath the light of the torch. A short while later a glimmer reached him from beyond the curve, gradually becoming more intense. Soon a bright glow flooded the passageway, making the torch unnecessary, and Doctor Pellicer heard the judge: "Follow the light, doctor!"

Again he did as he was told. He made his way around the bend and discovered that a few meters in front of him the passageway opened into a brightly-lit natural gallery. He entered it and came to a sudden halt, his mouth agape in astonishment.

His reaction was more than warranted. The short gallery gave way to a grotto of considerable size, large enough for the ceiling to vanish into the darkness overhead. The entire ground level, however—from the gallery to the end of the grotto—was brightly lit by lanterns that had been carefully placed two steps apart. There was not a single unlit corner.

In that light, Judge Carbonissa looked even taller and thinner than usual, and his shadow on the ground was as long as a wolf's howl in the dead of night. He stood there motionless, a nondescript expression on his gaunt face, beside a huge object covered top to bottom with white sheets.

The doctor looked around, pleased to discover a space in which a morgue, similar to the one in the Gothic

Quarter, seemed to have been combined with the work-
shop of a craftsman of exceptional skill. There were
neatly aligned and duly tagged morgue slabs, as well as
a couple of tables covered with crimson velvet cloths,
atop which were displayed a set of surgical instruments:
scissors, saws, scalpels, needles, drills, in every imagin-
able shape and size, ready to be used. The judge had
devoted one of the smoothest walls to three hanging
panels, each holding, respectively, the tools necessary
for a cabinetmaker, a blacksmith, and a woodcarver:
mallets, hammers, pliers, double-blade mason hammers,
awls, chisels, gouges, screws, saws, concave and convex
gouges, mortise chisels . . . There was even a forge and
an anvil for shaping metals, and a collection of templates
for pieces that would be made from the different kinds
of wood—oak, jacaranda, walnut, cedar, cherry—piled
in separate stacks in a hollow used as a woodshed. But
what most impressed Doctor Pellicer were the two huge
tubs filled with formaldehyde; he couldn't imagine how
they had managed to transport them from the outside
world down to those catacombs.

"I see it was no exaggeration when you said you had
left nothing to improvisation."

A slight nod. "Shall we proceed?"

"Please," replied the doctor, rubbing his hands with
glee.

The judge jerked the sheets off the object and let them
slide to the ground, uncovering an enormous black horse.

It was magnificent: a powerful neck and loin, perfect belly, long legs that seemed to have been shaped by a sculptor's chisel, and a dull-black mane and tail that contrasted admirably with the amber sheen of its coat. Its countenance, on the other hand, reflected a rigid stillness, and its eyes had a glassy, remote look, like the pupils of a dead horse. *Flesh of misfortune.* The phrase again crossed the doctor's mind. But he couldn't avoid an irrepressible emotion, a mixture of pride, admiration and gratitude that flooded his thoughts and spirit.

"My dear Doctor Pellicer—I give you Hadaly!" the judge exclaimed.

The doctor slowly circled the beautiful animal, stopping frequently to admire certain details—the precise contours of the thighs and legs, the meticulous outline of the ear, the texture of the horsehair, the delicate crafting of the muzzle and nostrils—and to hail its perfection by articulating occasional, indecipherable sounds.

"So?" Judge Carbonissa asked, curious.

"It's . . ." stammered Doctor Pellicer without taking his eyes off the horse. "It's even more perfect than I had dreamed . . . I . . ."

The judge took the doctor by the arm and tugged on him gently. He picked up a scalpel from one of the tables with surgical instruments and held it to the horse's ribs, as the animal stood there scrutinizing the void with eyes of ice.

"Our automaton, dear doctor, has four constituent parts. The first, the internal one, is what I refer to as the living system, comprising balance, the capacity for movement, the voice, the flexing of limbs, the various reactions to basic stimuli, and so forth. In a word, what in a horse we could call the soul, if it had one."

Doctor Pellicer followed the judge's explanations with great attention.

"The second part," he continued, "is the plastic insulation, a covering that is designed to function as a frame, separated from the flesh and the dermis. It is a structure with flexible articulations and holds the living system firmly in place."

"A frame for the skeleton of sorts."

"Precisely," the judge corroborated. "And, moving right along, the third part is the flesh and all that goes with it: the bone structure, venous network, muscles, digestive and sexual organs—in short all bodily systems. This is where the human remains proved to be essential, doctor, the parts you were kind enough to offer me, selected and classified. I have combined them with animal offal from slaughterhouses and farms, although, since the war began, human remains are more plentiful and easier to come by than animal matter." He shrugged in resignation. "So, you see, the flesh covers the insulation and adheres to it, emulating the features of the body on which it is modeled: a three-time winner in the trotting category at the Ascot racecourse."

"A perfect cybernetic organism," murmured Doctor Pellicer, nodding in admiration.

"Yes, indeed." Judge Carbonissa smiled and cleared his throat. "And now we come to the fourth and final component of the automaton, which is none other than the dermis. Here we find resolved outer aspects such as the coat and the oral system, as well as facial expressions, the mimicking of muzzle movements, every aspect related to the eyes and the animal's gaze . . ."

"The only flaw I detect," interrupted the doctor, "is that its gaze is so inanimate, so . . ."

". . . so dead, perhaps?" the judge suggested. "Yours is a valid observation, but that's because you haven't witnessed our creature in action."

"A feat I'm impatient to see!"

"You will shortly, doctor," the judge said, shifting his scalpel a few centimeters. "But first I would like to mention Hadaly's lungs, made from an alloy of gold and aluminum. They are in fact two phonographs placed at a convex angle so as to coincide with the center of the animal's thorax. They function like the cylinders of a printing press through which a roll of paper is circulated; in this case, however, what is transmitted between the phonographs is the entire spectrum of sounds characteristic of an adult horse, recorded on a strip of tin: Hadaly thus neighs, paws the ground, snorts, in perfect concert with his movements and the situation." Judge Carbonissa stood on tiptoes. "Forgive my vanity, but I am especially proud of this mechanism."

"I am very impressed," Doctor Pellicer conceded.

"Would you mind waiting a few more moments? The most impressive thing is yet to come."

He ran his hand along the horse's back, stopping at a certain point to flip a switch; the clicking sound was clearly audible to the doctor in the silence of the grotto. The automaton emerged from its dormancy at once and with the elegance and grace of a fine competition horse shook its head and feet as though loosening them up. It pawed the ground and neighed briefly with what sounded like impatience. Doctor Humbert Pellicer, who did not miss a detail, was especially fascinated by the brusque transformation of the eyes: the gelid deathliness that had troubled him only a moment before had given way to undeniable vivacity. And yet . . . The doctor planted himself in front of the horse; he thought he had noticed a reflection in Hadaly's pupils and wanted to investigate. Hadaly lowered his majestic head with well-tamed docility and gave the doctor a look he would have been hard-pressed to describe: that gaze, he would have said, was not completely animal, nor was it exactly human. Suddenly his brain lit up with the word he was searching for, the objectionable word that had been haunting him since he had first seen the automaton: monster.

"Hadaly! Let's go, Hadaly!" cried the judge.

As if it were the meekest, best-trained saddle horse, Hadaly broke into a slow, graceful trot and made his way around the perimeter of the grotto. The great empty space reverberated with the echo of horseshoes clopping against the ground, and Hadaly raised his neck with a distinction that revealed perhaps a trace of petulance. The glow of the lanterns illuminated the automaton's gait and multiplied its shadow on the ground and walls of the grotto. No one on this earth, thought the doctor, would have been able to distinguish Hadaly from a real horse: After all, what exactly was a real horse? Why were the only true forms and conditions those that man found already created, never the ones he himself might create? What could this magnificent animal—whose evolution filled him with pride—possibly begrudge any horse, in any stable in the world? Could it not be that creation was simply a blueprint, a rough draft, and the mission of the human species was none other than to perfect and complete the divine template? Be fruitful and multiply and subdue the earth.

Hadaly had moved to the entrance of the gallery in order to gain speed before racing at a gallop to the far end of the grotto, from which he emerged again at a trot, arrogant and lordly.

Yes, some would dare to label Hadaly a monster. Many would consider Judge Carbonissa and Doctor Pellicer monsters for making use of human remains to build Hadaly. They would fail to understand that the glory of the project lay precisely therein: that its beauty resided in taking discarded human body parts, preserving it from putrefaction, and transforming it into raw material for the creation of new life.

The doctor lit a cigarette and, as if the smoke from the first draw had got into his eyes, a couple of tears rolled down his reddened cheeks to his double-chin. He dried them with a linen handkerchief he took from his pocket. "We have fulfilled the mandate of the species, my esteemed judge. Wasn't this what Darwin was referring to? At a time when everyone insists on death, we have summoned life . . ."

". . . and the resurrection of the flesh," added the judge with a wry smile.

"Well, well!" exclaimed Doctor Pellicer, blowing a thin stream of smoke out of his mouth. "Here we go again, my dear judge."

"We stand in the presence of a living being created from other, dead beings, doctor; we have devised it and created it. And you still dare question the existence of phenomena that unfold at the threshold between life and death?"

"Not in the least. I am simply respecting another threshold: the one that separates science from magic. Hadaly is the fruit of science, not of some form of obscurantism. You and I both know that to be a fact."

The automaton approached the two men and started circling them like an attentive pet.

"Precisely," Judge Carbonissa agreed, still smiling. "What I meant is that I believe I am in a position to state that the success of Hadaly cannot be explained by purely scientific means."

"Is that so?" asked the doctor, who also maintained a patient smile. "And what other logic is in play here? Have you consulted a glass ball? Have you had your palms read, your cards, perhaps?"

The judge gestured to indicate that the conversation was futile. He walked over to the automaton and stroked its back again; once more a click was heard, and Hadaly's body instantly froze. Having admired him in the glory of motion, Doctor Pelliver was even more troubled now by the stiffness of his limbs and the return of the icy lack of expression in the eyes. But that did not keep him from pressing the matter.

"You see? It is a switch that allows you to activate and deactivate Hadaly. Not some spell, not some ritualistic formula."

The judge pressed his tongue against the roof of his mouth. "You're determined to make fun of me, doctor. I don't reproach you for this, but I can't say I agree either." He pointed the scalpel at the doctor before adding: "I am merely heeding the precept that no possibility should be dismissed out of hand. For example, in the case of the murder the other day in Pension Capell . . ."

The doctor opened his eyes wide and raised his eyebrows. "Yes, I know what you mean. And you also know my opinion on that."

"It's not exactly a matter of subjective opinion, doctor. Testimonies regarding the existence of vampires abound in all known cultures and go back to the earliest of times."

"Fine, fine." The doctor lingered over the last of his cigarette. "But I still believe that this vampire of yours, the one that killed Brother Gendrau and the boy and drank their blood, is not some creature from the afterlife, but a flesh-and-blood degenerate very much of this world. Like all the other cases of vampirism we hear about. The rest are simply tales to frighten small children. You want to bet?"

"I would never make a bet with you, doctor," exclaimed the judge with a hearty laugh. "Besides, this is a matter for our dear Superintendent Muñoz and our dear Brother Darder to elucidate, isn't it?"

"You're right," conceded the doctor. "And, then of course," he glanced at the automaton and had to repress a shudder, "we have Hadaly. Our hands are full."

"It's a real shame that this stupid war had to get in the way of Hadaly's progress."

"You're right again, judge. Do you think the bombing has stopped now?"

"**COMRADE! TELL THE** busboy to come and take our order; when we're parched we're good for nothing!"

The militiaman made a snorting sound as he sniffled, rose from the table and left the private dining room to look for a waiter.

"And tell him to make it snappy, our brothers here don't have all day either. Isn't that so?"

The man giving orders was Antoni Ordaz, pleased with his role of big wheel. He was running the show at the meeting at the Tostadero, and he exuded satisfaction. Ordaz was accompanied by the militiaman who had just stood up—a young volunteer in the surveillance patrols, a man everyone called "Burntface" because he had fallen into the brazier when he was little and half of his face was scarred—and by Comrade Gil Portela from Safe-Conducts. They represented Aureli Fernández, who had delegated the running of the meeting to Antoni Ordaz.

"Actually, we aren't in very much of a hurry." Brother Lacunza dared a smile that attempted—in vain—to transmit cordiality.

Silence again prevailed in the private room. The men were seated on either side of a rectangular table with chairs around it. None of them seemed to have anything to say. Finally Gil Portela spoke up. "I thought there would only be three of them," he said brusquely, without addressing anyone in particular.

He was referring to the presence of Brother Darder, who in the end had decided to accompany Brothers Plana and Lacunza and Adjutant Émile Aragou to the meeting with the FAI representatives. Actually, Brother Plana had already notified the anarchists the previous day that Brother Darder would be joining them, and he took the opportunity to inform them that the religious was related to the Republican mayor of Palma de Mallorca. So Gil Portela was in fact abreast of this addition and was merely trying to put more pressure on his interlocutors. And he succeeded.

Brother Darder, his voice hoarse, offered, "If my presence is an inconvenience, you have only—"

Brother Lacunza hurried to interrupt: "Brother Darder is—"

But both men were cut short by Antoni Ordaz, who made a hand gesture dismissing the matter. Brother Plana was hunched over, as always, a vague, vacant look on his face. The pale, sullen adjutant remained hieratic at his end of the table.

Burntface returned with a waiter and they all ordered drinks and coffee. When the waiter had left, Ordaz resumed speaking, his expression hardened. "Senyors," he said, solemnly, "I assume that the persons here present assert that they are who they say they are, and that this meeting takes place in the absence of observers and spies."

Before Antoni Ordaz had finished speaking, Gil Portela had reached into the inner pocket of his jacket and removed a revolver which he placed on the table. Burntface, standing beside him, also took out the gun he was carrying at his waist and placed it beside Gil Portela's. The weapons were identical—nine millimeter Astra 400s—and their appearance was galvanizing. Brother Darder glanced at Brother Plana with alarm, but the latter looked away. Adjutant Aragou cleared his throat.

"I think that is unnecessary," Brother Lacunza said, chin-pointing to the weapons.

Antoni Ordaz sat up stiffly in his chair. "It's not a matter of what you think, brother. I want all of you to know that we're not fooling around here. Many of our comrades are paying for fascist injustices with prison and torture, and your Church gives these dealings their blessing. Many others have paid with their lives. Our desire for retaliation against the powerful is great. And it is just."

A silence as thick as tar came over the room again. The waiter entered with the drinks and froze when he saw the guns on the table.

"You," Gil Portela snapped at him, "serve the drinks and scram."

His forehead and sideburns pearling with drops of sweat, the boy set each glass and cup in front of the correct person, without making any mistakes, then turned and left. The drinks and the two guns in the center of the table formed a sinister still life. Silence continued to rule the meeting, as if each participant was locked inside a bell jar.

"Very well, then!" Antoni Ordaz suddenly pounded the table, making the cups clink. "Now that we've gotten the introductions out of the way, what do you have to say, senyors?"

Brother Lacunza breathed out through his nose and unfolded a paper he had prepared. Circumspectly, he read the statement that the Marist Congregation of Barcelona had composed the previous evening:

"We come to the meeting requested by the FAI with the hope of reaching an agreement. In the last few days we

have received news that thirty-six Marists have been
taken prisoners in various locations, and our community fears and prays for their fate. Before negotiations
may proceed, as a preliminary condition, we must
insist that surveillance patrols cease conducting arrests
and that they free the prisoners presently being held
in the Generalitat's detention centers. Furthermore, we
demand that the safety of the brothers lodged in pen-
sions or private homes be ensured; we suspect that the
Department of Investigations has blacklisted them and
we fear that sooner or later they will all suffer the same
fate. If you agree to our conditions, we are willing to
reach an economic arrangement whereby the Marist
Brothers will be allowed to leave the country, along
with the seminarians and students who so desire."

He had read the communiqué fast, with no pauses, as
a child might recite a poem, but with a steady voice.
Antoni Ordaz looped one thumb around the other, seemingly pleased by what he had just heard. As no one spoke,
Brother Lacunza believed it necessary to broach the main
argument.

"I would like to reiterate the loyalty of our congregation
to the institutions of the Catalan government. Adjutant
Émile Aragou and I, in the name of our Provincial Superior,
guarantee the delivery in cash of the amount of money
decided upon here at this table, up to a maximum of two
hundred thousand French francs."

Burntface let out a whistle. Gil Portela couldn't help

but reveal an incipient smile. Antoni Ordaz breathed deeply and squinted, as if looking into the sun. Taking evil pleasure in the religious's predicament, he said, "Well then, brothers. You might be selling your skin, but you are selling it at a good price. No doubt about it."

None of the Marists said a word, knowing they could not allow themselves the luxury of responding to provocations. Gil Portela pulled a cigar out of thin air and lit it ostentatiously; the room quickly filled with smoke.

Brother Lacunza plopped his elbows on the table. "This is all we are able to offer you, senyors."

Enveloped by the smoke from Gil Portela's cigar, Ordaz delivered his judgment: "It should suffice."

Brothers Lacunza and Darder exchanged looks of relief. Brother Plana raised his eyes to the ceiling as if thanking God, thereby exposing his short, delicate neck, which recalled that of a ferret or a genet.

As if he had just received the awaited signal, Adjutant Aragou broke his silence to address the anarchists: "The FAI, or perhaps even the Generalitat itself, will need to resolve the issue of bank controls."

"That shouldn't be a problem," said Gil Portela scornfully. "When the time comes, we could open up the border crossing at La Jonquera. Under strict surveillance, naturally."

"Hold on, don't be in such a rush." Antoni Ordaz was annoyed that Gil Portela had taken the reins. "I assume, brothers, that you have already given some thought to the evacuation procedure."

Brother Lacunza nodded. "The students and seminarians must be given priority. The ones in Casa de Les Avellanes in Balaguer should be the first to leave in view of their desperate situation. The second evacuation would be for all the religious we are able to locate and who wish to join us."

"How many people are we speaking of?" asked Gil Portela.

"Before the beginning of the war the provincial community had seven hundred and seventeen religious. We have no way of knowing exactly how many there are now."

"Bloody hell!" exclaimed Burntface, furious. "We got to get all these blasted crows out of Spain? Come on, now. Let's take the money and tell'em to beat it."

The florid outburst unnerved Brother Lacunza.

"We do not have the money at present," he said. "Only if we reach an agreement will Adjutant Aragou return to Lyon to procure it at the headquarters of the Marist institution and bring the money back to Barcelona to make the payment." Then, in a quick, low voice, as if saying the rosary, he added: "And if it wouldn't be too much to ask, would you kindly refrain from using such language?"

Suddenly, as if in a dream, Burntface emerged from within the effluvia of his cigar, grabbed one of the pistols lying on the table, sat down next to Brother Lacunza and, pointing it at his head, whispered: "Mind repeating what you just said, you little bastard? I'm not sure I understood you, and right now I'm wondering if you are worth the bullet that would blow your brains out."

"Enough, comrade," ordered Antoni Ordaz. "Put the gun down and return to your place. Now."

But instead, in one sweeping motion Gil Portela seized his own gun and aimed it between Brother Plana's eyes.

"Portela, what are you doing? Not me . . ." Brother Plana stuttered.

Gil Portela exhaled a puff of smoke along with a corrosive laugh. Killing off a couple of those fools and letting the other two walk so they could convey the FAI's conditions to their provincial superior suddenly struck him as the best way to conclude the ridiculous meeting. Portela was unaware that Brother Plana was an FAI informant; it was all the same to him to shoot Plana or one of the other Marists.

Ordaz saw he was rapidly losing control of the situation. "You pig-headed idiots! Are you deaf? Guns on the table and everyone back to their seats!"

"Do as he orders, guns down, comrades." No one had noticed Manuel Escorza's arrival; he was standing at the door to the private dining room, leaning on his crutches. Nor had they noticed Sirga, who trailed him like a faithful dog. Burntface quietly put his gun away and Gil Portela placed his on the table again. As for Antoni Ordaz, he silently cursed Escorza for the gift of ubiquity that he loved to brag about.

"Comrade Escorza! To what do we owe this

unexpected pleasure?" Ordaz asked in a sarcastic tone that was clearly inappropriate. He was still hesitant to accept the obvious turn in the situation.

"You're not going to ask me to take a seat?" inquired the impassive Escorza.

Antoni Ordaz was forced to surrender his chair; he stood up and flattened himself against the wall to allow Manuel Escorza to get past him and sit down, which he did with considerable difficulty. Ordaz remained standing, as did Sirga and Burntface; he realized it was futile to expect Gil Portela—who had snuffed out his cigar in case it bothered Escorza—to offer him his chair. Just like that, Ordaz had been demoted in the chain of command, and in such an organic, irrevocable manner that it took him a few seconds to realize what had happened. Even so, he still had the guts to hazard another question: "I assume that Comrade Fernández is aware of your presence here . . ."

The grimace that contorted Manuel Escorza's knobby face might have been read as a sardonic smile in any normal person, but in him it seemed more like an expression of pain, and it intimidated Antoni Ordaz all the more. Brother Darder was examining with fascination the ugliness of the man whom nature had mocked, while Brothers Plana and Lacunza preferred to avoid observing his features. Adjutant Aragou remained silent. As far as Ordaz's inappropriateness, Manuel Escorza did not consider it necessary to dignify it with his opinion regarding Aureli

Fernández and the criteria used to run the Department of Investigations. He simply gave a long, loud burp.

"These gentlemen here must be the Marists with whom we have begun negotiations, no?" he asked.

"That is correct, comrade," confirmed Antoni Ordaz, like a pupil chastised by his teacher.

Brother Lacunza surmised he was in the presence of a high-ranking officer and immediately tried to establish direct communication with him. "Senyor, my name is Trifón Lacunza. I am here as the spokesman representing the Marist congregation in Barcelona. We would like—"

"I have no interest in knowing who you are or what you do, and none whatsoever in discovering what you and your people are after," Manuel Escorza spat out. "You," he said, pointing to Gil Portela, expressly ignoring Antoni Ordaz, "what are the conditions?"

"Two sets of evacuations, first the kids in Balaguer, then the cassocks. We are speaking of two hundred thousand francs, but Mister Fuckface," he said pointing to Adjutant Aragou, "has to go to Lyon to get the dough."

Manuel Escorza's moved his large head slightly, in a gesture of understanding. He turned to Burntface. "Problems?" He glanced at the gun the militiaman was carrying in his waistband.

"Nothing much." Burntface's mottled face tensed. "These here brothers think they're real clever," and he gave Brother Plana a hard slap on the back of his neck, making the religious coil like a caterpillar, "and they needed to be reminded of how things work."

Escorza nodded again, making disagreeable slurping sounds with his mouth. He studied the four Marist brothers seated opposite him at the table. "You."

"Are you talking to me?" asked Brother Darder, shaken.

Escorza went straight to the point. "I presume you're the nephew of the mayor of Palma de Mallorca, from the Republican Left Party. Am I right?"

Brother Darder realized his age had given him away. "That's correct."

"They told me about you yesterday, and that's when I decided to show up at today's meeting. I have to admit I was curious about you. So, tell me, how does someone with a godfather like yours end up becoming a priest?"

All eyes were fixed on Brother Darder, expectant. He shifted in his chair, as if each glance were a pinprick, and finally replied, "To be honest, I don't see any contradiction between the two, senyor."

"You don't, huh? And what does your uncle have to say about it?"

"He was the one who paid for my studies at the seminary, senyor. When my father died, his brother, my godfather, took care of my education."

"What's your name?

"Pau Darder."

"Pau Darder and what else?"

"Pau Darder i Serra d'Orfila, senyor."

"Pau Darder i Serra d'Orfila, you are a disgrace to your family . . ."

Brother Darder found the epithet amusing and couldn't repress a sardonic smile.

". . . a disgrace to your family and the scum of the earth," added Manuel Escorza. "You find that amusing? You should know not to laugh, Pau Darder i Serra d'Orfila. Our revolution will crush your filthy, rotten Church, and soon the proletarian brothers of this country will spit on your tombs. You will piss blood, Pau Darder i Serra d'Orfila. Not so funny anymore, huh?"

Brother Darder was silent, as were the others in the dining room. Both factions—even Gil Portela seemed petrified. Manuel Escorza allowed a few moments of silence to lend weight to his words, then said, "We accept your conditions, but we will keep the mayor's little nephew as hostage. We will return him to you safe and sound once you deliver the two hundred thousand francs; if for any reason the money does not arrive, we will kill him. You and you," he said pointing to Burntface and Sirga, "take him away to a safe place and set up shifts to watch him."

Brother Darder opened his mouth to speak, but he was incapable of articulating a single word. Brother Lacunza started to protest, but Burntface silenced him with a slap across the mouth. Adjutant Aragou remained quiet; Brother Plana was in a cold sweat.

"You," Manuel Escorza said, addressing Gil Portela,

"you're in charge of seeing that the Frenchie here goes to Lyon and returns with the money. Work it out with Aureli Fernández and with him," and he pointed to Antoni Ordaz, who stood forgotten in the corner. "From now on I want to be kept informed of all the details of this operation."

Manuel Escorza had not yet finished giving orders when his voice was drowned out by the loud wailing of the air-raid sirens on the street. The meeting was over, the bombing had begun.

HE WROTE:

I heard it coming, the sound gaining on me little by little.

Thirst had brought me out of hiding, the urge to quench it compelling me to show myself on the city's streets.

Aircraft carriers were flying low over downtown Barcelona, dropping bombs like enormous dead animals on Passeig de Gràcia and Gran Via, Plaça de Catalunya and Plaça Urquinaona, on La Rambla, Pelai and Bergara, on Bonsuccés and Tallers. Throngs of people scurried from one place to the next in a furious, meaningless stampede. Bricks and large stones fell from the ruined façades of buildings—rubble projectiles, entire balconies, shattered windows that crushed and dismembered the poor souls below. The fortunate escaped with wounds; others writhed on the ground, moaning as they tried in vain to stanch the bleeding. Soon they were engulfed by the cloud of dust raised by a new deflagration, as thousands of pavement fragments sailed through the air, mixing with mortar and shrapnel, lethal. The smell of charred flesh and fecal waters from burst sewer lines combined into an unbearable stench.

I sheltered in the portal of the Church of Bethlehem on the corner of Carrer del Carme, not so much to shield myself from the bullets as to keep a discreet watch on things.

And then I heard it coming.

Growing more and more audible above the hissing of the bombs.

Above the crackling of the flames.

Above the moans of the dying.

The sound of a galloping horse.

I did not believe it until I had it in front of me: it *was* a galloping horse.

A horse with no horseman. Pounding the ravaged streets, skirting the bodies and mutilated body parts that were strewn everywhere, jumping across the still-smoking craters caused by the explosions, traversing the streets at great speed.

A powerful, swift-moving beast that advanced as though oblivious to the air attack and the demolition of the city. It was a magnificent animal, a great black creature with a powerful neck and back, a perfect belly, long legs that seemed to have been chiseled by the burin of an exceptional sculptor, and a mane and tail a dull shade of ebony that contrasted sublimely with the jet-black of its coat.

As it passed, everything seemed to slow for a fraction of a second, as though even the turmoil of the air strike had been delayed to allow that improbable animal to flaunt itself, granting the dying that lay on the sidewalks one final, privileged sight before breathing their last.

And then it moved in my direction.

Its pace slowed from a gallop to a trot, and it began to circle around as though searching for something.

Suddenly, it looked at me and snorted. And then it came toward me.

It pranced onto the steps of the portal with a solemn gait and lowered its majestic head as it stopped in front of me.

Then it looked me in the eyes.

A long, steady gaze.

A gaze that wasn't exactly that of an animal.

I held it and for a long time we studied each other.

The clamor of war was now muted, distant, as though the droning of airplane engines and the lamentations of its victims issued from another world.

And they did.

For monsters are not part of this world—we do not dwell in a fixed physical plane.

And nevertheless there we stood, beneath the portal of the Church of Bethlehem, on the corner of Carrer del Carme, in plain sight of whoever cared to catch a glimpse of us. But no one did.

We monsters are not part of this world, but we exist and intervene in it, making our way among men, fashioning ourselves through them. Inside them.

The black horse's languid eyes spoke to me of these things. It had recognized me, as I had recognized it.

Poor beast, in the hands of a mocking angel, poor sad, wayward soul.

That artificial body was as imposing as the tragedy it contained.

What kind of mind had deemed it necessary to give life to a monster? What terrible destiny, what infinite sadness, what colossal nostalgia.

The horse finally averted its gaze, took a few steps, and used its head to push open the door that led inside the church.

On the street men continued to die as if on another planet.

I followed the horse into the cool dampness of the temple.

The light that penetrated the nave through the stained glass windows fractured the darkness that reigned inside.

In a side chapel with its wrought-iron grille ajar, an iron mite box awaited donations near a great candle holder that now stood empty. Before the war, candles had burned there for the souls of the faithful departed.

Flicker, flicker, a small flame quivered.

Then I spotted three men and two women.

They had entered the church fleeing the air raid and they now encircled the altar, frightened by our intrusion—mine and the animal's. By the intrusion of the beasts.

The black horse slowly paced the length of the church's central nave, stopping to contemplate the side chapels as if a vestige of comprehension in some recess of its being allowed it to recognize the effigies of the saints.

From time to time it pawed the ground or began to neigh, but then would stop.

The sound of the horseshoes on the marble floor broke the dreary silence that enveloped everything.

Outside, the explosions seemed to have stopped.

The animal approached the altar.

It paused for a few seconds in front of a clergyman's tomb and lowered its head to the grave marker, as though wanting to read the Latin inscription.

Then it turned its attention to the three men and the two women who stood trembling around the altar.

For a moment time stood still.

"Scram! Go away! Scram!"

One of the men, driven not so much by courage as desperation, started shouting and flinging his arms about in an attempt to drive the horse away.

As though heeding the message, the animal slowly turned around and began to move away. It had not taken three steps when it stopped again.

It seemed stunned.

The frenzied man intensified his screaming and approached the horse.

This proved to be a fatal error.

The man's shouting was cut short by a kick that crushed his ribs and sent him flying. He landed on one of the pews of apricot wood arranged in rows in the main nave. His body lay draped over the backrest like a disheveled ragdoll.

He was dead.

The women began to weep; the two remaining men were silent.

The horse gave them a look of boundless sadness.

Then it turned around and slowly walked the length of the aisle in the opposite direction, toward the portal. The grainy light that filtered through the stained glass windows bounced off its back, lending the blackness of its coat a ruby-like sheen.

There was such elegance in its gait, such aplomb in its movements.

Before stepping outside it paused before me once more.

I saw its mouth full of saliva, the death wish in its eyes.

The thought came to me that I wanted to live forever.

I will live forever.

But I understood the tedium that assailed the beast, the exhaustion and disgust of living.

It crossed the threshold of the church into streets sowed with dust and death.

An explosion shook the ground and the stained glass windows.

The bombardment was not over.

I turned toward the altar.

The two men and the two women were still there, weeping and defeated.

I felt a burning thirst.

BROTHER PAU DARDER looked through the iron bars across the lone window in the stifling cell where he was being held and saw the rubble and trash piled up in the alleyway outside. He had no notion of where he was, or whether he was still in Barcelona or outside the city. He had no way of tracking time, and his grasp on it was starting to slip. He had become lost in the confines of a space that did not exceed ten square meters. He was a prisoner in his cell.

The chamber's only furnishings were a straw mattress and a chamber pot. When night fell and darkness overtook the room, Brother Darder's only means of lighting the place was the nub of an altar candle which stood on the cement floor propped against one of the exposed brick walls, the combustion of the wick having left a black streak on the rough surface. Brother Darder found it terribly disconcerting that such a small space could hold such desolation.

During the day, a bit of sunlight found its way into the cell through the glassless window that left him exposed to the elements. Fortunately, a mild autumn was expected and temperatures had thus far not been unmerciful, though, roused by the mistral winds of dawn, he awoke each morning trembling and curled up on the straw mattress. He endured moments of desperation when he would have given anything to see his mother appear in that hellhole, hold him against her fragrant, bountiful breast and, with that comforting smile, whisper to him the adage that had epitomized her approach to life:

If God so deems it . . .

But his mother was not to appear, and Brother Pau Darder was left with no consolation other than to tighten his grip around the gold and silver medallion of Saint Michael his parents had given him for his first communion, which he had worn around his neck since that day more than twenty years ago. He grasped the medallion— in the image, an undefeated Saint Michael the Archangel straddled a serpent speared by his sword—and recited the Lord's Prayer, or the Creed, or the Salve Regina, again and again, until he was able to appease the disquiet that gnawed at him, whereupon he would rise from his pallet and stand in the middle of his cell. But was it all real or had he dreamed it? Every time he fell asleep he entered a nightmare in which he suffered a captivity identical to the one he endured in his waking life. When was he awake and when asleep? When most awake and most asleep? Couldn't it all be a dream? Awake or asleep, could life itself be a dream?

The worst was the hunger. On the first day, he had been left a pot of half-boiled garbanzos and another with water. Neither Sirga nor Burntface, who took turns as watchmen, had thought to tell him he would do well to make them last. By going thirsty, he still had a finger left of water, rarefied and with a tinny taste; the garbanzos, however, were all gone, and his stomach and bowels churned with increasingly painful spasms, as though infested with parasites. At times he chastised himself for having eaten the chickpeas too quickly, but he found comfort in the thought that he couldn't have done otherwise, for in the end he had had to vie for the remaining beans with a pack of small, shiny worms that frequented the pot with an excess of insolence.

The rats, meanwhile, ruled the alleyway that the young Marist glimpsed through the window, scurrying amid the debris and large sacks. Big and fleshy, there were so many of them that they seemed to be constantly multiplying— by bipartition perhaps, thought Brother Darder, like a vast family of oversized amoebas.

A scream coming from outside drew him to the window. For an instant he had hoped to find someone in the alleyway whom he could call on for help. But he understood at once that the sound was just the squealing of a rat bitten by one of its kind in a struggle over a putrid piece of rubbish. The wounded rat tried to fend off its aggressor only to receive another bite to the neck, which was left raw. This did not dissuade it from attempting a counterattack: hobbled and rabid, again and again the rat charged its adversary, who easily dodged the onslaught, waiting for the moment to deliver the final blow.

Presently a multitude of rats appeared and came together in an almost perfect circle around the two combatants. Brother Darder calculated that there were at least thirty rats, fifty, sixty—perhaps a hundred. They had surrounded the wounded rat, which moved in circles, sniffing the air as though trying to quantify the danger.

Finally there was another squeal, from the winner of the combat. It was the awaited signal: the rats pounced on their ill-fated comrade. The victim struggled to defend itself for a few seconds, it bit back at random, now gouging out an eye, now tearing off an ear. But its efforts were in vain. In less than a minute it lay on its back, disemboweled. The voracity of its companions was of a chilling efficacy, but the rat was not yet dead, and from the window Brother Darder could hear its dying groan. In the end, the animal was reduced to a formless, bloody mass that a large, mangy, mottled rat placed in its mouth, no doubt intending to save it for later.

"YOU LOOK UNWELL, superintendent."

"It's that rubbish you're smoking. It makes me nauseous."

Superintendent Muñoz strode to a chair, sat down, and

stretched out his legs. The morgue was illuminated by an oil lamp that hung from a hook and gave off a milky light, like the skin of a cadaver. Doctor Pellicer took another drag on his cigarette.

"Are you on the vampire's trail yet, superintendent?" he inquired in a tone that could have been one of mocking or of sincere interest, it was impossible to tell.

"It's not the cigarette."

"Excuse me?"

The superintendent took a deep breath. "It's not the cigarette that's making me dizzy. It's that I'm not sleeping at night."

The doctor lowered his head in a gesture of understanding. Without putting his cigarette down, he grasped another chair and sat facing the police officer. A pair of feet protruded from a slab, close to his face.

"Suffering from insomnia again? Are you fatigued?"

A speck of badly-ground tobacco crackled. Superintendent Muñoz pressed his brow into his hands and closed his eyes. "It's not insomnia, doctor. I force myself to stay awake."

Doctor Humbert Pellicer looked at him wide-eyed. "What do you mean?"

"I don't want to fall asleep. When I do, the nightmare returns."

The doctor was silent, waiting for an explanation. As it was not forthcoming, he said: "What nightmare?"

The police officer removed his hand from his forehead

and waved it as if swatting away a fly. "Would you mind putting out that cigarette?"

Doctor Pellicer let out a moan of resignation and tossed the half-smoked cigarette on the floor; he squashed it with his shoe, as though it were a poisonous insect. "I'm all ears, superintendent."

"I'm walking in the countryside at night," began Superintendent Muñoz, holding his head in his hands again, his eyes fixed on his knees, his voice monotonous. "Not cultivated land, but wild, open fields. The stones and holes in my path make me trip. It's very cold, a damp, biting cold that soaks through to your bones.

"It's the dead of night, starless, moonless, and I grope my way forward. Every now and then I trip and fall. I hold my hands in front of me to protect my face; they are begrimed with earth. I stand up again and continue walking.

"I hear sounds around me, some I'm able to identify, others not. I think I detect a barn owl, or perhaps it is a long-eared owl, I'm not sure. There's also a murmur, as of human voices, though it could also be the wind. And a gurgling sound, like a pot of boiling water. Other things, too, but none make me uneasy; on the contrary, it's as if they are keeping me company. But the only sound I'm able to clearly distinguish does frighten me, and that is the howling of a hound. Sometimes it appears to be coming from afar, others from nearby, and it is always a long, afflicted howl, like a ghost's lament. But it's no specter, it is a flesh-and-bones dog, and that is precisely what frightens me. I shiver from cold and apprehension. I keep walking.

"All of a sudden I come to a wall. It's the façade of a house, or, more accurately, the exterior of a shack made of mud, stone, and reeds. I grope my way around it until I find an opening with a wooden door. The dog's howling has ceased, the silence and darkness are complete. I push the door with my hands, but it won't yield. I lose heart and sit on the ground with my back against the door. With all my being, I wish to enter the shack so I can rest and be safe from the hound, which is now quiet but I know is lurking nearby, spying me.

"When I'm least expecting it, the door suddenly opens and I fall backward. I am blinded by the white light inside the shack. There's a great commotion: shrieking and laughter, as though someone were having a party. I rise and, as my eyes adjust to the excess of light, I see the crowd gathered inside the shack. They are laughing in a riotous, uncouth manner, and they point their fingers at me. Some are even writhing on the floor from laughter. And they are all pointing at me. Then I realize that I'm naked and the crowd is laughing at me. I cover my private parts with my hands; I feel humiliated and exposed. Many of the faces are of strangers, but others I recognize; some are living people, others are dead. There's the slaughtered child from Pension Capell, laughing through his mouth and his slit throat. There's a bigwig from the Iberian

Anarchist Federation who I know suspects me of treason.
They call him the Cripple of Sant Elies; he's laughing
under his breath, his body shaking as if he were sobbing.
You're also there, doctor, and you are mocking me just
like the others; you shout something to me but I can't
make it out above the ruckus. I can't take such taunting
any longer.

"I leave the shack and slam the door behind me. The
uproar instantly dies down and the unbearable bright-
ness is also extinguished. I find myself alone again in the
whispering night that envelops me with murmurs.
Things are better now, because despite the moonless
sky, a tenuous light has swept across the land, allowing
me to see as though on a clear winter night. The shack
has vanished, along with all the wickedness it contained,
as though it had never existed. I am still naked from the
waist down; my chest, though, is covered with a jacket
that has appeared from out of nowhere. It's thick like a
military coat, but the material is soft, gentle to the touch.
I bundle up to shield myself from the biting air, and
despite my cold-stiffened legs, I feel much better than
before I entered the cabin. I close my eyes and breathe
in deeply.

"I open them again when the sound of growling alerts
me to the hound's presence. It's directly in front of me,
its head as big as a bull's, its fur white, as though coated
in snow. It looks me in the eye and lets out an uninterrupted, menacing growl that indicates it is about to

pounce on me, attack me, kill me. It bares its sharp, yellow teeth, a rabid foaming at the mouth.

"I consider bolting, but I immediately realize that I have no chance of escaping. Instead, I make an effort to hold its gaze and slowly begin to take off my jacket. The hound observes me; its growling does not let up. The maneuver seems to go on forever.

"Finally, it jumps. No, it flies. I see it coming, immense, above me, as though I were floating in the middle of the ocean and a killer wave were about to engulf me. In one breath, I wrap my jacket around my left arm and offer it to the hound. It accepts it and sinks its teeth into the cloth, ripping it, its fangs cutting through to my skin. It clamps its jaws and bites with more and more strength, furious, amid gasps and slobber. I hold my arm as firmly as I can, but the dog appears to be on the verge of severing it. I raise my other arm, and with a clenched fist I slog it on its enormous head. I hear the crushing sound of the skull as it cracks and see the animal's eyes bulge in their sockets.

"It loosens its bite, releases me, and takes four steps on trembling legs. Then it falls, heavy and inert.

"I unwrap my arm from inside the jacket and examine the blood from the bite. Superficial wounds, I think to myself. I approach the dog, which is lying with its back to me, and crouch down to ascertain it's dead.

"With a swift heave I turn the animal on its back. Then I see that it has my mother's face."

Iuxta crucem tecum stare
et me tibi sociari
in planctu desidero
Virgo virginum praeclara
mihi iam non sis amara
fac me tecum plangere
Fac ut portem Christi mortem
passionis fac consortem
et plagas recolere
Fac me plages vulnerari
fac me cruce inebriari
et cruore filii
Flaminis ne urar succensus,
per te, Virgo, sim defensus
in die judicii
Christi cum sit hinc exire
da per matrem me venire
ad palmam victoriae.

Sister Concepció read and reread the words of Jacopone da Todi until the letters danced before her eyes and assumed the shape of insects that buzzed about the hymnal before setting off like a swarm of scattering moths, flying through the stale air of her cell, drawing imaginary spirals in their path. The transmutation led her to the presentiment, the impression, that she was not alone in her cell, but accompanied by a presence she could not define, one that manifested itself by a sound that was nearly imperceptible but was nevertheless there: in the great solitude of her stark cell she could sense it . . .

Was she going insane? Was she losing her mind, or was she being forced to atone for an offense against God? Was it all a torment such as what Saint Eulàlia had endured? Saint Eulàlia with her thirteen geese that pastured the Desert of Sarrià . . .

The blood anguished her more than anything else, the hemorrhaging between her legs that had lasted so many days now and had given her a chill, a bellyache, and a diffuse sadness tinged with shame. With her usual kindness, Sister Encarnació had explained to her that it was the price women had to pay for their part in the original sin. She spoke to her of Eve, the first mother of humanity, and of the cunning with which she had turned Adam away from God's plan. She told her about the Lord's anger, the banishment from Paradise, about the just demand that every one of Eve's female descendants give their blood to satisfy that offense. She showed the novice how to apply and wash the rags on the days of the month when the blood flowed. Sister Encarnació had ended up hugging her and trying to console her, telling her that although being female meant they were small, unclean, and prone to sin, they themselves had nothing to fear because their husband was not of this earth, but dwelled up above in the sheltering sky, and this fact redeemed them and allowed them to pray for the redemption of all of mankind.

To Sister Concepció this was a paltry consolation. Her imagination turned to Paradise, to the garden the Bible described it as at the beginning of the world. What must it have been like? If she had had the chance, if she had been able to travel back in time to any place and era, she would have asked to go to Paradise. She would have warned Adam and Eve against the serpent's temptations, and then there would have been no original sin, and women wouldn't have to bleed to atone for it. She would have assisted Adam and Eve in the task of naming things and animals—a task Bishop Perugorría had mentioned the day he commissioned her to compose the Stabat Mater—and she would have been able to decide, for instance, that geese should not be named geese. If it had been up to her, geese would have been ducks because they resembled ducks and there was no need to waste words on such similar creatures. The word goose would have been reserved for another, more original animal. Nor was there any need to apply the name to an animal: she could bestow it on a parsnip, if she liked. That would mean, of course, that the word parsnip would become available, so it would need to be assigned to something else. Could the bishop's spindly fingers be considered parsnips? They did resemble them, come to think of it...

These thoughts amused her and, hearing the sound of her own laughter, she realized it had been a long time since she had laughed. Laughing made her feel better. But now it had conjured memories of her mother, whom she missed terribly, and of Emília, a friend she hadn't heard from in a long time and for whom she often prayed, wishing her and her family well. She and Emília had laughed a lot in their class at the Orfeó Català, as Master Millet tried to sharpen their sense of melody by having them intone a little song that went:

It's rainy and sunny,
And witches are combing their hair.
It's rainy and sunny,
And witches are laying an egg.

For her and her friend Emília, the image of witches laying eggs brought on peals of laughter; they were often forced to interrupt the song because they couldn't refrain from giggling and Master Millet would scold them. When their lesson was over, the girls would find their mothers waiting for them outside the Palau de la Música; they would sing to them the song about the witches who laid eggs and they would all laugh heartily. She remembered having once asked her mother if it was true that witches laid eggs and, smiling, her mother had responded that it could not be true because witches did not exist. Witches did not exist, and neither did ghosts, or the bogeyman, or demons who speared mischievous children with their pitchforks and hoisted them away, or Maria Enganxa, who hooked them by their necks and made them vanish in the depths of water tanks. Monstrous creatures such as those did not exist, and in life, the most important thing was not to be afraid.

Not to be afraid: those words were etched in her memory, as was her mother's smile when she spoke them. But now she was very much afraid. Perhaps it was true that neither witches nor the bogeyman existed, but she had learned on her own that gloom was real. The convent was full of it; it was at the root of the revulsion she felt, of her fear of going mad, of her senses departing and not snapping back: the gloom, the shadows that pervaded everything, abolishing light and devouring the world, silencing music and little girls' laughter. Gloom in the always-strained expression on the mother abbess's face, gloom in the glassy eyes of His Excellency the bishop. How could she not be afraid? Mater Dolorosa by the cross. Was her own mother also experiencing fear? No, she couldn't be—not her. Sister Concepció wanted to pray, she needed to pray, for her mother— who must also be praying for her—and for Emília, whose whereabouts were known only to God. And she prayed that one day she would leave the convent and find her mother standing at the door, and she would hug her tight and sing her the song about the witches and they would laugh until she would again remind her that witches do not exist and that only Paradise awaits us beyond death.

She again tried to concentrate on the lyrics of the Stabat Mater, but it was hopeless. She was uneasy and couldn't banish the feeling that animals and strange creatures were all around her, stalking her.

Bishop Perugorría's fingers brushed against the door as he plodded toward his chambers, having devoted a few minutes—once more—to spying on Sister Concepció through the keyhole.

"**YOUR MOTHER . . .**" repeated the doctor after a few moments of silence.

Superintendent Muñoz's gaze was lost amid the light and shadows that flooded the morgue. He saw only cadavers, or parts of cadavers. Then, Doctor Pellicer's face studying his own as if seeing it for the first time.

"Yes," he said. "My mother lying in place of the dog, her head bashed in. By a blow from my fist."

Doctor Pellicer nodded. "That's quite the nightmare."

"It repeats itself every time I fall asleep."

"Always the same?"

"The differences are imperceptible."

"Such as?"

"Sometimes it's as though I awake inside the nightmare. I mean I'm conscious that I'm dreaming, but I can't do anything to interrupt the nightmare and rouse myself. It continues to unfold until the end."

"Until you see your dead mother."

"Precisely."

"Is there anything relevant you can tell me about your mother?"

"Yes. She committed suicide."

The doctor waited a moment. Then he asked, "For any particular reason?"

"Yes. My father used to hit her. I remember the beatings."

"He beat her like a dog."

"Yes."

"And she . . ."

"One day my sisters and I came home from school and found her at the bottom of the stairs, in the entrance to the building. She had climbed over the banister and thrown herself down. She had broken her neck."

"And your father?"

"He left, abandoned us. But it was better that way. He used to beat my sisters too. And me. We all breathed a sigh of relief when he disappeared. We never heard from him again."

"And you and your sisters . . ."

"We ended up in a orphanage. We were also beaten there, though not as much. We looked out for each other as much as we could, until we each reached an age when we became independent. For me, joining the police force meant fulfilling the only childhood dream I could recall. I had always wanted to be in uniform and carry a gun. So, you see, doctor, I'm just your typical embittered soul."

"You shouldn't speak that way, superintendent."

"It's the truth. The parish rector wouldn't allow my

mother to be buried in the cemetery because suicides couldn't be buried on hallowed ground. We were forced to dump her at a morgue much like this, and I suppose a doctor like you must have chopped her up into bits . . . By the way, what becomes of all this butchery? Once the forensic analysis has been conducted, I mean."

The doctor thought of Hadaly and swallowed.

"Well, it's none of my business, I guess," the superintendent answered himself. "Science has its reasons, religion has even more. That is precisely why I told you that I, too, have my reasons for not having much empathy for the Holy Mother Church. As I've said, I'm your typical embittered man."

Superintendent Muñoz smiled for the first time since the conversation had begun. Doctor Pellicer celebrated the fact by lighting another cigarette. They were silent for a long time, surrounded by the discreet attentiveness of the dead. Finally, the police officer opened his mouth again.

"I can't continue my investigation into the Pension Capell murder. I'm being watched, we have a sleeper agent at the precinct."

"You can't be serious," said the doctor.

"It's Sirga, the officer who accompanied me the day I was at the pension. He's an FAI operative."

"Are you sure?"

"He has a taste for whoring. With his salary, he couldn't possibly afford it. Not being the sharpest knife in the drawer he's incapable of concealing the fact that he's making a haul somewhere else."

"All right, but that . . ."

"You're right. That doesn't mean anything. But I smell a rat."

"And your suspicions . . . ?"

"Have been confirmed. I had a man tail him and what he discovered was quite interesting. Not only as regards Sirga, but also our good friends at Pension Capell."

Behind his spectacles, Doctor Pellicer's small rabbit eyes widened.

"They are Marists," said Superintendent Muñoz. "They are negotiating with the FAI for safe passage into France. The other day, just before the air raid, they had a face-to-face meeting in a bar downtown. Everyone from Pension Capell was present, including the nephew of that mayor from Palma de Mallorca. Representing the FAI was a group of big fish from the Department of Investigations. Altogether, a real cross-section of beasts. Then they were joined by Manuel Escorza—the Cripple of Sant Elies, they call him—the biggest, most loathsome big fish of them all."

"The man in your nightmare."

"One of them, yes. I forgot to mention that Escorza arrived at the meeting accompanied by Sirga."

"I'm beginning to catch on."

"That's not all: as a bargaining chip, they took a hostage, who turned out to be that blasted young Mallorcan. Sirga and another goon led him away, prisoner."

"Where?"

"I don't know. My man saw them leaving the bar, but the bombing started and he wasn't able to follow them."

Doctor Pellicer considered the fact that, while bombs rained over Barcelona, Hadaly had been trotting gracefully through the grotto beneath Judge Carbonissa's house. Afterward, they had committed the sin of arrogance by letting him out onto the street, where the incident at the Church of Bethlehem had taken place.

"In any event," continued the superintendent, "it's obvious that Sirga has already informed Escorza, or Aureli Fernández, or whichever one of those bastards it was, that I turned a blind eye on a group of Marists. And so, by now my name is probably on the Department's black list of traitors and abettors. I can't continue with the investigation."

"And this causes you nightmares and keeps you from sleeping?" asked the doctor.

"No," said the superintendent. "What keeps me from sleeping is the thought that Sirga and three or four of his henchmen might whisk me away in a car, blindfolded, and tomorrow I might turn up on Carretera de l'Arrabassada with a bullet in my back and another in my head. I admit the thought unnerves me. I regret all this; I would have liked to become better acquainted with your vampire, but it'll have to be on another occasion."

Doctor Pellicer managed a somber half-smile. He

empathized with the officer's distress, but he could have done without the mockery.

"Personally," insisted Superintendent Muñoz, "I'm inclined to think that Brother Gendrau was dispatched by the FAI so the Marists would get the message that the negotiation was in earnest, if you know I mean. The boy must have been thrown in as a sort of gratuity, these folks are generous that way. At least I hope it wasn't Sirga who did the honors."

Doctor Pellicer snuffed out his cigarette with the tip of his shoe. He valued the superintendent's frankness and thought he should repay him in kind.

"Superintendent," he began, "the only positive effect of war is that it brings to the surface everything that is secretly circulating underground. The good and the bad."

"Not sure what to say to that . . ." the officer said distractedly.

"I imagine," continued the physician, "that you haven't heard about the man found dead at the Church of Bethlehem after the air raid. It's rumored that it wasn't the bombs that killed him, but a horse that entered the temple, its provenance still a mystery."

Superintendent Muñoz raised his eyebrows by way of response.

SISTER CONCEPCIÓ HEARD muffled screams filled with such evident desperation that they gave her goosebumps. At first, she froze in the middle of her cell, arms folded across her chest; then she heard running in the corridor and decided to take a peek, even though she was not allowed to step outside without permission. She cracked her door and caught a glimpse of scrawny Sister Anunciació from the back, hiking up her habit with both hands to be less encumbered; as though possessed, she flew down the stairs that led to the refectory, where the screams seemed to be issuing from.

Without thinking twice, Sister Concepció followed her. As she rushed down the stairs, she saw other nuns running along the hallway off the refectory toward the door to the vegetable garden: the disturbance was coming from there. Did the screaming voice belong to one of the sisters? She couldn't be sure; the nature of the shriek made the voice impossible to identify. What could be the cause of it? Her heartbeat accelerated with every passing instant but it seemed to slow again when she went out into the vegetable garden and realized that it was early morning and the sun was starting to come out. Shut inside her cell, she lost all sense of time and, in the end, she didn't know if it was night or day. She was pleased to realize it was neither: the night was coming to an end, but day had not yet dawned. The cool air—when not excessive—always had an invigorating effect on her. She stopped to breathe deeply and, as she did, she detected the well-water freshness condensed in the air. For a few seconds, the mortification caused by the Stabat Mater verses was compensated by that salutary inhalation that made her feel rejuvenated. But then another disconsolate scream rent the morning.

"They're dead! They're dead."

Now that she finally understood what the voice was saying, her stomach was suddenly in knots. Who was dead? She raced to the palm tree and, in the patches of morning light, she saw a group of sisters huddled together in a circle by the pigsty. She approached as the screams grew hoarse and syncopated, as though whoever was making them was losing her voice. She spotted Sister Anunciació a few steps from the circle, together with the chubby Sisters Benedicció, Dormició and Visitació, the ancient Ascensió and Adoració, and others who were flailing their arms toward the heavens gesturing wildly and causing a great commotion. Mother Superior was there, too, looking as stiff as though she were carved in stone, and, a bit farther away, Bishop Perugorría, equally impenetrable, plunged in faraway thoughts. They were like two gargoyles, and this resemblance made Sister Concepció's heart sink even more.

The person doing the screaming was none other than Sister Encarnació, who stood in the middle of the circle, her face contorted, hands gnarled, eyes like saucers—as though she were seeing a monstrous apparition. Her body twitched spasmodically as she made vaguely menacing gestures that the other sisters deflected by stretching out their arms and brandishing rosaries and crucifixes before the woman's face.

"They're dead! They're dead!" she repeated over and over, her voice ever weaker, more guttural.

"She's possessed!" clucked Sister Benedicció as the roll of fat around her wizened body quivered.

"She carries the devil within!" came cries from around the circle. The crucifixes bobbed in a maniacal dance.

"Deaaad! They're deaaad!" bellowed Sister Encarnació, deranged, pointing to the pigsty with her gnarly fingers.

The novice had retreated and stood several steps from the commotion. Sister Encarnació's fit had nothing to do with diabolical possession, she thought; rather, it was a nervous breakdown much like the one her Aunt Enriqueta—one of her father's sisters—had once suffered after a fight in the drawing room over something to do with her grandparents' will. On that occasion, her aunt had gone as far as scratching up her own face and hurling a porcelain teapot, which had shattered on the floor. Compared to that memory of Aunt Enriqueta, Sister Encarnació seemed less frightening, or in any case not nearly as much as the rest of the community, which was in the grip of hysteria. Sister Concepció again glanced at Mother Superior; she remained hieratic, absent, as though she were at a cosmic remove and Sister Concepció were seeing her through a telescope. For his part, His Excellency the bishop returned the novice's glance with that look of his that always seemed to precede a calamity. Frightened and confused, Sister Concepció lowered her head, not knowing where to look.

"The devil, the devil!" shouted the nuns of every age and shape, in a frenzy.

"Deaaad!" droned the ghostly Sister Encarnació.

Sister Concepció summoned her willpower and decided to take a look in the pigsty. She walked haltingly toward it, making her way little by little, as though entering a sick person's room. She glanced at the feeding troughs first and saw only the slop that, every morning before prayers, Sister Encarnació fed the two pigs that Manuel Escorza had delivered to the convent, to be slaughtered over the winter. The actual slaughter would be a task for Sirga, and afterward the sisters would prepare the meat and make the sausages. Sister Concepció had never dirtied her hands during the yearly pig slaughter, but Sister Encarnació had already announced that, when the day came, she would teach her how to cut, mince, mix, fill and sew the casings.

She entered the pen, treading carefully because the timid light of dawn was not sufficient to illuminate the place and the floor was slippery from the mixture of hay and excrements that covered it. She was surprised not to hear any noise or grunts: the pigs were unusually silent. Outside, the nuns continued clamoring around Sister Encarnació.

The novice waited for her eyes to grow accustomed to the penumbra and then discovered that the hay and excrements were not the only substance scattered across the pigpen. All around there were dark puddles of sludge, a mixture of muck and blood that had also splattered the walls and was dribbling to the ground, forming a design that recalled a kind of macabre calligraphy.

When she finally saw them a chill ran up and down her spine: the pigs lay on a bed of straw, limbs disjointed, eyes glassy. Dead, as Sister Encarnació breathlessly repeated. Their necks and guts were ravaged, as though the animals had been attacked by a wild beast capable of jumping the five-meter wall around the convent and slipping inside the pen to quench its thirst and hunger.

"Hey. Hey."

"Mmm . . ."

"Wake up. Open your eyes. Hey."

"Mmm? Where . . . ?"

"Over here. Open your eyes."

"Where . . . am I?"

"In the clink. Wake up, little priest. I got news you'll like."

Brother Pau Darder rubbed his eyes and opened them. The first thing he saw was a pock-marked face belonging to Sirga, who was sitting on the straw mattress beside him. He spotted the chamber pot in one corner of the cell, by the candle nub that was leaning against the wall. Then, in front of him, the iron-bar door. Then, the empty pots of garbanzos and water. His slumber had been devoid of dreams, and waking again inside that den, Sirga's repulsive face so close to his own, made him feel the most miserable of men.

"I'm hungry. I'm thirsty," he murmured, like a sick person regaining consciousness.

Sirga grinned. "Sorry to hear that, little priest; I'm afraid I forgot to bring you a snack. At least I hope you slept comfortably—you can't take issue with the bed, now, can you?"

Brother Darder tightened his grip around the medal of Saint Michael that he held in his right fist. "So you've come to mock me, then," he gasped, sitting up on the cot.

"No," said Sirga. "I've already told you, I have news that will bring you great joy. Your uncle, the one who was mayor of Palma, is dead."

Brother Darder felt his entire body tense up. He heard the voice inside his head: *Emili will bring shame on his family.*

"He was executed by firing squad," Sirga added. "The fascists' doing—your people's doing, that is. Congratulations, little priest."

Without another word, Sirga rose from the cot, walked to the metal door, opened it and then closed it behind him with a violent clang that ricocheted through the emptiness of the cell.

"Wait!" Brother Darder called after him, but Sirga was no longer listening. No one was.

He stood and started pacing the length of his cell, faster and faster. He was trying to remember his uncle, but the only thing that came to mind was a strange figure seemingly molded in ice: transparent and unsteady, colorless, odorless, mute. The image of Uncle Emili, dead. Murdered, like Brother Pere Gendrau. The two men who had been father figures to him: one killed by one faction, the other by its foe. And his biological father, Don Gabriel: long dead, not in the war but from life itself. Pawns fallen off the board, puppets no longer of any use in the game plotted by God the Creator.

And his mother? Was she still alive? Yes, it was quite possible she was; after all, in the midst of chaos, the simple-minded are more likely to survive, as they are better able to adapt to folly and senselessness.

If God so deems it . . . he could hear her whispering in his ear.

And Brother Darder had to admit that he would have given anything to hear from his mother's lips those words of utter resignation that had once displeased him. Yes, he would have given anything to be by her side, embrace her, and let her know that he was also alive, that he would protect her and keep her safe. That he was a man now, capable of making his own decisions, and he didn't need a tutor to attend to his future. That he was responsible for himself and his mother and would remain firm in his determination however much the world around him insisted on falling to pieces until it was transformed into a different, nameless landscape full of rubble and debris. "If God so deems it . . ." would chirp his mother, self-satisfied, in her singsong voice.

Brother Darder would not have known how to respond now; he had learned that God's views were no more relevant than rat's carrion.

He looked out the window at the filth piling up in the street. He was hungry and thirsty. He had to get out of there.

"YOU CAN GO in now. Don Aureli is expecting you in his office."

The secretary, a ruddy-faced girl not yet twenty-five, smiled at Brothers Lacunza and Plana and at Adjutant Émile Aragou, who was guarding with both hands the calfskin satchel that rested on his knees. The three religious rose from the faux-leather armchairs and followed the secretary down a corridor inside the Generalitat de Catalunya's Department of Investigations and Patrols. The girl proceeded at a quick trot, like a ballerina about to perform a dance step. When they were in front of the door to Don Aureli's office, the secretary, dutiful, tapped on it with her knuckles and gently opened it.

"Good day and welcome, senyors," exclaimed Aureli Fernández, as he approached the three Marists and cheerfully shook their hands.

"A pleasure to see you again," came another greeting, this one in a mocking tone, from the depths of the office. All three men immediately recognized the voice: it was Gil Portela, ensconced in a beige velvet armchair and smoking a cigar.

"I'm afraid I can't say the same," retorted Brother Lacunza. Gil Portela looked him over as though taking his measurements.

Aureli Fernández thought it a good idea to intervene. "Pay no heed," he said, resting his hand on Brother Lacunza's shoulders in a conciliatory manner. "I realize you gentlemen had some sort of . . . disagreement at the Tostadero meeting, but there'll be no hiccups now."

"It's just that our brothers here are so very witty," quipped Gil Portela.

"I wouldn't describe what took place as a mere disagreement," responded Brother Lacunza, ignoring Gil Portela. "What can you tell us about Brother Darder?"

Aureli Fernández and Gil Portela exchanged a glance.

"He's in a good place, safe and sound," responded Aureli Fernández, unfazed. "We'll discuss it all now. Sit, please."

He pointed to a sofa upholstered in the same beige velvet as the armchair. Brother Lacunza noted that the room was furnished with as much luxury as bad taste; nevertheless, Aureli Fernández (Don Aureli, his secretary had called him), had an agreeable disposition and gave off a cordiality that appeared sincere. He was smartly dressed and had an easy, appreciative smile, his gestures reflecting a decisive nature that conveyed self-assurance and inspired trust. He waited for the three Marists to be seated on the sofa before he settled himself on a leather armchair behind an oversized desk. Brother Lacunza noticed the two flags to Don Aureli's left: the Catalan flag and the red-and-black emblem of the anarcho-syndicalists. Aureli Fernández drummed his fingers on the table and began: "I think we can come straight to the point. Senyor Escorza and Senyor Ordaz have filled me in on the Tostadero meeting and the terms and conditions that were negotiated."

It was Aureli Fernández's attempt to diminish Manuel Escorza's standing and present himself to the Marists as the highest authority they could appeal to. Gil Portela gave him a look of disapproval but also of commiseration. Meanwhile, Brother Plana shifted nervously in his seat on the sofa and Adjutant Aragou clutched his brown leather bag as though he had been shipwrecked and it was a float. Brother Lacunza was trying to capture every detail.

"I'm pleased to inform you," continued Aureli Fernández, "that a couple of days ago, the FAI's Investigations Committee sent confirmation that they have accepted your proposal." He smiled again and opened his arms like a magician who had just pulled a rabbit out of a hat.

"Excellent news," murmured Brother Lacunza.

"No need to thank me." Aureli Fernández tilted his head a little. "The whole matter is of great interest to both parties, as I'm sure you understand . . ."

"Of course," said Gil Portela from his armchair, which seemed to be spewing smoke from all sides. "Especially for you, *hermanos*. Was the Frenchie's trip profitable? He better have returned with the money, don't want you thinking it was easy to grant him safe passage through La Jonquera without getting himself clipped . . ."

It was true. However legitimate the whole thing was, checkpoint patrols had a hard time believing a priest would be in possession of a safe-passage to reach France; they suspected the document was forged. Gil Portela had had to keep a constant watch on Adjuntant Aragou to ensure he wasn't killed at one of the stops.

"Let's watch our tone, please," said Aureli Fernández. The comment was intended for Gil Portela, who appeared to be enjoying the situation. "If it's all right with you, gentlemen, let's talk specifics. The agreed-upon sum is two hundred thousand French francs. Are you in a position to satisfy that amount?"

All eyes turned to Adjutant Aragou; seated at the tip of the sofa, he appeared to be shrinking. "The money . . . is . . . is here," he stuttered, lifting the brown leather bag with shaky hands. "It's all here."

"Let's count it," exclaimed Gil Portela, rising and reaching out his arms for the bag.

"Not yet," Brother Lacunza said, grasping the satchel by the handle. "First, we need the hostage to be returned. Where is Brother Darder?"

"I'm afraid you haven't understood how this works, *hermanos*," said Gil Portela, stressing each syllable, annoyed.

"If your aim is to pull a handgun on us," Brother

Lacunza said, defiant, "I must say it will take more than that to intimidate us. We've gotten used to it."

Gil Portela removed the cigar from his mouth and leaned forward, as though he were about to rise. "I'm getting tired of all this posturing."

"Enough," ordered Aureli Fernández, and Gil Portela grudgingly fell back. "Brother Darder will be reunited with you on the day of the evacuation. Safe and sound, as I said earlier. But it will be on the day of the departure, not before that. Now you must hand over the money. If you would, senyor . . ."

"Aragou," the adjutant supplied.

"That's it. Please hand the bag over to Senyor Gil Portela so he can verify the contents."

"Don't get ahead of yourselves, gentlemen," Brother Lacunza intervened. "The first half, now, the second half the day of the evacuation. If we can't have the hostage, you can't expect us to hand over the entire amount now."

Aureli Fernández stiffened behind his desk. Brother Plana went pale. Gil Portela made a dismissive gesture with his hand.

"Two thirds now, the rest, the day of the departure," Aureli Fernández finally said, trying to appear firm.

"Half and half," insisted Brother Lacunza.

"I don't advise this kind of stubbornness, *hermanos*," said Gil Portela, feigning indifference. "Frankly, you have much more to lose here than we do."

Adjutant Aragou clutched the bag as a child would a

toy. Brother Plana took Brother Lacunza by the arm, as though imploring him to yield.

"Senyor Gil Portela is right," declared Aureli Fernández. "Do as you please."

Brother Lacunza scanned the room and read the intimidation in Adjutant Aragou's eyes and the anguish in Brother Plana's. And he gave in. "All right then, two thirds up front."

"Much better," said Aureli Fernández, relieved. "The bag, please."

"One moment," the Marist said. "Brother Aragou, please open the bag and divide the money into thirds yourself."

"But... what does this mean?" asked Aureli Fernández, growing impatient.

Gil Portela huffed, as though none of it had anything to do with him.

"Go ahead, Brother Aragou," instructed Brother Lacunza.

Adjutant Aragou unfastened the buckles, zipped open the bag, slipped his hands in, and began to remove wads of bills held together with elastic bands. He licked the tip of his thumb and index finger and counted the money with the skill of a seasoned banker. He did not raise his head for even an instant. When he finished, he set aside a stack of bills and slipped the rest inside the bag, which he handed over to Brother Lacunza. Lacunza rose, walked over to the armchair where Gil Portela was seated, and offered him the brown leather bag. The goon grabbed it with both hands, his eyes on the Marist's strained face.

"Check to see if it's all there, if you want," said Brother Lacunza.

"That won't be necessary," said Aureli Fernández. "Sit back down, please."

Brother Lacunza obeyed. Once seated, he turned to Aragou. "Anything else regarding the money, brother?"

"Well," the adjutant said, "there is still the question of banking controls . . ."

"Don't worry about that," said Aureli Fernández, seemingly revived. He addressed Gil Portela: "Let's be sure to call the Ministry so they'll take care of it as soon as possible. Agreed?"

"Should I speak with Tarradellas?"

Aureli Fernández made a gesture of discomfort. "No, not him. I'll inform the minister myself," he lied, Escorza being his only contact. "On the contrary, don't even mention Tarradellas or use his name under any circumstances, understood?"

"Understood, Senyor Secretary General, understood," Girl Portela mocked him, as he grasped the bag and made as if to leave; before stepping outside the office, however, he turned to the Marists: "You'll see, *hermanos*, everything will go smooth as silk." He slammed the door on his way out, leaving behind him a frayed trail of smoke.

Aureli Fernández recovered his most comforting smile.

"Please excuse his rough ways. Comrade Gil Portela might be a bit brusque, but he's a good comrade."

"We have no doubt about it," sighed Brother Lacunza, beginning to feel more at ease. "May I ask what your plan is for the evacuations?"

Aureli Fernández again drummed his fingers on the table to the rhythm in his head. "That's not your concern," he said. "The Department of Investigations will take care of the logistics. What we need to know is how many people we are talking about here so we can calculate the number of trucks that will be needed, as well as the water and food provisions."

"We have circulated an announcement to let the brothers decide if they want to accept the evacuation offer. It's not an easy task because the community is scattered and we have no way of reaching certain people. But, in any event, we will be closing the list in a couple of days and will be able to give you an exact headcount."

"Excellent. We'll continue to work on establishing the fastest, safest route through La Jonquera with the information we receive from the front."

"When will the students and seminarians be able to leave Casa de les Avellanes?" inquired Aragou, recovering some of his poise. "They are in dire need."

"As soon as we have cleared up the bank issue. I'm guessing in three or four days. In the meantime, Comrade Gil Portela will expedite the processing of departure permits."

A morose silence came over the office, as if each of the four men had withdrawn into his own thoughts. Brother Lacunza shuffled his feet, unable to conceal his impatience; Adjutant Aragou rested his eyes on the anarchist flag; Brother Plana remained mum and grew paler and paler. Finally, Aureli Fernández clapped his hands and declared the meeting over.

"Very well, gentlemen, it appears that, at the moment, that is all there is to discuss. We will be in touch over the next few days and we will make sure that everything proceeds as swiftly as possible." He paused, looked at Brother Lacunza, and added: "You have nothing to fear. Everything will be all right. You have my word."

September 29, 1936
Orders issued by Manuel Escorza of the
inbestigaiton services CNT—FAI.

As per the comuniqué, a raide and arrests were made at Calle Valencia 225 following a report that some Carlists were using it as a hyding place.

We aperhended the owner of the house, the lawyer Joaquin de bruguera de Sarriera, 52 years of age, we also detained the others who had takin shelter there Roberto Llanza de Bruguera, 17, the lawyer Jose Benito de alas de Mateo, 52, the lawyer

Francisco Javier de alas, 55, former Marquis of
Dou. Our Squads had already informed us they
were on this individual's trale since he fled his
house on Calle Baja de San Pedro 29-31 which had
already been siezed last July.

I hereby order a trip to the montcada cematary
for the 7 deetanees in the San Elias stationhouse,
on the wey back we shall deliver 4 of them to the
glue Factory.

Manuel Escorza reread the search and arrest warrant, which he had penned himself, and was about to stamp his signature on it when someone knocked on the glass pane of the door to his office.

"Come in," he said distractedly.

The door opened and Sirga appeared, a grimace of alarm on his pock-marked face.

"Comrade Escorza," he said, clicking his heels together. "We've had word from the convent. From the mother abbess."

"Right," sighed Manuel Escorza, setting his pen down on the table. "What's eating the good sister now?"

"A strange occurrence has taken place at the convent. The mother abbess requests a meeting with you, Comrade."

"Again? What happened?"

"It's the pigs, Comrade Escorza. The two pigs you had sent over to the convent. They were found dead this morning. It appears they were attacked by some kind of animal. A wild beast, it seems."

Manuel Escorza's eyes darkened. "What you're saying makes no sense at all, Sirga."

"That's what I thought, Comrade Escorza, but the mother abbess insists that they were bitten to death. They were found in their pen, the blood drained from their bodies and with wounds to their necks and heads."

"And the bishop?"

"I inquired after him. He's safe and sound, comrade."

Manuel Escorza huffed. "It's essential that the bishop's safety continue to receive the utmost priority. Orders from high up. They want to exchange him for some head honcho on the Republican side, and if anything happens to him, we'll be taken to the woodshed."

"Yes, comrade. I am aware of that."

Escorza became withdrawn, adopting an expression that made it seem as though thinking was a great effort. Finally he said, as if talking to himself: "It is impossible for anyone to break into the convent—the place is like a fortress. It must have been someone inside. And this has given me an idea."

"Bravo, Comrade Escorza," said Sirga, obsequious.

"Tell the mother abbess I'll call on her this evening. Right now we have work to do—Here." He handed Sirga the arrest warrant. "Give this to Aureli Fernández so he can take care of it at once."

———

SISTER CONCEPCIÓ THOUGHT she might have found a method of composition that would at least allow her to begin work on the Stabat Mater. Bishop Perugorría's assignment had become an obsession, a heavy weight that oppressed her in body and spirit, mortifying her like a cilice. And things had gotten worse after the episode with the two dead pigs and since the mother abbess had meted out her punishment for having abandoned her cell without permission. She was not allowed to leave her cell until further notice, and the other nuns had been banned from entering her room to visit or talk to her. They were to limit themselves to two knocks on her door when they left her food, nothing more. This ordeal had already lasted a day and a half. The complete seclusion— her only company the few little sounds that reached her—deepened her anguish over the task she had been assigned. Her mind often filled with thoughts of Saint Eulàlia pasturing her geese amid the trees of the Desert of Sarrià, which had been cypresses until an angel transformed them into palm trees, a sign that the little girl had been chosen by Heaven. Singled out for torment.

The harder she tried to concentrate on the task at hand the more lost she felt, and it occurred to her that chance might help her find a way to begin. She considered tackling the Stabat Mater in C-sharp minor—Beethoven's *Clair de Lune* as a reference point—but she was all too aware that it was an odd choice, which made it more attractive but at the same time filled her with self-doubt. She also debated working in A major, a key that Schubert—she recalled from her lessons with Master Millet—had described as the best suited for expressions of youthful joy and faith in God, which is what she supposed His Excellency the bishop expected of her piece. But what youthful joy could she feel or convey, isolated and sequestered as though in a prison?

She was incapable of making a choice, and so decided once again to disobey the mother abbess. She had been banned from leaving her cell, but, curiously, the door had not been locked. It was as if the Mother Abbes wanted to test her, and Sister Concepció decided to use the test to her advantage. She would go to the chapterhouse and resort to the vase method: if she got a bean, C-sharp minor, if an almond, A major. Once the initial hurdle was overcome, perhaps she would find a thread she could follow to help her fabricate a suitable receptacle for the words of Jacopone da Todi.

Sister Concepció waited until after Night Prayer, and around eleven o'clock, when the whole convent was asleep, she cracked the door and slipped silently down the hall. She descended the stairs in the dark, crossed the refectory, went out into the vegetable garden, and from there she dashed in the direction of the cloister. She passed the pigpen and was unable to avoid a shudder. The night was luminous and placid under the full moon, as though the war had long been over. Unhurried and aloof, the cats that roamed the cloister turned for an instant to observe Sister Concepció as she passed.

The great door to the chapterhouse was locked and bolted, but her thin white arm had no trouble slipping between the latticework of the window that gave onto the cloister and releasing the latch. Sister Concepció climbed onto the windowsill, jumped down, and carefully shut the window behind her. The moonlight that streamed through the jalousie allowed her eyes to quickly adjust to the darkness. The great table in the center of the room resembled a large sleeping beast. She walked past it and went straight to the glass cabinet that held the two black-clay urns; she opened it and chose the same vase she recalled the mother abbess taking on the day of their interview. She could tell there was something inside the container and fished out the bean and the almond that were to help her decide the key of her Stabat Mater.

Suddenly, the doorknob made a sound. It had to be the mother abbess—she was the only person who had the keys. Sister Concepció felt her heart climb to her mouth; as fast as she could, she returned the vase—the almond and bean back inside—to the cabinet, shut the glass door, and frantically scrambled in search of a hiding place. The only one she could find was beneath the long, dark, austere center table.

She curled up like a dog in front of a lit fireplace and, from her hideout, she trained her eyes along the floor and toward the entrance; the door opened slowly, with a certain affected solemnity and not a single creak. It was, indeed, the mother abbess who entered. Sister Concepció glimpsed the purple strip along the hem of her black habit, the unmistakable shoes, also black, her feet curiously small for a woman of her height.

The mother abbess was not alone. Behind her followed a pair of shapeless boots, greasy, raised on enormous lifts, which dragged clumsily across the tile floor driven by a pair of crutches. Terrified, shrinking more and more into herself, it occurred to Sister Concepció that those feet could have been Saint Eulàlia's after her martyrdom, but she tried to quiet her mind by thinking they had to belong to a man. A man she had never seen before. Perhaps he was the one who had killed the pigs the other night?

The mother abbess's small feet and the stranger's disturbing hooves approached the table without a sound. Sister Concepció saw a chair being dragged backward and heard the mother abbess's voice: "Please, sit."

She heard the stranger huffing as he heaved himself into his chair. When the man's body finally settled into it, it moaned like a branch of a tree breaking. The mother abbess walked around the table, pulled out another chair and sat down facing the stranger. Her small feet and his bulky ones rested on the floor just a few centimeters from Sister Concepció's head. The light-colored wood of the stranger's crutches, which rested against the table, was also visible from beneath the table. Afraid that her breathing would give her away, Sister Concepció tried to hold her breath, taking in air only through her nose. Aside from a small tremor that coursed up and down her body, the novice didn't have to make any effort to hold completely still. She was paralyzed by terror.

"So? What is it you want from me now, little sister?"

The voice sounded rasping yet waterlogged, as though the stranger was grinding his teeth as he spoke, his mouth full of foam. Sister Concepció had never heard anything like it. It was repulsive.

"You already know the answer, Manuel," said the mother abbess, her voice quiet despite the stranger's forcefulness. "I want you to remove him. He can't stay here."

A few moments of silence followed. Then came that rasping sound again: "You've always been a bore, little sister." The growl created a faint echo inside the chapter-house. "What's the matter, or did I not make myself clear the other day? I thought I expressed myself well enough."

"I beg you, Manuel."

"I'll remove him when the moment comes, and I'll be the one to decide when that is. There is no use insisting."

"The man is unwell, Manuel. He will bring us trouble. Actually, he already has."

Sister Concepció heard bubbles bursting and identified the sound as the stranger's laughter. "What has he done now?" he snarled. "Has His Excellency taken to chasing nuns behind the confessional?"

The mother abbess's tiny feet twitched as though with

a life of their own, and Sister Concepció had to lie flat so they wouldn't bump into her. She breathed in deeply and tried to recite a Hail Mary, praying she wouldn't be discovered.

"I explained the incident with the pigs over the phone. That's the reason I asked you here. You know I do my best not to bother you."

"Do you mean to tell me, dear sister, that our beloved bishop polished off two fat pigs in a couple of bites?"

"You can poke fun all you want, but I'm not able to come up with any other explanation. We haven't detected the presence of any other animals, and it's impossible for someone to have entered the convent from outside."

"Are you in the middle of a fast? Perhaps the dinner you served left some of the sisters hungry . . ."

"Furthermore," the mother abbess continued, ignoring the comment, "there is still the problem with the novice I mentioned. I've been forced to place her in isolation and have forbidden her to leave her cell. But I had her key left in the lock in case she had to flee. He hasn't stopped stalking her and doesn't even bother to conceal the fact anymore. It's like a fixation."

Sister Concepció had to bite the insides of her cheeks to prevent a scream from escaping her mouth. The man let out a boorish laugh.

"I'm frightened, Manuel. Something is going to happen, I just know it. I'm asking you, no, I am begging you once again to remove him. Please."

The stranger's voice grew deep.

"I think you're forgetting the fact that you are in no position to ask for anything, little sister. Not even to beg. You and your fanatics don't even exist, remember? You wanted a life of enclosure and sacrifice. Well, that's what you got."

"Precisely," replied the mother abbess, her barely-contained rage unprecedented as far as Sister Concepció was concerned. "It would be easy enough to let people in the city know we are here, that the great Manuel Escorza has betrayed his revolutionary principles to hide away the bishop of Barcelona in the very convent that houses his sister the nun."

Silence.

"Careful, little sister," said the stranger, dragging out each syllable. "It wouldn't take much encouragement to send a group of trigger-happy militiamen your way. You'd all end up like those mummies you've got buried who knows where, but before that you would endure a long, unpleasant ordeal. And that includes you, the bishop, and that little girl you have locked in her cell."

More silence. Big, warm tears rolled down the novice's cheeks. She was hardly breathing; she could feel the beginnings of a burning sensation in her chest.

"Here's what we'll do," added the man, squeaking like nails on a chalkboard. "I've already said I will not take the bishop, but neither am I particularly keen to see you get killed. For the time being at least. What I can do is place the convent under surveillance. You'll get the Catalan police, no less; after all, they *are* under my command. What do you say to that, little sister?" The mother abbess said nothing. "That should also help us verify what happened with the pigs. You can't complain, now can you? Go on then, help me up, little sister. I have a lot to do and war waits for no one."

Sister Concepció did not take another breath until she heard the key turning in the lock. She let out the air she had been holding and began to pant like a castaway suspended between life and death.

"THE BASIC IDEA," explained a circumspect Judge Miquel Carbonissa, "is to take advantage of the cycle that follows the arc of nature. Continually, from dead bodies new ones are born—living bodies. The earth is nourished by animal and human carrion, by the remains of trees and vegetables. Bury a body, plant a seed above it, and soon you will see a tree growing. In a way, that's what we've done with Hadaly."

The words of the magistrate ricocheted through the walls of the grotto and vanished into the dampness beneath the natural vault. With a look of awe, Superintendent Gregori Muñoz listened as the judge spoke; Doctor Humbert Pellicer observed both men with growing impatience. A few steps from the three men, the great black horse, illuminated by the glow of the lanterns, cut a haughty, indifferent figure.

"What the judge has done here," said the doctor, "is take human remains and give them new life by means of electric devices. It is life itself that has benefitted from our experiment."

"Life . . ." murmured the superintendent, not addressing anyone in particular. He contemplated the animal, transfixed, without daring to approach it.

"See for yourself," urged the doctor. "Your Honor, if you would kindly . . ."

Judge Carbonissa approached Hadaly, felt the animal's back for the switch, and flipped it. The animal's eyes lit up at once; it stomped and moved its legs. It slowly made its way toward the end of the grotto, but seemed to change its mind and it turned around and returned to the judge's side. It lowered its head tamely and allowed the man to caress it.

"There you have it," exclaimed Doctor Pellicer, smiling triumphantly at the police officer. "Isn't it marvelous?"

Superintendent Muñoz had gone from astonishment to consternation. "What is the origin of this monstrosity?" His curt tone earned him a reproachful glance from Judge Carbonissa.

"It would take too long to explain," replied Doctor Pellicer, who, in contrast, seemed utterly delighted. "Let's just say that our friend Judge Carbonissa has dedicated many days of his life to the study of automatons and had long toyed with the idea of building one that would go a step beyond a merely mechanical engine and include organic matter in its makeup. As for me, you already know that my profession entails a quotidian dealing with death, and, over the years, this can become abhorrent even to the hardiest of spirits. I felt that contributing even modestly to Judge Carbonissa's endeavor might help offset my malaise . . ."

"But this is a monster!" repeated Superintendent Muñoz, pointing at the horse.

"This notion of monstrosity seems to be a fixation with you," said Doctor Pellicer, assuming a professorial expression. "That is understandable to a certain point, but our goal here is not to mimic nature, but to improve upon it. The word for it is science, superintendent. It is an application of reason, a sign of humanity's capacity for progress. Even though our friend the judge would probably have something to add to this argument."

Judge Carbonissa smiled vaguely. "Let's not confuse the superintendent further with our little squabbles, doctor," he said somewhat condescendingly. "You entrust everything to the dictates of progress and science, which you practically sanctify as though they were a new religion. For my part, I will simply point out that in the tension between life and death, in the transition from one to the other, certain forces intervene which escape the boundaries of our rational understanding. It is a question of nuance, really, but the nuance is significant because, in the end, we are speaking about what sets apart an inert body from an animated one—that is, what we conventionally refer to as the soul . . ."

The superintendent hissed like an angry cat. "What on earth are you babbling about? So far, based on what you yourself have revealed"—he turned to Doctor Pellicer—"your . . ."—he hesitated—"your creature has already killed a man. This does not appear to be a very auspicious beginning, not for the progress of humanity, not for the knowledge of the soul."

Doctor Pellicer slowly lit the cigarette he had just finished rolling and made a grimace of distress. "It was an accident. The copper sheets inscribed with the synchronization of Hadaly's movements include a self-protection command. The man must have somehow frightened the animal, and, sadly, he paid the consequences."

"Sadly. But what were you thinking when you allowed this beast to roam freely through the city's downtown in the middle of an air raid?" inquired the superintendent.

"That was precisely our intent," Judge Carbonissa said softly, as Hadaly shifted its head as though listening. "We wanted to set a human feat, a proclamation of life's supremacy over death—a proclamation, therefore, of hope—in the midst of the destruction and brutality by which our species debases itself. No doubt we allowed ourselves to be carried away by the euphoria that seized us after watching Hadaly gallop for the first time, but we had no intention of causing any harm. Just the opposite."

The superintendent, who was starting to look pale, cast a bitter look at Doctor Pellicer's cigarette. "You are all crazy," he said flatly. "I thought I had seen it all, but you take the prize. Completely looney."

"Exactly what Galileo was called after he declared that the Earth revolved around the Sun," objected the doctor, smoking calmly. "And Paracelsus, too, when he described the causes of syphilis. Or Servetus, when he discovered the circulatory system by studying the lungs. I will not pretend I am not disheartened by your reaction, superintendent. I thought I would discover in you a keen intellect, but I was obviously mistaken."

"Great. Now you insinuate that I am dull simply because I am not jumping for joy before the sight of Doctor Frankenstein here and his hunchback friend. What will you do, have your creature kill me, too?"

"For the love of God," sighed Doctor Pellicer, crestfallen.

Hadaly neighed briefly, the sound like an admonition. Out of the corner of his eye the superintendent glanced at the animal with apprehension.

"Superintendent," Judge Carbonissa said somewhat shyly, "you have nothing to fear from us or from Hadaly. We don't wish anyone harm. As I've said, our goal is quite the opposite. At the risk of sounding immodest, I would say that Doctor Pellicer and I might be considered philanthropists."

"Go tell that to the fellow at the Church of Bethlehem," replied the superintendent. Then he had an idea: "What are you, masons?"

Judge Carbonissa and Doctor Pellicer exchanged a quick glance.

"That is not a matter we need to clarify now," said the doctor. "It is a policeman's job to ask questions, but this one, if you don't mind my saying, is irrelevant."

The superintendent raised a hand, then let it drop, conveying his lack of interest in the matter.

"Superintendent," the judge again addressed the officer. "Allow me to pose the question. Wouldn't you agree that the real monstrosity is not to be found within this cave but outside, in the streets and homes of this city, where men are killing men, where fury, hatred and rage have poisoned people's souls? Don't you see that the true danger comes from the beasts running wild among us, not from Hadaly, who is merely the brainchild of two men who yearn to come closer to understanding life?"

The superintendent couldn't say whether the judge's reasoning was absurd or whether it forced him to think, but the fact was he didn't know how to respond.

He looked at Judge Carbonissa and Doctor Pellicer and thought that although they might be crazy, not only were they harmless, but their behavior and mode of expression reflected a rare kind of goodness. He hadn't encountered goodness in anyone since his mother's death. I hope I'm not mistaken, he told himself.

He waved away the cigarette smoke, gave the judge and the doctor his back and took a few steps, until he was in front of Hadaly. The horse observed him with a look that sent chills through him: What was in those eyes? Who was looking at him, exhausted, from the depths of those pupils, as though imploring his help?

He caressed Hadaly's muzzle and nodded. Then he turned to the men: "Could you please tell me how you reached this point?"

"HEY. HEY."

"Mmm?"

"Wake up. Open your eyes. Hey."

"Mmm? Where . . . ?"

"Over here. Open your eyes."

"Where . . . am I?"

"In the big house. Rise and shine, little priest."

Brother Pau Darder rubbed his eyes and opened them. The first thing he saw was Burntface standing at the foot of the cot, his scalded mug observing him, then the chamber pot in a corner of the room, next to the candle butt that was against the wall. Then, in front of him, the iron grille extending from wall to wall. He had been asleep but he couldn't recall his dreams. It was as though he were already dead.

"You do sleep a lot, little priest," Burntface reprimanded him in his hoarse voice.

Brother Darder covered his eyes with the palm of his hand. "I'm thirsty and hungry," he said slowly. "When I sleep, at least I forget."

The Marist raised his head and saw, on the floor by the

straw mattress, a pot full of brownish water and another that contained a few lumpy garbanzos. He started to spring for it but an intense nausea made him pause; he sat on the cot unable to move, queasy, his head spinning. A spasm made his stomach churn; he tried to vomit, but only succeeded in coughing and strings of saliva oozed from his mouth.

"What a spectacle," Burntface taunted him. "Aren't you ashamed of welcoming guests in this manner, little priest?"

"I don't feel well. I need to get out of here," murmured Brother Darder, wiping his mouth with the back of his hand.

Burntface grinned. "Of course you do. You're right, you need to beat it. But in order to do that you got to get your strength back. Go on, eat up."

Burntface crouched and grasped the pot of water in one hand and the garbanzos in the other. Very slowly, he brought them closer to Brother Darder, until they hovered beside his emaciated face. With his back resting against the wall, Brother Darder lifted a hand to grasp the garbanzos, but when his fingers were about to touch the tin pot, Burntface suddenly withdrew it.

"You want your meals in bed, I got to put the fucking food in your mouth? You're a spoiled brat from moneyed folks, little priest. You want the chow, you get up and get it."

Burntface turned around and walked to the other side

of the cell. He placed the garbanzos on the floor by the chamber pot and peeked inside.

"Son of a bitch, your insides rotten or what, little priest? You know you're shitting green, don't you?"

Brother Darder didn't say anything. He remained seated on the straw mattress, his back glued to the brick wall, his head canted to the side, on his shoulder.

"No response?" asked Burntface, turning to him. "C'mon now. Come and get your grub."

The spots on Burntface's face gathered into a scowl, as though he were staring at the sun.

"Why are you doing this to me?" asked Brother Darder with a thread of a voice.

With two steps, Burntface planted himself in front of the Marist, extended his arm, and slapped him with the palm of his hand, knocking his head against the wall.

"Why am I doing what to you?" Burntface screamed, enraged. "What is it exactly that I am doing to you, stupid little priest?"

He grabbed Brother Darder's ear between his thumb and index fingers and jerked on it with such violence that the priest fell off the cot and onto the floor. Brother Darder felt as though something had exploded inside his skull.

"Go get the food!" ordered the militiaman. "Go get it, dammit! Are you deaf?"

Pressing one hand against the cot, the other against the wall, Brother Darder slowly gained his footing. His head throbbed; sharp pains cut through him, as though he had been pierced through with one of those sackcloth needles his father used to stitch together the sacks of grain in his warehouse.

Emili will bring shame on his family.

He took one step and tottered. He thought about the rats outside his window.

"What's the matter, little priest? I thought you were hungry. You're three steps away from the food. You can't take three sorry steps?"

Three steps. It would be more than that—his steps were small now. And he was tormented by the pain. He took one more step, then another. He was shivering as though from a fever. Come to think of it, it probably was a fever.

Suddenly he found himself back on the floor. He had lost his balance. No—Burntface had tripped him.

"That won't do, little priest!" Burntface shouted above him. Brother Darder shifted his head and saw his tormentor's boots. "Better watch your step! Go on, get up and eat!"

A blow to his nape made him kiss the ground again. Another of Burntface's caresses, this time delivered with the side of his hand.

"What's keeping you? Get moving, we don't have all day, dammit!"

Brother Darder's head boomed; it felt as though it was about to explode. His teeth ached as well and he recognized the greasy texture and the unmistakable taste of blood; he started to run his tongue over them but the pain stopped him.

"You better get up, little priest, or I'll have to give you a real beating. You hear me?"

Fear. Fear. He didn't want to be beaten again. He couldn't take any more blows from that singed-face beast. He propped himself up on his elbows and flexed his legs until he was in a kneeling position. Then another push, and he was up. He looked straight in front of him: two small steps and he would be at the pots. He glimpsed the chamber pot and its revolting contents, no longer disgusted. He felt only pain—and fear. He couldn't take any more thrashing.

His first step was more assured than he had expected.

"Good, little priest. You're almost there." Burntface was breathing down his back, whispering in his ear.

The shivering started again and he paused for an instant. He breathed deeply and swallowed some blood. One more step. He put his right foot forward, but before it came to rest on the floor, Burntface had knocked him off balance with a knee-jab to his left calf and a shove to his back that threw him against the wall. He held his hands out in front of him as he hit the wall, but he couldn't keep from tumbling to the floor again. He lay there, curled up in a fetal position, within reach of the pots of water and garbanzo beans and the chamber pot.

"See how you were able to make it to the food, little priest? You only needed a little push, didn't you? A little push was all it took to get you there. Are you not hungry anymore, little priest? Are you not thirsty?"

Brother Darder coughed and spat out blood. Perhaps he had broken a tooth—there was a sharp pain in his mouth. Slowly, he stretched his body to reach the pot of water. He had to have a sip.

But it was not to be. Burntface bounded forward and, with a kick, knocked over the pots and the chamber pot. The water and garbanzo beans lay scattered across the floor next to a pool of greenish fecal matter. Some of it splattered on Brother Darder's clothes and on his face, which wore a blank expression.

"See what you've done now, little priest. You're a real mess, aren't you?" Burntface taunted him. "There'll be no slop for you now. You'll have to wait for me to bring you some more. And, to tell you the truth, I don't know when that will be. Oh—wait—you could just eat it as is, seasoned with a bit of your own crap! Don't you like eating shit, little priest?"

Brother Darder recalled the rats.

He thought about Brother Gendrau, killed next to a child, and about the blood puddle that had formed beneath their bodies.

He wouldn't have been able to say where he got the strength: it was as though he were a puppet and someone were making him go this way and that. He jumped up and pounced on Burntface, grabbing him by the waist. The militiaman was caught off guard and fell backward.

"Son of a bitch!" he screamed as his hand went to his waist, in search of his gun.

He didn't make it in time. Brother Darder raised his

fist and delivered a ferocious blow to the militiaman's crotch and he doubled over and wailed in pain. His hand continued to fumble at his waist, but Brother Darder grabbed it and bit into it as hard as he could, drawing blood.

Burntface scrambled to get away from the Marist and managed to half-sit up to defend himself. But Brother Darder was so filled with rage that he seemed to have taken on the strength of two men. He moved frantically, eyes bulging, mouth full of blood, and swooped down on his jailer, grabbed him by the neck with one hand, and pounded his pocked face with the other, the fury of his actions emanating from the depths of his soul or from some other, unknown source. Another punch, and another. And another. Each harder, wilder.

The men fought in a silence disturbed only by the dull sound of flesh being pounded. Burntface punched Brother Darder in the face, the neck, the abdomen, and drove his knees into his opponent's back. But the Marist took the blows in stride, as though suddenly desensitized to pain, and he kept up the speed and brutality of his attack. Like a jackhammer, he hit and hit, until his jailer's face was a deformed, bloodied mass. At some point he heard the crunching sound of bones breaking and he smiled when he realized they weren't his own.

He suddenly understood the rodents' pleasure as they tore at the body of their dying comrade.

Burntface had not moved for a while. Brother Darder

stopped when he finally realized how tired he was. The priest huffed like the engine of an old, overheated car, but he was exultant. The militiaman mumbled something—he was still alive.

Brother Darder stood up with a lightness that only minutes before would have been unthinkable, and then he crouched down again, maneuvered his hand under Burntface's ribcage and flipped him over so that he lay face down. The militiaman made guttural sounds, muttering incoherently like a drunk sleeping off a hangover. Still panting, Brother Darder sat on Burntface's back, grabbed him by his hair and lifted his head. Then, with all the strength he was still able to marshal, he slammed it against the floor. Again and again—and again. On the seventh time his skull cracked, a sound like glass falling on stone. Burntface's body writhed a couple of times. Then it was still.

Brother Darder rose and observed the blood oozing from his jailer's bashed skull, mixing with the paste formed by the garbanzos, the water and the feces.

He thought: *If God so deems it . . .*

God had done nothing to prevent it.

He rummaged through the militiaman's uniform and found thirty pesetas in paper money and a bunch of keys. He opened the door to that hellhole, stepped out onto the stifling, low-ceilinged landing, and bolted the door with two turns of the key.

PART 3
Stabat Mater

HE WROTE:

I am comfortable here.

I like the coolness of the chapel in the middle of the night when everyone is asleep and I can be there alone, contemplating the images of the saints.

I like the smell of clean clothes hung out to dry on the small terrace by the laundry room; I get close and breathe in the soap and bleach-scented air.

I like the gothic arcade of the gallery in the cloister. So simple, so delicate, so elegant.

I like to sit in a corner by the woodshed and wait for the mice to come out. I enjoy catching them.

I feel good here. Protected by these stone walls, sheltered from the incessant clamoring of war. In the company of the Holy Ghost. In the company of monsters.

I am but a poor chimney sweep who has left his coffin and now wanders aimlessly through a city that is bathed in blood.

When the moon is high, I enjoy walking silently down

the hall where the cells are, watching over the nuns' sleep.

I am fond of the sleepless young girl confined in her small alcove, striving to compose a piece of sacred music. There is a certain beauty to such futile efforts.

The convent is an orderly world, oblivious to the chaos that governs the city. A world in which everyone performs the task assigned them and fulfills it in the best possible manner.

I could easily grow accustomed to such a place. A place where I can rest, protected by the shadows. A place where I am well taken care of.

I have made a foolish mistake.

Oh, yes, it was foolish, but there are times when a vampire is unable to tame his thirst no matter how hard he tries. And the pigs were right there, nice and warm, nestled in the straw and dung, lying on their bed of fruit skins and potato peels, sleeping.

I had only to sink my teeth into them.

The first one was easy because I caught it deep in slumber. The second, not so much: it was roused by the squeals from the first (just the one squeal, really—I snapped its neck at once) and tried to defend itself. Pigs are ferocious fighters.

But I knew how to grapple with them. It had been a long time since I had feasted on the blood of barnyard animals, but I remembered the method well.

I started by slowly removing my jacket without

glancing away from the animal's eyes, the creature observing me, gauging how best to tackle me. We were locked in that stance for a long time; removing my jacket seemed to take forever.

Finally, the pig charged toward me. I saw it flying at me, enormous.

In one breath, I wrapped my left arm in my jacket—a thick jacket like a military coat, but soft and pleasant to the touch—and offered it to the pig. The animal's canines sank into the cloth, tearing through it down to the flesh. It clamped its jaws and bit harder and harder, furious, grunting, slobbering. I held out my arm as firmly as I could, though the pig kept jerking and it felt as though my arm was on the point of being severed. I raised my other arm, fist clenched, and delivered a hard, blunt blow to the animal's head. Its eyes bulged; the sound of its skull cracking thrilled me. Its bite slackened; it released me and took a few steps on shaky legs. Then it collapsed, heavy. Inert.

I unwrapped the jacket from around my arm and observed the blood. I sucked on it greedily. I approached the pig, lying with its back to me, and crouched to make sure it was dead. With a swift motion, I flipped the animal over, belly up. Then I saw it had my own face. I felt an unspeakable anger. I threw myself on the pigs, sank my teeth into them and drank their blood until I was sated.

"WHAT A PLEASURE, Superintendent Muñoz."

Manuel Escorza uttered the words with an affability

that seemed almost sincere. Seated in an armchair in his office at the Department of Investigations, he resembled an oversized puppet that someone had left as a prank intended for whoever happened to be passing by. He was flanked by Aureli Fernández and Antoni Ordaz, who sat silently in upholstered armchairs, the three of them forming a semicircle. In the center, at a rather formal distance, sat Superintendent Gregori Muñoz.

"Likewise, sir."

Escorza flicked his hand as though waving away a fly. "Let's do away with bourgeois formalities. To you, superintendent, I am a comrade."

"As you wish, sir—that is, comrade."

"The two men joining us," said Escorza, "are Comrades Aureli Fernández, who heads our Committee of Antifascist Militias, and Comrade Antoni Ordaz, who works with him."

"Pleased to meet you, comrades," said the superintendent. Ordinarily he would have laughed at hearing himself utter those words, but now he did not find it amusing. He was tense and intimidated.

"Pleasure," responded Aureli Fernández. Antoni Ordaz muttered something inaudible.

Manuel Escorza drew out the pause in conversation, and Superintendent Muñoz lowered his eyes to the floor.

"Thank you for agreeing to grant us some of your valuable time," Escorza said at last. "The goal of this meeting is to establish a direct rapport between us. We are conducting a round of meetings with the heads of the

Barcelona police precincts for this very purpose. As you are well aware, we are living through difficult times, and we believe this calls for closer collaboration between our Department and your most valuable men, those who, like yourself, are in daily contact with life on the streets."

"The gesture is appreciated, comrade," said Superintendent Muñoz, raising his eyes again.

"I have been perusing your file," said Escorza, opening a folder, "and it is truly remarkable. More than twenty years on the force, steadily rising through the ranks. You joined the service as an officer in 1914; two years later you'd been promoted to corporal and, merely a year after that, to sergeant. In 1920 you were again promoted to lieutenant and, four years later, to inspector. In 1926 you passed the state exam to become chief inspector and, in 1931 the Department of Home Affairs of Catalunya appointed you superintendent. And it just goes on. Any day now, we will have to promote you to commissioner. A brilliant career, no doubt about it. Congratulations are in order."

"Much appreciated, comrade."

"You are also decorated. You were awarded the bronze medal for your role in the arrest of a band of miscreants who sold smuggled goods on the black market. They were armed and opened fire, but the two deaths that resulted from the showdown were criminals. No police officer was wounded. And that was thanks to your skill and valor as the leader of the operation, superintendent. You put your neck on the line. A well-deserved medal."

"You flatter me, sir. I mean, comrade. Again, thank you."

"A first-rate officer, is he not?" Escorza inquired of Fernández and Ordaz, who nodded as one man.

Muñoz swallowed. He could almost feel the incoming tempest.

"In any case, superintendent, we need men like you," continued Escorza. "You are what the revolution needs, I mean. Intelligent, determined men. Honest and hard-working. The fascists want to wipe us out, along with our country, but we must best them and wipe them out first. Do you agree, superintendent?"

"To the fullest, comrade," Muñoz responded without hesitation.

"Yes, I felt sure of it. I only wanted to emphasize that in each police jurisdiction we must approach the issue of unauthorized assemblies with extra zeal. You never know where insurgents might congregate to plot against the legitimate authority of the Republic and the Generalitat government. Basements, warehouses, abandoned or semi-demolished office buildings—that type of thing."

"Absolutely, comrade."

"Absolutely," parroted Manuel Escorza, pausing for a moment, as if trying to remember something. "Fantastic, superintendent. That will be all then. Again, it has been a pleasure speaking with you. Carry on as you have until now, superintendent."

"May I go?" asked Muñoz with a measure of involuntary disbelief.

"Back to work, yes, where this country needs you most," said Escorza with a grin he had intended to be beatific.

"In that case, gentlemen, that is, comrades, if you'll excuse me . . ."

Muñoz rose from his armchair, performed the customary salute, and headed for the door. His hand was already on the doorknob when he heard Manuel Escorza`s voice behind him.

"Superintendent."

It could not have gone so smoothly.

"Yes, comrade?"

"There is one question I forgot to put to you."

The superintendent stiffened. He noticed Aureli Fernández and Antoni Ordaz darkly scrutinizing him.

"I'll do my best to answer . . ."

"Of course you will," said Escorza, condescendingly. "It regards the removal of two bodies from a crime scene at a pension on Carrer Ferran—a boy and an old man, apparently. Do you know what I'm referring to?"

"Indeed, comrade."

"Indeed. It appears you neglected to include in your report that both the old man and the three witnesses at the time of the removal were priests."

Sons of bitches. The superintendent's thoughts paraded through the darkest curses he could level at Sirga and his entire family.

"And? Have you anything to say about it?" inquired Escorza.

"It's true. They were wearing street clothes and I didn't recognize them as religious men."

"Despite what you say, I have been made aware that during the course of your conversation with the witnesses this fact came out. You're sharp, superintendent. You don't miss a trick."

Muñoz bit his top lip. "I didn't think it was relevant to the report."

"Of course," replied Escorza, as though talking to a child, "you did not think it relevant. And yet, you are aware of the world you are living in, superintendent, are you not?"

"Yes," conceded Muñoz. "Yes I am, comrade."

He stood tall, almost at attention. This was a trial. A summary trial. His gaze moved from one man to another. In Aureli Fernández's eyes he saw a thirst for vengeance; in Antoni Ordaz's he recognized the executioner. Manuel Escorza's were inscrutable.

"Anyone can make a mistake, superintendent," said the cripple, laconic. "But in these agitated times, everyone must pay for their mistakes. Your slipup, shall we call it, leaves me with two options. The first is to add high treason to your distinguished credentials and instruct Fernández and Ordaz to take the appropriate measures. The second is to grant you a second chance and put you in charge of a special mission. After all, it is true that men of your caliber are not a dime a dozen, and it would be a shame to be forced to . . . Well, it hardly needs to be said, does it? You help me decide, superintendent. Which of the two options do you think is best?"

Muñoz breathed in deeply through his nose. "Tell me what I can do for you, Comrade Escorza. And for the revolution," he said, his voice barely audible.

Escorza again bared that obscene grin of his. "It is a delicate job, superintendent, in an unexpected place—the Capuchin Convent in Sarrià. Comrades Fernández and Ordaz will fill you in on the details and an officer from your precinct—he goes by the name of Sirga—will give you the rest of the information."

SHE STILL DIDN'T know where to begin; she continued to debate between C-sharp minor and A major. The eruption in the chapterhouse of the mother abbess and the stranger named Manuel had prevented her from carrying out the test with the vase, and she hadn't been able to reach a decision. Neither bean nor almond.

She continued, then, her study of the poem by Jacopone da Todi, which increasingly resembled an unsolvable hieroglyphic. The more she read and reread it the less sense it made to her, as though the words were dimming little by little, losing their meaning. Abstruse blots on a piece of paper. In the end she always returned to the first verses, the only ones that still commanded her attention:

Stabat Mater dolorosa
Iuxta crucem lacrimosa
Dum pendebat Filius

The mother weeping beneath her son on the cross. The image played over and over in her imagination, in her dreams and waking life. That was her theme, the theme she must translate into a musical score. But how?

Her mother had told her not to be afraid, but she hadn't warned her of the abominations she would encounter in life. Even inside the convent.

Who was this Manuel who had the power to decide whether Bishop Perugorría was to be removed from the convent? And what had mother abbess meant when she said that the bishop was stalking her? What could His Excellency the bishop possibly want with a humble novice such as herself? And what was there to fear, what was the danger that troubled the mother abbess so much?

Why didn't her own mother come to fetch her so they could leave and travel far from the Desert of Sarrià where thirteen-year-old girls were doomed to torment?

She tried to guide her concentration back to the Stabat Mater, but found she could only focus on the translucent glimmers that floated across her eyes like a mirage. It must have been the effect of exhaustion, or perhaps hunger. She had learned that fear, when sufficiently intense, trumped bodily urges. But that didn't mean she had no need to eat or rest.

She rose from the spot on the floor where she had been sitting, her legs weak and tingly. She took several steps and was relieved to find that the cramp slowly diminished, then disappeared. She stretched out on the cot; it creaked slightly under the weight of her small body.

When she raised her eyes she had a strange perspective: the crucifix over her bed looked like a projectile about to be launched. The hanged son for whom his mother wept. She was so unsettled that she had even neglected her prayers of late. In moments of affliction praying had always brought her solace, ever since she was a child. But until she entered that shadowy convent, what afflictions had she experienced? In any event, it was never the wrong moment to seek the warmth of our Heavenly Father, His Son, and the Holy Ghost. Three people in one, her mother had tried to explain, though she never truly understood. How could three people exist in one? Nevertheless, without shifting her position on the cot, she made the sign of the cross over her brow, mouth, and chest, and moving her lips without making a sound, she began to recite:

Our Father, who art in heaven,
Hallowed be thy name,
Thy kingdom come,
Thy will be done . . .

She paused. Again that murmur she could not identify, a brief, faint rustling that was nevertheless audible, as though someone at a great remove was trying to tell her something. Those little noises she kept hearing—were they voices trying to speak to her? Or were they figments of her feverish imagination? More acutely than ever, she felt the need for the comfort of prayer; she shut her eyes tightly, as she used to do when she was little and was afraid the bogeyman was hiding under her bed, and she continued:

> *Thy will be done*
> *On Earth as it is in Heaven.*
> *Give us this day our daily bread . . .*

Another sound disturbed her, and this time it wasn't a murmur, but the sharp, clear sound of knocking on the door to her cell. She heard someone leaving something on the floor, then footsteps scurrying down the hall. Her meal had been brought. The Lord's Prayer had had an immediate effect, she thought, and this notion made her smile.

She rose from her cot, walked to the door, turned the key in the lock and opened the door. She looked down, but there was no tray with a plate of food and a pitcher of water. In their place she saw a pair of over-sized black shoes and, scanning upward, a cassock and, atop that, the head of Bishop Perugorría in his stiff white clerical collar, staring at her with vitreous eyes and a terse smile.

She stood at the door, mute and petrified, as though she had taken a strong poison. The bishop spoke in a mellifluous voice: "My dear, I was wondering if you would have a moment to speak with me."

"ARE YOU TELLING me that a priest has bolted from the brig after killing a militiaman with his bare hands? Is that what you are saying?"

Manuel Escorza had risen from the table and, using his crutches, limped toward Sirga until less than a span separated the men. At such a short distance, Sirga could see the tiny saliva bubbles that exploded between Escorza's lips as he spoke. Out of the corner of his eye, he glimpsed Aureli Fernández looking as if he had just been smacked and Gil Portela looking as if he had just caught a whiff of shit.

Sirga scratched his jaw. "That's right, comrade."

With saucer eyes, as though startled by a large, poisonous frog that had just leapt into his office, Manuel Escorza looked the young man up and down, then stood there for a moment before giving a big, sonorous laugh. He returned to his place, his boot lifts screeching along the plank flooring, and let himself drop into his armchair.

"Goddammit."

"How long has it been since you say you found Burntface's body?" asked Aureli Fernández without losing his sullen grimace.

"Less than an hour, Comrade Fernández—the time it took to contact the squad on duty and have them collect the body and get rid of it. After that, I came straight here to inform you."

"And how long had he been dead?" inquired Gil Portela with his customary apathy.

"I don't know. I never touched him." Sirga ran his fingers through his hair and scratched his scalp. "Since last night, I suppose, when he was on guard duty. I had the morning shift and when I got there I found him splayed on the floor."

"With his head bashed in," added Gil Portela.

"With his head bashed in," confirmed Sirga.

Aureli Fernández and Gil Portela exchanged glances. Fernández spoke: "It's hard to believe that Marist brother could have done such a thing. He was shitting himself back at the Tostadero."

"Burntface didn't have many friends," added Gil Portela. "He had too much pent-up resentment, was too much of a neanderthal. Quite a few had it in for him."

"So who could have done this?" asked Sirga. "Only he and I had the key—only Burntface and I knew the priest was being held there."

There was a thick silence. Aureli Fernández looked at Gil Portela again. Portela spoke:

"You, perhaps?"

Sirga's hands jerked as if he'd just touched a live wire. "Me? How can you even say that?" He tried to make eye contact with the rest of the men, but they all averted their gazes. "How can you think that? But I . . . it's ridiculous! Absurd! Tell me you don't believe that!"

He looked as though he was on the verge of tears.

Manuel Escorza breathed in ostentatiously until a snort came out. "Leave him alone. No need to dig where there's nothing to find." He opened his arms. "Let's try to fix this mess. Fernández, what's the news from Balaguer?"

"Everything went fine. The buses were dispatched yesterday to collect the first batch of brothers; a car was sent with Ordaz on our side and that Lacunza person on theirs. Brother Plana, the fellow who's in charge of keeping us abreast of developments, also went along for the ride. When they arrived at the Convent of Bellpuig de les Avellanes the seminarians were already waiting, standing single file like in a procession. Apparently the hardest thing was to round up the teachers who were hiding out in the mountains, but the farmers had spread the news and in the end everyone turned up."

"So, how many have already left?" inquired Manuel Escorza without turning around.

"Only the seminarians," Gil Portela replied. "Just as we had requested of them, the folks from the Puigcerdà committee were pigheaded and refused to let anyone through except the young boys. Ordaz play-acted for a while trying to make it seem like he wanted to get everyone out. In the end, the ones who are of age were sent back to Barcelona on buses with the promise that they'll be part of the second evacuation. Lacunza is fuming, from what I hear, but he'll do as we tell him. He wants to get across the border at any cost."

"I can imagine," said Manuel Escorza. "What's the story with the Frenchie?"

"He's being held at Sant Elies," Aureli Fernández said. "As soon as Lacunza and Plana were on their way back to Barcelona, we sent a squad to Pension Capell with search and arrest warrants. We have the rest of the money."

"And why have I yet to see it?" shouted Manuel Escorza. "Bring it to me at once! And the Frenchman—take him up to Carretera de l'Arrabassada and shoot him in the back of the head." He hesitated. "No, just throw him in the Modelo prison. Maybe we can exchange him for ransom once we have gotten rid of this riffraff."

Aureli Fernández made a grimace of disapproval. "Listen, comrade, I still don't think it's necessary to—"

"Dead dogs don't bite," Gil Portela interrupted with a smile.

"Precisely," said Manuel Escorza. "And besides, this ordeal with Burntface adds new urgency. Get moving with the second evacuation and round up the Marists—including the ones who are coming with Ordaz—and take them to the Capuchin convent. Since we already have the money, let's wind this thing up as soon as possible. And while we're at it, let's close down our dear little nuns' convent; I've run out of patience." He paused for a moment, perhaps considering his sister's fate, perhaps just to cough. "We'll stick the bishop somewhere else; I'll think of something. Let's get things out of the way, understood?"

"Understood," agreed Gil Portela with a satisfied smile.

"Comrade, listen, please," insisted Aureli Fernández. "Do you really think it's necessary to—?"

"Understood?" repeated Manuel Escorza, angry.

"Okay, okay, goddammit."

"Turn everything upside down and find this damn Marist brother who's absconded," ordered Manuel Escorza. "Take him to Sant Elies and let the boys have their way with him. As for you . . ."

Sirga had been trembling for a while. Manuel Escorza studied him with those same saucer eyes. Then he smiled.

". . . you have a mission to carry out with your superintendent."

"IT'S A MOUSETRAP," said Superintendent Muñoz, waving away Doctor Pellicer's smoke. "They have seized the Capuchin convent with all the nuns inside, and they are sending me to investigate something to do with a couple of dead pigs. To make things worse, they are making me take along that rat Sirga, presumably with orders to take me out. Exciting prospect, don't you think?"

They were in Judge Carbonissa's library; the judge had already brought out his diminutive liqueur glasses and a bottle of Armagnac. He and Doctor Pellicer were sprawled in gutta-percha wing chairs while Superintendent Muñoz slowly paced back and forth in front of the high, crammed bookcases, his hands in his pockets, a grave look on his face. From behind the heavy velvet curtains that blocked the large windows came the jagged-thunder sounds of a late-summer storm. A summer that had been warm— Superintendent Muñoz recalled—with clear skies and a resplendent sunlight above the bombed houses and the bodies scattered on the streets of Barcelona.

Something Muñoz had said brought the judge out of a state of absorption that at times seemed almost constitutional. Leaning forward, he asked, "Do you know how these animals died, superintendent?"

"Pardon?" said the officer, not sure he'd understood the question.

"The pigs. I was asking if you were privy to the details of the case."

"It appears they were attacked by some kind of beast. They were found dead inside their pen, bitten to death."

"Bitten to death. Interesting."

"Interesting? What can I say? It's merely an excuse to force me to go to the convent. Who knows—Escorza himself probably ordered them killed."

"In the treatise *De masticatione mortuorum*," said the judge, turning to look at Doctor Pellicer, not appearing to have heard what Muñoz had said, "Rehrius recounts that in a Hungarian village called Kisolova, this man Plogojovits turned up one day two months after his own burial. His wife declared that her deceased husband had appeared at the house and asked to be handed his shoes, which left her so horrified that soon afterward she left the village and never returned. The thing is that Plogojovits continued to appear to the farmers of Kisolova, or, more accurately, to their livestock. At night, he would raid the farmers' pigpens and kill the animals by strangling them with his own hands and biting them on the neck and, once they were dead, he would drink their blood. In the end, the parish rector and an officer in the Emperor's service exhumed Plogojovits's body, drove a sharp stake into his chest, and threw him into a burning pyre where he was reduced to ashes . . ."

Superintendent Muñoz raised his eyebrows. "For Christ's sake," he said. "I tell you that the FAI has decided to take me out and you react by coming up with these vampire tales?"

Judge Carbonissa turned and looked at the superintendent as though he had just arrived. Doctor Pellicer said, "Our dear judge's erudition sometimes gets the best of him, superintendent." The judge mumbled something as he sipped on his Armagnac. "Nevertheless, and given the circumstances surrounding the case, the judge has pointed to a hypothesis that you would do well not to dismiss out of hand. Remember what I told you about vampiric disorders."

The superintendent nodded several times. "I remember it well, doctor, but I don't think you gentlemen understand me. My concern is . . ."

". . . staying alive," the doctor completed the sentence. "It is a reasonable concern. Do you think we might be of any help in that regard, superintendent? If so, don't hesitate to tell us how. Might Hadaly be of use?"

The police officer bit his lips and then he smiled. They truly were a lost cause, the pair of them. "I appreciate it, doctor, but I really can't see how a mechanical horse could help me in this situation. I'll figure it out."

"Mechanical, but with organic elements," Judge Carbonissa pointed out. "It is the principle of life that—"

"Yes, whatever you say," the superintendent said impatiently. "I didn't come here for that, but to entrust you with something I would like you to keep."

He took his hand out of his pocket and produced a small object. It was the spinning top. He walked to the coffee table and put it down beside the liqueur glasses.

"It belonged to the boy in Pension Capell," he explained. "In case I . . . well, in case I don't make it."

"*Memento mori*, huh?" said the judge.

Muñoz tried to muster a smile. "I suppose so," he admitted.

"We are honored by your trust, superintendent. Judge Carbonissa and I appreciate it most sincerely."

"Well, you are welcome," the officer replied drily. "I don't really know who else to approach. If I get killed, perhaps you will one day be able to establish who killed the boy. The truth is I haven't been able to take my mind off it."

"The *Manducus*," muttered Judge Carbonissa, absorbed in his Armagnac. But he stopped and didn't complete his thought.

The superintendent sighed and slipped his hands back

into his pockets. A bolt of lightning lit up the edges of the large windows as though someone had switched on a searchlight. Loud thunder followed; sheets of rain lashed against the window panes.

AGAIN THAT ACHE in her belly.

"Why don't you sing, dear? You have such a lovely voice. Please sing to me again."

She felt the heavy ache, like a brick inside her, like a cobblestone she had swallowed and was now sitting right there in the pit of her stomach, oppressive. She felt the ache, and also the chill that was penetrating the cellar—a rank, humid chill, with a stale smell. And fear, a great fear. She was trembling and she did not know whether it was from cold or fear.

"Sing for me, my dear. You were doing wonderfully only a moment ago. Why did you stop? Sing again."

Shelves stocked with food were all around her. Here, the lard; there, the butter; a bit farther along, the pots of jam—plum, apricot, cherry—and a hook with salt cod. Sister Concepció stood at the bottom of the cellar, where the ceiling was lower and the wall became concave and had a recess with an image of Saint Galderic, patron saint of farmers, guarding the food. Wearing a floor-length clerical robe and looking like a large ghost, His Excellency Bishop Perugorría sat atop a barrel of herring in front of her in semi-darkness. Behind the bishop some steps led down to the well and, to his side, others went up to the courtyard: he had positioned himself in the middle, cornering her, thwarting any chance she had to escape. He peered at her with lachrymose eyes and requested again and again that she sing. Earlier, and only by mustering every ounce of courage she possessed, the novice had managed to intone the beginning of Fauré's *Pie Jesu Domine*, but fear had soon strangled her like a knobby, long-fingered hand around her neck, and she had stopped.

The bishop continued to stare at her, unrelenting: "Sing, sweet child. Sing in praise of our Christian faith, by which the Lord, Our Father, will lead us to ecstasy and glory. Sing, my dear."

She recalled the canticles to Saint Galderic that her mother used to sing at that time of year, when summer was coming to an end and she was preparing to go back to school. Her mother had learned the canticles when she was a girl of her age. They had a lovely melody, and she remembered the beginning:

> *Legitimate and ancient Patron*
> *of our farmers,*
> *Saint Galderic every day*
> *watches over fruit and seed . . .*

She had to stop again: the pain in her belly, the choking sensation in her throat, her weak voice that kept breaking up, and that unbearable longing for the sweetness of her mother's song. Why had she not come to collect her? Sister Concepció's eyes filled with big, warm tears like benign drops of rain and she started sobbing like a little girl who had lost a toy. She rested her back against the whitewashed wall and let herself drop to the ground. She continued to weep, and the more she did the greater the onrush of tears; she found it was rather enjoyable—it made her feel that her mother would appear at any moment and tenderly wrap her arms around her, soothe her, tell her there was nothing to fear.

"What is all this now? Is this how you show your faith, my child? Is this how you honor your torment?"

The bishop's booming voice ricocheted against the walls of the cellar and returned to Sister Concepció's ears, amplified. She looked up and saw that he had risen and was standing in front of her, gesturing as though he were a puppeteer at a street fair. She stopped crying as suddenly as she had begun. The bishop had also regained his calm, and now he offered her his woody hand along with an inscrutable smile.

"Get up, dear child. There's something that you *can* do. Something you must do for me and for the glory of your deceased mother."

"Is this Barcelona?"

With every step Brother Darder asked himself the same question. Dazed and bewildered, he plodded along, his faltering steps taking him through a landscape of ruin he did not recognize. After his escape, he had found himself on a deserted street with four dilapidated houses and a strip of earth, sand, and debris ending in a vacant lot filled with refuse and weeds. The sky was thick and sooty.

He took a sloping street that led away from the vacant lot and, a bit later, he arrived at an area of low, small shanty houses. There was no one around; the houses seemed abandoned. He did not recognize anything that would indicate his whereabouts: perhaps he had been taken out of the city, he thought. Then he spotted a man riding a bicycle up a hill. He hastened to catch up with him, and when he was abreast of him, he asked: "Is this Barcelona?"

The man on the bicycle turned around with a look of scorn and started pedaling harder. Brother Darder was left standing in the middle of the sloping road, panting as he watched the cyclist grow smaller as he sped away.

He had killed a man.

His whole body ached from the beating Burntface had given him, and he had painful cramps in his stomach. He was famished, thirsty, spent.

After wandering the empty streets for a long time, he spotted a garage in the distance with people moving about inside. He drew closer. Three men wearing caps were working on an engine mounted on a lathe; when they noticed his presence they studied him with marked hostility.

"Is this Barcelona?" he asked them.

"Go away, you looney," one of them said.

He turned around and started walking again. He had killed a man. His legs could scarcely hold him and felt stultified, as from a coating of rust and gasoline.

He recalled something and turned around to convey it to the men in the garage. It seemed important to do so.

Suddenly everything turned black; he did not feel his head hit the ground.

When he opened his eyes again his vision was blurred and his mouth full of a viscous paste. The sensation scared him, but then he realized it was only his spit. Slowly, his eyes began to regain focus.

"Is this Barcelona?"

And, yes, it was: he was on the corner of Carrer Aribau, by the university. In front of him was the square, the ground gutted by bombs, and the closured Tostadero, its façade partially demolished. He had come full circle, then. The men in the garage must have taken pity on him, carted him to the center of town and, not knowing what to do with him, dumped him on that corner, leaving him on the sidewalk like a drunk or a beggar.

... *shame on his family*.

He had been robbed of his shoes. Or perhaps he wasn't wearing them when he left the prison cell. He wasn't sure, but his feet were as filthy as if he had waded through a quagmire.

This reminded him that he hadn't seen his own

reflection for a long time. He rose and, steadying himself on the wall, verified that his legs could support him, in spite of his dizziness. He spotted a tailor shop on the corner across the street, its counter intact, the dressed mannequins still inside. The sight of the undamaged store surrounded by half-dilapidated, shrapnel-wounded houses put him in an uncomfortable, vague state of mind somewhere between incredulity and despondency.

He crossed the street and approached the shop. He was saddened by the reflection he saw in the window; he looked even worse than he had expected: emaciated, his body scrawny and ungainly, his face gaunt, his cheeks overtaken by a madman's beard. His clothes hung from his frame like a sad rag, and he was so soiled he could have been mistaken for an enfeebled beggar. He was covered with stains, some of excrement, others of blood—his own and Burntface's.

It occurred to him that what he saw in the window was no longer his own image but that of a criminal. He bowed his head and leaned forward as though about to pray. But Brother Darder no longer prayed. He was simply trying to accept that he was now a criminal.

If God so deems it . . .

He started walking, crossed Plaça Universitat and headed down Carrer Tallers toward La Rambla. He passed Plaça Castella and saw a group of men and women who were living on the street: they wore rags and had built a makeshift shelter from empty boxes and debris. As he passed by they shouted out to him: they had recognized him as one of their own. He ignored them and walked on, encountering with each step insufferable signs of misery and devastation. Balconies ripped away, broken windows, bomb craters between the buildings and the cobblestones. The sky was still bleak and the few people moving up and down La Rambla dragged their feet and held their heads low, avoiding each other's gaze. *Am I in Barcelona?* Brother Darder again asked himself, the question merely a reflex now, for he knew full well it was Barcelona. What remained of it, in any event: the ghost of its former self.

He walked up Carrer Ferran until he reached Pension Capell. The building was undamaged, the door locked. He pulled the doorbell chain. He waited a minute, two, three. No answer. He tugged on the chain again, harder now, more insistently. A boy walked by and looked at him with distrust. Then he heard a woman's voice behind the door: "Who is it?"

"Senyora Gertrudis? It's . . ." He lowered his voice so passersby wouldn't hear him. "it's Brother Darder. Do you remember me?"

Silence.

"Do you remember me, Senyora Gertrudis? Please let me in."

The key turned in the lock, the door cracked open and the tip of Senyora Gertrudis's nose protruded. She looked Brother Darder up and down, brought her hands to her face, and began to weep. He had not expected her reaction, and the pang of affection and compassion he felt for the woman made him push the door open, step inside, and embrace her with a tenderness that seemed almost improper but that comforted them both. Senyora Gertrudis was small, a tiny sack of bones, and she smelled pleasantly of talcum powder. She didn't seem to mind the stench from Brother Darder's clothes.

Without releasing the woman from his embrace, he peered down the hallway. The stairs leading to the bedroom were dark.

"Are they gone?" he asked.

Senyora Gertrudis raised her tear-streaked face. "They have been taken away, Brother Darder," she sobbed. "Brother Plana came by a couple of hours ago with FAI militiamen and a bus. He said the evacuation was starting and they were rounding up the brothers who had been dispersed and taking them to the Capuchin convent in Sarrià. They climbed into the bus and left. I am terrified they might claim I was covering up for them. Do you think the people from the FAI will come back for me?

Brother Plana, he thought. "At the Capuchin convent, you say?"

"That's what they told me."

He released the woman and rubbed his hands together, as though preparing to undertake a difficult task.

The parable of the Good Samaritan came to Senyora Gertrudis's mind. "Won't you wash? You are so dirty and ragged . . . I still have the clothes and shoes that belonged to my husband, may he rest in peace. They should be your size, more or less."

Brother Darder tried to smile, but he could not. "I must leave now, Senyora Gertrudis."

"Are you going to look for them? Please tell Brother Plana to explain to the FAI that I was not abetting them."

"Don't worry—I will."

Senyora Gertrudis clasped one of his hands between hers. "May God protect you, brother."

Now he smiled. "Perhaps it would be better if He didn't."

Brother Darder opened the door and went out into the street. He continued up Carrer Ferran as far as Plaça Sant Jaume, where some sort of checkpoint patrol had set up. He counted about a dozen men, as he felt his stomach rise to his throat. He didn't want to backtrack because they had already seen him, so he continued plodding along, his bare feet on the shrapnel-gnawed cobblestones. As he was walking by, one of the militiamen addressed him: "Where are you going, pal?"

Brother Darder stopped and, fixing his wild gaze on some unspecified spot, he shouted as loud as he could: "Comrades, Visca la Revolució!"

The militiamen looked at him as though he were an exotic creature. He wondered how his uncle Emili would have reacted had he seen the deplorable condition he had been reduced to. A few seconds later one of the militiamen burst out laughing and the rest followed suit. Without a doubt, it was better to make them laugh than to anger them, he thought to himself. They were even younger than he, probably none of them over twenty, their appearance strong, arrogant, beautiful. It saddened him to imagine them dead in some back alley, riddled with bullets or killed by an Italian bomb.

The one who had stopped him spoke again: "Excellent, pal. We need more men like you. How about you sing something for us? Do you know 'To the Barricades'? Go on, I'll start it for you.

> *"Our only wealth lies in freedom*
> *Which we defend with courage and boldness.*
> *Raise the flag of revolution . . ."*

The others laughed heartily, while Brother Darder, not knowing the words, lowered his head and stared at his toenails. Finally, another militiaman, half choking on his own laughter, said to the one who was singing: "Leave him alone, man, can't you see he is an outcast?" He turned to look at Brother Darder. "Run along, comrade—and long live the revolution!"

Brother Darder said nothing and moved away from the patrol without haste and without looking back, not even when he heard the militiamen proffer another insult and break out laughing. Freedom, courage, and boldness, went the song, and it sounded like sarcasm to Brother Darder. Though, come to think of it, war was a colossal macabre joke. Brothers sacrificing brothers, parents informing on children, and children killing parents or having them killed; merchants of misery and whoremasters of death, gossipmongers of crime and peddlers of depravation.

He remembered Brother Plana's ridiculous face as he came into his room in Pension Capell to ask him to again hear his confession of having taken a sweet potato from the pantry. Brother Plana who must have already collected his thirty pieces of silver. War created no heroes—only traitors. War was a great rubbish-filled courtyard crawling with rats that devoured each other alive.

He wanted to head to the Capuchin convent, arrive in time to expose and publicly shame Brother Plana before he was killed. Had an evacuation finally been negotiated? It was hard to believe that Brother Lacunza and Adjutant Aragou could have been so naive. Had they paid money to be led to their deaths?

He wanted to head to the Capuchin convent, but instead he wandered like a lost soul through the narrow streets of Barri Gòtic. He still had that sticky paste in his mouth and his innards churned from thirst and hunger. He was exhausted and debated between walking to Sarrià or simply lying down in some corner and letting himself die.

Comrades, Visca la Revolució.

He entered a particularly long and narrow street and came to a building with a great façade and a limestone portal with large wooden doors, the Republican flag flying above it. A public building. MORTUARY, read the plaque on one side of the door, above smaller lettering he could not decipher because his vision blurred.

It seemed like a good idea.

He sat by the door, rested his head on a stone ledge, and fell asleep a few seconds later.

He couldn't tell how long he had slept when he felt someone shaking him by the shoulders, waking him up.

He half opened his eyes and saw a large bespectacled man crouching over him. The smoke from the man's cigarette hit him in the face.

"*Hola*," said the man. "Aren't you the Marist brother from Pension Capell, the Majorcan? I'm Doctor Humbert Pelllicer. I was at the pension to oversee the removal of the bodies. Can you hear me?"

"I killed a man," responded Brother Darder, feeling his head bobbing from side to side.

"SO, THEN," SAID the mother abbess, "my brother hasn't mentioned the presence of His Excellency the bishop here at the convent?"

Superintendent Muñoz arched his eyebrows in surprise, his gaze hardening. His reaction did not go unnoticed by the mother abbess, who was seated in front of him at the great table in the chapterhouse. Sirga, standing in front of the solid wood door to the chapterhouse in his police uniform, also took notice.

The superintendent, however, had no intention of concealing his feelings. "What bishop are you referring to? And who exactly is this brother of yours?"

The mother abbess took a hand to her mouth, as though to prevent what she was about to say from being heard. "Good God. You know nothing." She lowered her eyes and for a moment it seemed she was about to weep.

The superintendent turned to Sirga, who looked away, trying to appear undaunted. "What is it, Mother Abbess?" he said impatiently. "What do I not know?"

The mother abbess brushed her brow with the tips of her fingers. "My secular name is Isabel Escorza. My brother is Manuel Escorza, and, for reasons unknown to me, he is forcing me to keep His Excellency Monsignor Gabriel Perugorría, bishop of Barcelona, hidden away in this convent."

The superintendent was silent. The mousetrap was far more poisoned than he had imagined. Like in his dream, he had entered a shack in the middle of the night only to discover that he was naked, the shack infested with people who were mocking him.

"You were aware of all this, Sirga?" he inquired without turning around.

"No . . . absolutely not, senyor. I—"

"Of course you were," said the mother abbess, her voice trembling with rage and bewilderment. "He was the one who—"

"Damn you, nun!" shouted Sirga, putting his hand on his gun holster.

It only took a second. A shot like a clap of thunder rang out inside the chapterhouse, its jagged echo muffling the knife-sharp scream the mother abbess's let out. Sirga staggered, then fell with his back against the doorframe, one hand on his stomach, the other still intimating the motion of drawing his gun. Standing by the table, the superintendent was holding his own weapon, the barrel still smoking.

"Dammit," he sighed. "What a lousy, rotten mess."

He kicked away the chair that had toppled when he stood up, and he walked over to Sirga, still pointing his gun at him. The mother abbess had started weeping, disconsolate. Muñoz saw the blood oozing through Sirga's fingers as he clutched at his ruptured abdomen. A small puddle of urine was forming on the tiles beneath the officer.

"Oh God," moaned Sirga, his cheeks wet with tears.

"Shut up, you idiot," the superintendent cut him off.

"Oh my God, oh my God," cried the mother abbess, her voice breaking.

The superintendent looked at her. "You're an expert in these matters," he said. "Say a prayer for his soul."

Sirga was trembling like an infant waking from a bad dream. Muñoz knelt beside him and, taking care not to soil himself in the puddle of urine, he put his arms around Sirga so that the man's head rested against the superintendent's leg. Moving him caused him to moan with pain, and Muñoz could hear a gurgling rattle in his throat. He pressed the barrel of his gun against Sirga's chest, aiming at his heart. The sound of the shot was muffled this time. Muñoz released his embrace and stood up again, as Sirga's dead body slid to the floor.

"What a horrid war," he said in a resigned tone, as though complaining about the weather.

The mother abbess was leaning against the display cabinet that housed the clay urns, whimpering. She looked at him, her eyes filled with horror.

"I have only spared him some suffering," said the superintendent. "If I had not done this he would have agonized for hours. I am very sorry you had to witness it, but it was either him or us."

"Oh God. Oh, my God," the woman repeated again and again, lost in her litany.

The superintendent snorted, annoyed. "I could use some help, but it doesn't seem we can count on your God very much, does it? Where is the bishop?"

The mother abbess took a deep breath and tried to compose herself. "I don't know," she answered between sobs. "I haven't seen him since yesterday at dusk. Perhaps in his cell, or in the chapel . . ."

"Please listen to me, senyora," interrupted the officer. "We must get out of here as soon as possible, before the militia squad sent by your brother gets here and kills us all. There is no time to waste. Have all the nuns gather in the cloister. I'll locate the bishop."

"Superintendent," said the mother abbess, drying her face with a kerchief, "there is still something about His Excellency that you don't know. He . . ."

"It will have to wait until after we have left, ma'am. We must act swiftly. Do you understand? Round up the sisters and meet me in the courtyard in five minutes. Which way to the chapel?"

"WHERE IS ADJUTANT Aragou?" asked Brother Lacunza, a bump in the road making him shift in his seat. "And what's the latest on Brother Darder?"

"The adjutant is riding in another car with comrades Escorza and Gil Portela," lied Brother Plana, who was sitting beside him rubbing his sweaty hands. "Brother Darder is on one of the buses. We will all meet up at the Capuchin convent. Am I right, comrades?"

"That's right, comrade!" shouted Antoni Ordaz from the driver's seat, and he burst out laughing. He found it amusing to be addressed as comrade by that pompous Marist. In the copilot's seat, Aureli Fernández was quiet. He would have liked for things to unfold differently, but Escorza had managed to convince Minister Tarradellas, and even President Companys, to turn a blind eye on the operation. He must remain silent and follow orders, he had no other choice. War, after all, had its own logic.

Brother Lacunza, in the back seat, did not look much better. Disguised as a patrolman—leather jacket, corduroy trousers, militiaman's cap, espadrilles fastened with a black ribbon, a red-and-black scarf—he cut a grotesque image, thought Fernández, and this opinion was only reinforced by the sight of Brother Plana, who was dressed in the same attire and looked just as ridiculous. Who were they trying to fool? Any dimwit could see they were no anarchists. But Ordaz had insisted on this attire; he said it might ease things at the border. He wanted to avoid what had happened with the first group, he said. Brother Lacunza still fumed every time he thought about it; more and more he was beginning to doubt the FAI's word. He had a terrible foreboding and was tortured by the thought that he might be leading one hundred and seventy-two brothers from the community into a death trap. But he soothed himself by thinking of the seminarians from Balaguer whom he had managed to get across the border in the first evacuation. He had received news of the boys' reunion with their families. He had imagined motherly hugs, tears of joy, and he had been thankful that everything had ended well for them.

Their car had just started up Major de Sarrià, which meant they were nearing the convent. The car with Manuel Escorza and Gil Portela and—according to Brother Plana—Adjutant Aragou, must already be there. Behind them were the buses transporting the brothers: those who had not been able to cross into France during the first expedition, those still living at Pension Capell, and those who had answered the call that had been put out from various towns around Barcelona. They would gather at the convent, do a head count, climb back onto the buses, and begin their journey to the border at La Jonquera. Everything should be fine. Everything would be fine.

"Comrade Fernández," said Brother Lacunza.

"Yes?"

"The two of you sure are looking like proper comrades, *hermanos!*" Antoni Ordaz interrupted, laughing again. "Starting to enjoy our revolutionary mission, huh?"

"That's enough, dammit," said Aureli Fernández. Ordaz immediately fell silent. "Go on, brother."

"You gave us your word."

"Excuse me?"

"Your word, Comrade Fernández. The day we made the payment you gave us your word that everything would go smoothly. Are you prepared to give it again now?"

Aureli Fernández took a deep breath. With his eyes on the hood of the car, he replied, "I don't see why I should. If I gave my word, that should suffice."

"You gave us your word and the first evacuation did not go according to plan. Give us your word that everything will go well this time, comrade."

Antoni Ordaz gave Aureli Fernández a sidelong look and saw that he was clenching his teeth. Fernández turned around; speaking slowly, he said: "Everything will go well, brother. You have my word."

Brother Lacunza nodded. He did not notice that

Brother Plana had turned away and was looking out the car window. Farther ahead, at the top of the hill they were now ascending, the walls that encircled the grounds of the Capuchin convent of the Desert of Sarrià were beginning to come into view. The day was bright, the skies clear and limpid after the recent rains.

"I CANNOT FIND the bishop anywhere. I searched the cells, the refectory, and the chapel, but there is no one there. Where else should I look?"

Superintendent Muñoz was coming from the refectory hall and had just stepped into the courtyard off the cloister where the nuns had assembled following the mother abbess's orders. There was Sister Ascensió with her blotchy skin and Sister Adoració holding her cane—both of them centenarians. There were also Sisters Benedicció, Dormició, and Visitació, looking beatific in their obesity. There was Sister Encarnació, who had a bad presentiment, her fingers compulsively telling the beads of her rosary. The mother abbess had given them no explanation, yet every one of them understood something extraordinary was unfolding, as on the day of the false arrests, when the mummies had been dug up. The superintendent considered the twenty-seven religious and wondered what he was to do with them. But, more than anything else, it was imperative that he find Monsignor Perugorría.

The mother abbess looked pained; she took the

superintendent by the arm and led him a few steps away
from the group.

"We are missing someone too," she said, lowering her
voice. "Sister Concepció; she is a novice, a girl of
thirteen."

"And why is she not here, this Sister Concepció?" asked
the superintendent, also whispering but making no
attempt to hide his disgruntlement. "Do you know where
she is?"

The mother abbess looked like she was about to
resume her weeping. "With His Excellency the bishop, I
suppose. It's what I was trying to tell you earlier."

The mother abbess continued to whisper for a couple
of minutes, as the nuns sat motionless in the sun and the
superintendent's face deepened in color as though a
bonfire were starting to burn at his feet.

"I will find them," he said. "Wait here with the sisters
and be ready to depart at once. Do not take anything with
you, no objects or clothes. We will need to move fast."

He left the courtyard taking big strides, practically
running, intent on further inspecting the premises. A
perturbed bishop in the habit of chasing after little girls—
that was just what he needed. He reached the pigpen and
peered inside. There was no one there, but he saw the
animals' blood still darkening the walls. So it was true,
something had happened there. He would question the
mother abbess about it after they had left. It had probably
been another courteous attempt of her brother Manuel's

to summon him to the convent along with Sirga. But why would Escorza go to such trouble? His thinking was fired up with intuitions and half-formed ideas, but he could not thread them together.

He inspected the toolshed and took a look inside the stone oven, troubled by the thought that he might discover Sister Concepció's remains. But there was nothing there. For some reason, he could not banish from his mind the image of the little boy murdered near Pension Capell. He arrived at the laundry facility and he found only washbasins, bars of soap, and linens hung out to dry.

He backtracked, running this time. He had to find them at once. Sirga's tears as he understood he was dying came into his mind. Poor idiot. It wasn't the first time he had killed a man, but that thought did nothing to ease his conscience. He felt terrible. Dirty, debased. What would his mother say if she knew? He hadn't joined the police force to kill men, but to prevent them from being killed. But it seemed it could not be avoided. Did every person have a killer inside them? He had to find the bishop and the novice before Escorza's men arrived at the convent to check whether Sirga had carried out his orders.

He went down to the woodshed; there was no one there either, only the mice scurrying to hide behind the wood.

He knew what he had to do. He would leave with the nuns, the bishop—the whole lot—and escort them to parliament. There he would request the protection of the

Generalitat government until things calmed down. Crossing the entire city would be no easy task with that flock in tow, but at least he knew where he needed to go to avoid having himself and the nuns executed in a corner up on Montjuïc or on the Arrabassada.

He reached the door to the cellar and had to crouch in order to enter. He glimpsed the dark stairs, the uneven steps. From the penumbra suddenly came a moan that sounded like a wounded dog.

He gripped his gun and slowly descended a few steps, holding his breath. The sound stopped but started again a few seconds later, no longer a dog's whimper but a voice that was saying something. A small, weak, little girl's voice. He stopped and listened more intently.

> *Stabat mater dolorosa*
> *Iuxta crucem . . .*

He was able to make out the words, but then the voice broke and gave way to moaning. Was it moaning or weeping?

He descended four more steps, then the stairs spiraled, then he saw them. A large, heavyset man atop a herring barrel, wearing a clerical robe that fell on either side of the barrel like drapes. Cornered against the wall in front of him, a girl was crying, her face buried in her hands. She was completely naked, her thighs covered with blood.

———

"**Good morning, little** sister! Well, well, it looks like there's a community meeting here. I hope we are not interrupting!"

Manuel Escorza strode into the cloister with the nonchalance of someone paying a courtesy call. Despite his crutches and boot lifts, he was surprisingly nimble; Gil Portela, walking beside him, quickened his pace in order to keep up. Three militiamen armed with rifles and looking rather hung over followed behind. Lined up in the center of the courtyard, the Capuchin nuns observed the men's arrival with curiosity, but without apprehension. The mother abbess, on the other hand, looked like she had seen a ghost.

"What are you doing here?"

The militiamen and Gil Portela stopped beneath the arcade in the cloister. Manuel Escorza continued on to the courtyard, propelling himself on his crutches until he was standing in front of his sister.

"I've only come to make sure you were all right, little sister," he replied with that contorted smile of his. "Strange things are going on in this convent... By the way, a group of friends we have unfinished business with are about to arrive any minute now. I'm afraid it'll be a bit noisy for a while. But tell me: Are you well, little sister? Everything all right?"

"A group of friends? What are you talking about, Manuel?"

Like a drying stain, Manuel Escorza's smile shrank

until it finally disappeared. "You don't seem very glad to see me, little sister. Frankly, I was expecting a warmer welcome. Aren't you pleased with the men I sent you?"

"The men?" stuttered the mother abbess, barely able to speak.

"Yes, Sirga and a police superintendent who is a prime example of diligence and uprightness, little sister." He smiled again. "Why aren't they here with you? Have they solved the mystery of the pigs?"

The mother abbess stared at the ground, stunned. A cat inched closer and sniffed at Manuel Escorza's boots. "I don't know what men you are talking about, Manuel," she whimpered. "I . . ."

"Don't mess with me, little sister. Where are Sirga and the superintendent? And the bishop—where have you put the bishop? And what are you all doing out here?"

A militiaman who had walked back to the convent's main entrance now reappeared in the cloister, approached Gil Portela, and said something to him. Gil Portela cleared his throat and spoke to Manuel Escorza: "Comrade, the buses with the patrolmen and the brothers have arrived, as well as the car with Ordaz and Fernández."

"Good," replied Escorza without taking his eyes off the mother abbess. "As I've mentioned, we have work to do, little sister. Round up your wimpled fanatics and shut them in the chapel; we have no need for them here. And come back immediately; you and I need to have a talk. I have something to show you that I'm sure will pique your interest. Understood?"

The mother abbess nodded.

"You," continued Manuel Escorza, turning to the soldiers, "go to the entrance and bring the religious here to the courtyard. And you, Gil, find out what's going on with Sirga, the superintendent, and our friend the bishop. There's something fishy here."

"MONSIGNOR, STEP AWAY from the girl."

The superintendent had reached the bottom of the stairs and was standing at a safe distance from the bishop, who had his back to him. From the steps behind him leading down to the well came a cold, damp blast of air. He could see the novice clearly now; she had removed her hands from her face and placed them between her legs, trying to cover her nakedness. She was stricken with terror and shame; the contrast of the menstrual blood on her pale thighs gave her a disturbing air. The superintendent noticed the recess with the image of Saint Galderic. Religious faith was just another form of folly, he thought.

The bishop did not respond, so the superintendent insisted, "Monsignor, I am a police superintendent. Please look at me and step away from the girl."

Superintendent Muñoz was holding his gun, but he was not pointing it at the bishop. Monsignor did not turn around; he remained perfectly still, his hunched shoulders blocking the officer's view of his hands. Keeping as much distance as the shelves of food and sacks of grains allowed, Superintendent Muñoz maneuvered around until he had the bishop in profile. Sister Concepció followed him with her eyes. She was still crying, her thick, abundant tears rolling down her face and neck and pooling on her budding breasts. But she no longer moaned, sobbed, or said a word. The girl's silence—and the bishop's—combined to give the scene a vaguely oneiric atmosphere. Yes, this could have been one of my nightmares, thought Superintendent Muñoz. Though this little girl is naked, not me, it's clear that someone is mocking me.

He observed the bishop's bloated profile carefully. Monsignor seemed lost in reverie. The superintendent could now see the bishop's hands: he had them crossed on his lap and he moved his thumbs every now and then, as though counting something. Monsignor had yet to look at him, nor was he looking at the girl. It was as though he were alone.

"Monsignor, we must leave immediately. Your life is in grave danger. The anarchists are coming to kill you and the nuns, the girl, and myself. They will kill us all, do you understand? Do you understand?"

The superintendent fell silent. The only sound that could be heard was the water trickling from the stone into the well. Sister Concepció began to weep again. For now, he could congratulate himself on having succeeded in scaring her even more.

Suddenly the bishop turned to the police officer with his arms extended and his mouth agape. The superintendent raised his weapon and pointed it at the bishop's head.

"Let them despoil me of riches and honor," intoned the bishop, eyes raised toward the heavens, "let illness deprive me of my strength; let me be parted from grace by succumbing to sin—not for this shall I lose hope, yet will I preserve it until my last breath. And vain will be the efforts of all the demons in hell to seize it from me, for with Your guidance I will rise above guilt. My trust rests entirely on the certainty with which I await Your guidance. For You, Oh Lord, have singularly confirmed me in my hope . . ."

He spoke in a falsetto tone, as though saying Mass. Then he abruptly stopped, rose from the barrel, and took a step toward the superintendent. Standing, and in those clothes, Bishop Perugorría looked like a dragon that was too fat and well-larded to take flight.

"Stand back, Monsignor," ordered the superintendent, gripping his gun. "Do not come near me or the girl or I will have to shoot you. Do you hear me? Stand back."

The bishop finally obeyed. He turned to his right, giving his back to the superintendent and Sister Concepció, and began walking toward the stairs to the well.

"Do not move. Stop where you are, Monsignor."

The bishop did as he was told. He stopped, spread his arms wide, and recited: "I know full well that, on my own,

I am fragile and inconstant. I understand that temptation overpowers the strongest of virtues, and yet this knowledge does not daunt me. If my faith remains strong I shall be safe from misfortune, and I shall faithfully await You always, as I have faith that You shall fulfill this hope . . ."

He paused again and lowered his head, as his body began to sway gently. His eyes were streaming with tears. The superintendent could hear the young girl crying behind him. The bishop plunged into a slow, measured weeping, devoid of histrionics; his tears were sincere, caused by a great sadness. He turned to the police officer, who was still pointing his gun at him. With his face contorted by grief, he sobbed: "My mother. My poor mother, weeping at home over the death of her son. The torment . . ."

He let himself go, and another kind of weeping began, convulsed, incensed. Devastated, he collapsed and continued to sob on the floor, pummeling his knees with his fists. The superintendent lowered his weapon; he would have liked to feel empathy but he could not. Who among them did not miss their mother?

Keeping an eye on him, he approached Sister Concepció. She had stopped crying, but she was still trembling. Her body was numb from cold and shame. She kept her hands over her crotch, but she couldn't hide the trickles of blood that reached down to her knees.

"Don't be scared, child," said the superintendent, his voice like a lullaby. "I'm with the police. We'll get you out of here now; I'm here to help you."

Sister Concepció looked at him intently and nodded.

"Has he touched you?" asked the superintendent, pointing at the bishop with his free hand. "Has he hit you or hurt you?"

She looked at him as though she didn't understand the question. She opened her mouth and blurted out, "I'm cold and I have a bellyache."

"Of course," said the superintendent.

He glanced at the bishop, who was still crying in the middle of the cellar, removed his jacket, and placed it around the novice's shoulders. Though he was a small, scrawny man, his jacket seemed enormous as it enveloped Sister Concepció's slight frame.

"Bundle up, child. We'll leave now, and then it will all be over. Don't be afraid."

Sister Concepció remembered her mother telling her not to be afraid. But His Excellency had said that her mother was dead. She wanted to ask that man if it was true, but just as she was about to pose the question there was a tremendous ruckus outside. The superintendent gestured for her to keep quiet while he listened intently for a few seconds.

"Don't budge," he ordered.

He walked past Bishop Perugorría, who seemed to have completely lost touch with reality, and bounded up the steps. From the threshold he could see part of the cloister and the courtyard.

"Shit."

He recognized Manuel Escorza, Aureli Fernández, and Antoni Ordaz, as well as two Marist brothers from Pension Capell, clumsily disguised as anarchists. Then he caught sight of a multitude of their brothers who were following the orders of a group of FAI militiamen. There were at least twenty of them.

"HAVE THE BROTHERS position themselves along the arcade, facing the north façade. And have the boys line up along the south façade with their rifles loaded and ready."

Antoni Ordaz and Aureli Fernández listened carefully to Manuel Escorza's instructions and then turned to the large group of people who had assembled and began to carry out the orders. The one hundred and seventy-two Marists who had responded to the evacuation call were still filing into the convent from the street, ushered by the soldiers who greeted them at the entrance. When they arrived at the cloister they were met by another group of soldiers, who informed them that they had reached the meeting point. The Marists quickly formed small groups and began to converse about their situation. Amid the chatter, it was not difficult to catch snippets of hopeful conversations.

"Why have they brought us here?" asked one fluty voice.

"Can't you see this is the meeting point?" replied a thicker voice. "People from all over are assembling here, and they need to make sure that everything unfolds according to plan. The evacuation will start soon."

"Will we sleep in France tonight?"

"Probably not tonight—look at the time—it's late already and it will still be a while before we head out. Tomorrow . . ."

Someone lowered his voice before posing a question. "What about the nuns who live here?"

"God knows where they are. The war . . ."

Taking advantage of the commotion, Brother Plana approached Antoni Ordaz. "Do you remember me?"

Ordaz looked at him as though he were facing a plaster saint. "Of course I do, *hermano*," he answered just to say something. "Now return to the line and find your place."

"I'm the one who brought Brother Darder to Tostadero for you," moaned the Marist, trembling.

"Yes, yes, don't worry—none of this has anything to do with you. Just get back to your place. Go on."

Antoni Ordaz and Aureli Fernández flitted about trying to keep the Marists from lingering in idle conversation and to have them make their way to the arcade and line up along its perimeter. They were going to conduct a roll call, they said. Everyone happily acquiesced; there was even some joking and elbowing to grab a spot in the first row. Like a couple of Catalan sheepdogs, Ordaz and Fernández busied themselves correcting their placement. When the group was starting to look fairly organized, Manuel Escorza approached Aureli Fernández.

"Come with me for a moment, comrade."

Fernández moved away from the group and followed

Escorza, who led him to a corner of the courtyard. Once there, Escorza, using his crutches to hoist himself up, sat on the stone banister of the cloister's gallery. He wiped the sweat from his brow with the back of his hand.

"I'm listening," offered Aureli Fernández.

Manuel Escorza pointed with his head to the group of Marists, who were still lining up along the arcade.

"Which one of them killed Burntface?" he asked through a mouthful of saliva.

Aureli Fernández had feared the question. He shrugged. "None of them, comrade. We have yet to find our man."

Manuel Escorza's eyes grew smaller. "I assume you have a good excuse for that. You always do," he said, drawing out each syllable.

"There's no excuse. I can only say that I am sorry. As soon as . . ."—he hesitated for a moment—"we are finished here, I will assign more men to the task and we'll intensify our search. We'll find him."

Manuel Escorza again gestured with his head toward the men who stood along the perimeter of the cloister. "You disapprove of all this, don't you?"

Aureli Fernández felt cornered. He made an effort to sound steadfast: "No, comrade. Upon reflection, I have realized you're right. Revolution has a price, and one can't be wishy-washy about it."

Escorza spat out his most offensive laugh and climbed down from the banister. "I like that wishy-washy bit, Fernández," he said, steadying himself on his crutches.

"Try not to let it slip your mind; I would hate to have to remind you of it one day. Now find our little fugitive priest, as you said you would—and let it be soon."

Aureli Fernández felt a twinge of hatred in his stomach, but he swallowed and remained silent.

The mother abbess appeared in the hall that led to the Saint Agatha chapel, escorted by two militiamen.

"Comrade Escorza," one of them announced, "the nuns have been locked in the chapel until further orders from you."

"Good," replied Escorza. He noticed the panic in the mother abbess's face. He said: "So, what do you think, little sister? A nice little gathering we're having here, isn't it?"

"What does all of this mean, Manuel? What are your intentions?"

Manuel Escorza smiled again, enjoying himself. "Where are Sirga and the superintendent, little sister?"

The mother abbess was silent. She turned toward the Marists. Nearly all had found their place when one of them, dressed as a patrolman, stepped out of the line and began walking toward them.

"Hey, *hermano*, where do you think you're going?" shouted Antoni Ordaz. "Come back here immediately! Hey—comrade!"

Brother Lacunza played deaf and hurriedly crossed the courtyard to where Aureli Fernández and Manuel Escorza were standing.

"Where are Brother Darder and Adjutant Aragou?" he inquired, agitated.

"Our brother here is quite the character," Escorza laughed. "And, mind you, it's a good question: Where *are* they, Fernández?"

"They must . . . they must be about to arrive," he improvised. "There is still a van missing with some of the laggards."

"Do you take me for an imbecile?" exploded Brother Lacunza. "There is no one missing here except Adjutant Aragou and Brother Darder. Don't feed me any more of your excuses. You gave me your word back there . . ."

Manuel Escorza grasped both crutches in one of his hands and put the other on Brother Lacunza's shoulders in a friendly manner. "The man is right, Fernández." He patted Brother Lacunza's back as though it was a dog's head. "Besides, he has proven himself to be a skilled negotiator and a man of determination. He deserves to be spoken to with candor. Look, Lacunza"—he drew his face nearer—"your beloved Adjutant Aragou is locked up in the Modelo prison and we intend to approach your Marist institution for ransom. As for Brother Darder—he was causing us some trouble. So we had him detained, but he killed one of the men who was watching him and escaped. We have been left with no other choice but to find him and execute him. That is the whole shebang. Satisfied, Lacunza?"

Brother Lacunza wished to say something, but he couldn't speak—he could scarcely breathe. The oppression in his chest was choking him. For the first time in his life, he experienced fear, and he discovered that fear deprived him of his strength. Fear. And disgust. And horror at his own idiotic behavior. He succeeded only in exchanging glances with the mother abbess, who had also gone mute and was struggling to come to terms with what she was seeing and feeling.

Gil Portela came running toward them as though he were being chased, pushing his way through the throngs of Marists and militiamen gathered in the cloister.

"Comrade Escorza," he panted. "I've found Sirga. He's dead."

The smile on Manuel Escorza's face vanished.

"He's in a room over there," Gil Portela continued. "He has two bullets in his body and he's not looking good."

"Where's the superintendent, little sister?" grunted Manuel Escorza.

The mother abbess said nothing. She shook her head slightly, as though telling herself that what was happening could not be real.

"You hear me? Tell me where the superintendent and the bishop are, you filthy whore!"

He raised his free arm and with the flat of his hand slapped his sister so hard that she was knocked to the ground, and there she remained, seated, her cheek on fire and a ringing in her ear. A vacant expression had settled across her face; she looked like a little girl struggling to understand her punishment.

"Do you hear me, little sister? Tell me where they are!"

A wave of commotion swept through the Marists, who had witnessed the scene. Some of them stepped out of the line and tried to come to the mother abbess's aid, but Antoni Ordaz and some of the militiamen pushed them back.

"Nobody move!" Gil Portela shouted across the courtyard. "Ordaz, if anyone budges, put a bullet in him, got me? You hear that, you filthy priests?"

They had heard him clearly. The echo of the threat reverberated through the courtyard. The militiamen stood before the semicircle formed by the Marists, rifles in hand. Antoni Ordaz took his place on one side of the troops, expectant. Brother Plana tried to gesture to him, but it was useless—either Ordaz did not see him, or he pretended not to.

Brother Lacunza helped the mother abbess to her feet. She planted herself in front of Escorza.

"Manuel, you have always been despicable," she said in a clear voice. "You may think you're triumphant, but you were born a miserable good-for-nothing and will be one until the day you die. And when that happens, you can be certain I will pray that you burn in hell for all of eternity."

Aureli Fernández averted his face to conceal his satisfaction at the nun's words. Gil Portela, however, kept his eyes trained on Escorza, awaiting an order. But none came. The Cripple of Sant Elies twisted his mouth into a grimace, unable to hide his pain.

"Escorza! Over here!" cried a voice from across the courtyard.

Everyone turned in the direction of the voice, but there was nothing to see. Manuel Escorza suddenly emerged from his stupor and smiled. "Superintendent! Where are you, you son of a bitch?"

"I love you too, Escorza!" responded the police officer. "Over here! In the cellar, by the vegetable garden!"

Gil Portela made as if to head there, but Manuel Escorza motioned for him to stop. He didn't mind playing games for a while.

"Are you coming here or would you prefer for us to come and get you, superintendent?"

"Listen carefully, Escorza—I have the bishop with me! Either you and your men leave now, without harming anyone, or I'm knocking him off, and then you might have a real problem. What do you say?"

Manuel Escorza shook his head as at some childish remark. "You have *cojones*, superintendent, I have to hand it to you. But you're no idiot, so you probably know you are in no position to impose conditions. Come out with the bishop and I promise I will let you go!"

"That's right, Escorza, I'm no idiot. Either you do as I say or you won't have a bishop for long—your choice!"

"Superintendent, between the brothers and the nuns I have nearly two hundred hostages here, and if you don't come out of that hole, you will be responsible for their fate!"

A few seconds of silence followed. From across the courtyard Brother Lacunza observed his Marist brothers; they stood stiffly, as though immortalized in a photograph of desperation. The militiamen, with their weapons, also looked fossilized, as did Antoni Ordaz, who was as rigid as Gil Portela and Aureli Fernández. Only the mother abbess—who had repressed the urge to ask the superintendent about Sister Concepció and now bowed her head in prayer—and Manuel Escorza, standing in a corner of the courtyard barking commands, showed any signs of life. As for Muñoz, he was silently repenting for his sins and entrusting his soul to God, but he had to recognize that he had never felt more alive.

The answer finally arrived.

"Sorry, Escorza, I'm having none of it. You are the only one responsible here. And you know full well that your two hundred hostages matter far less to you than my one pawn. So tell me, what do you think will happen to you if he runs into trouble, Escorza?"

The Cripple of Saint Elies's patience had come to an end. High treason is what would happen to him. A court-martial and death by firing squad. He had ruffled more than a few feathers on his way up the FAI ranks, and now he had too many enemies. He could not afford to make a mistake—the superintendent wasn't bluffing.

"Send two boys to him," Escorza said to Gil Portela.

After this exchange, the superintendent retreated back

into the storage room. Sister Concepció was kneeling in front of the shrine to Saint Galderic, Muñoz's jacket still around her; Bishop Perugorría was where the superintendent had left him: lying atop the sacks of grain, his arms and feet bound and secured with a couple of reef knots he had learned in his youth. The prelate was half asleep and delirious.

"The Holy Ghost . . ." Muñoz heard him say. "The Holy Ghost . . ."

"Come with me," the superintendent said to Sister Concepció.

He took her by the hand and they went down to the well.

"Stay here and do not move or speak, no matter what happens. Is that clear?"

"Do you know if my mother is dead?" asked the girl.

The superintendent would have liked to answer, but just then he heard noises coming from above. Escorza had sent someone to fetch them. He bounded up the steps and hid behind a section of the wall that projected out behind the stairs that led up to the vegetable garden.

He listened intently and heard the sound of boots approaching. He couldn't tell if there were two or three men. He held his breath.

Just as he had anticipated, the shape of Bishop Perugorría's body on the sacks was the first thing the men's eyes encountered as they came around the curve in the stairs. That sight should distract them for an instant—at least in theory.

The superintendent caught a glimpse of someone's head. He lifted his weapon and, almost without aiming, pulled the trigger.

The shot rang out in the cloister's courtyard, the echo slowly fading into the morning light. Then, another shot—and another—nearly simultaneous. A final shot came a few seconds later.

Then, silence. Aureli Fernández and Gil Portela watched Manuel Escorza in a corner, engrossed in thought. Brother Lacunza was wringing his hands. The mother abbess was praying.

More than a minute went by, until Escorza grew tired of waiting.

"What happened?" he shouted in a shrill tone.

More silence. The Cripple snorted.

"Careful, Escorza!" Superintendent Muñoz's voice sounded grave. "This is a bottleneck here—the only thing I have to do is wait for the men you send over, and I have plenty of ammunition! They might end up getting me, but before that I will have taken out quite a few of yours. Are they really that brave, your men? Or do you think they might prefer to get rid of you instead?"

Manuel Escorza opened his mouth to reply but only a half-formed profanity came out. One of the militiamen cursed; the other seventeen remained silent.

"Escorza!" shouted the superintendent. "I will not repeat this again: leave the convent, you and your men, and forget about us, and I guarantee that nothing will happen to the bishop. What do you say?"

An unexpectedly cold gust of wind made the men shudder. Manuel Escorza seized his crutches, abandoned his corner, and stared at Gil Portela. Then he nodded toward Brother Lacunza, who was standing by the mother abbess with his forage cap in his hands.

Gil Portela drew his weapon from his jacket, pointed it at Brother Lacunza and shot him in the heart. Brother Lacunza gave what sounded like a belch, opened his eyes wide, and looked at Aureli Fernández, who averted his gaze. Then he collapsed onto the mother abbess, who embraced him as though he were a long-lost relative. His body slid to the ground, revealing the mother abbess's blood-stained habit.

"Superintendent!" barked Manuel Escorza. "I'm not sure if you saw that, but I just executed the *hermano* who was in charge here. Will you come out of your own free will now, or would you prefer for me to continue?"

The superintendent rushed down the stairs and ducked back into the cellar. He heard the bishop mumbling incoherently atop the sacks.

"Monsters," he said. "Poor chimney sweeps . . ."

Sister Concepció had returned to the niche that housed the image of Saint Galderic, and she was studying the bodies of the two soldiers the superintendent had shot: one had collapsed by the herring barrel, the other, two steps from the stairs. Curiously, the girl did not seem afraid anymore. She looked at him and said, "You didn't answer my question, senyor."

The blood trickling down her thighs now reached her feet. There was also blood on the floor—the soldiers' blood. Neither of the men appeared to be more than twenty; they could have been his sons, thought the superintendent. Or the novice's older brothers. A feeling of exhaustion swept over him, deep and sweet, as though he hadn't slept for days.

"I'm sorry, child," he said, "but I don't know anything about your mother. Funny thing is, I've been missing my own mother recently."

Sister Concepció lowered her head and said nothing more. She was starting to understand that, in life, the prospect of torment was at least as certain as that of joy, and encountering one or the other ultimately depended on chance. Bean or almond—C-sharp major or A minor. What she didn't understand is what faith had to do with any of it.

She felt a chill and bundled deeper into the jacket. She watched the superintendent as he dragged the two bodies by the well to clear the way. The bloody trails left on the floor reminded her of the blotches that formed across the lines of her sheet music when she knocked over an inkwell.

"I think we've waited too long already, comrade," said Gil Portela, squinting under the blinding sun that fell on his brow.

"Maybe he's thinking of surrendering. He has no way out," Aureli Fernández hesitantly pointed out.

The mother abbess was staring at the bloody streaks on her habit as though trying to read a map. Brother Lacunza lay sprawled at her feet, his mouth and eyes still open; the nun leaned down and closed them with a trembling hand.

There was murmuring among the Marists, forced by the militia to remain in line. Brother Plana continued to try to attract the attention of Antoni Ordaz by making increasingly bizarre grimaces. Ordaz steadfastly ignored him.

"Gil is right," said Manuel Escorza. "We will only get him out of there feet first."

"And we have no guarantee that the bishop is still alive," Gil Portela pointed out.

"Let's be methodic about this," said Escorza. "First we take care of the *hermanos*, then the superintendent. After that we'll decide what to do with the nuns."

He looked at the mother abbess, who was still bending over Brother Lacunza's body. She returned his gaze. Heavy with scorn. Drained.

Manuel Escorza swallowed, a bitter taste in his mouth.

"Proceed," he said.

Gil Portela crossed the courtyard, approached Antoni Ordaz, and conveyed the orders in a low voice.

Ordaz positioned himself in a corner of the courtyard, perpendicular to the squad.

"Lock and load!" he shouted to the militia.

The eighteen soldiers lifted their rifles in unison and stood ready.

"Superintendent, pay attention now!" said Manuel Escorza, relishing the moment.

"Take aim!"

The soldiers placed the buttstock of their rifles to their chests and pointed their rifles at the line of Marists. The idea was to aim for the heart to avoid the need for a *coup de grace*. The soldiers stood six steps from the religious and could see the horror in the faces of the doomed men. Some of the militia smiled. For others the rifle was heavy as stone.

A shriek of horror pierced the silence.

"No—not me!" cried the voice.

Brother Plana abandoned the line and started running aimlessly through the courtyard like a chicken with its head cut off.

"Not me. Don't kill me!" he repeated. "Don't kill me!"

Two of the soldiers fell out of formation and took aim at him, but they didn't dare to shoot without hearing the command. Brother Plana flailed his arms wildly and ran around in circles shrieking pitifully like a child who has burnt himself with the fireplace embers. Manuel Escorza clicked his tongue and shook his head. He looked at Gil Portela and gave the go-ahead with a hand signal. Gil Portela nodded back.

Brother Plana finally stopped in front of Antoni Ordaz and Gil Portela. He knelt before them.

"Not me!" he wailed. "I was told I would be spared! I delivered Brother Darder to the Tostadero for you . . ."

He began to weep—a snotty, resolute weeping. The rest of the Marists observed him with looks that ranged from rage to pity, revulsion, and indignation. Brother Plana curled up on the ground and wept.

"Not me . . ." he repeated in a nearly lifeless voice.

Standing beside him, Gil Portela again drew his gun and, as though swatting away an insect, shot him in the head. Brother Plana collapsed facedown, a large pool of blood immediately forming under his head. One of the Marists let out a cry, and the mother abbess covered her face with her hands.

"Enough fun and games!" shouted Manuel Escorza. "Let's get this over with!"

"Squad—attention!" commanded Antoni Ordaz.

The militia immediately obeyed and pointed their rifles at the religious. Someone among the Marists shouted: "Brothers—let us hold hands! *Ad Iesum per Mariam!*"

"Fire!"

In the cellar, Superintendent Muñoz wrapped his arms around Sister Concepció and covered her ears with his hands to muffle the sound of eighteen rifles going off at the same time. But it was to no avail—the discharge boomed with a force that was audible even beyond the convent walls.

"Monsters . . ." Bishop Perugorría repeated, reclining on the sacks with his eyes closed.

One hundred and seventy-two men for eighteen

militiamen. The weapons had to be reloaded, and ten times Antoni Ordaz had to repeat the command to fire. The execution lasted eight minutes; the survivors of each blast witnessed their slayed brothers falling to the ground. Piled one on top of the other, their bodies bled as one. The first did not have time to join hands, but the rest did. Some died with their hands clasped.

Gil Portela followed the development with keen interest and a smile. Manuel Escorza also smiled, especially after seeing the sadness on Aureli Fernández's face. The mother abbess felt weak in the knees and leaned against the railing by the arcade; she stared at her brother as though wishing to exterminate him with her gaze.

When it was all over, the pungent smell of gunpowder wafted through the air, thick and acrid, and the center of the courtyard was shrouded in the smoke from the fusillade. One of the soldiers fell out of formation, ran to lean over the banister, and vomited. From the pile of bodies came the sound of moaning and whimpering.

"Finish them off, dammit!" Manuel Escorza raged. "Can't you hear them?"

Antoni Ordaz, Gil Portela, and the soldiers took up their weapons and started groping through the bodies searching for the wounded. It was not an easy task; some of the men were buried two or three bodies deep, and more than one dead body received a redundant *coup de grace*. Antoni Ordaz looked away when he fired, but Gil Portela discharged his weapon with unnerving impassivity.

Finally there was no more moaning. Only silence.

The mother abbess thought of the twenty-seven sisters in the Saint Agatha chapel, who must have heard the commotion and were probably praying, expecting to be next. Yes, it was now their turn to die, she thought, and after them it would be the superintendent's. He wouldn't be able to withstand such ferocity. Her brother had finally released the beast he had inside him since infancy, the beast whose appetite had been repressed for so long. She thought also of Sister Concepció, and she prayed silently, fervently, that she was safe and that those savages would at least take pity on her. *Stabat Mater dolorosa*: without knowing why, those words now came to her mind.

"Superintendent!" Manuel Escorza boomed, facing in the direction of the cellar. "Did you enjoy that? They died for you, superintendent!"

The officer released Sister Concepció, trudged up the stairs and approached the door very cautiously in case one of Escorza's men was waiting for him. When he was sure no one was there, he peered out and glimpsed the cloud of gunpowder and the carnage. The bodies were strewn about on the rough ground of the cloister. He was feeling more and more exhausted.

"I think you are finished, Escorza, that is what I think!" he said. "I still have your bishop; come and get him, if you want him!"

He ducked back into the cold room and made Sister

Concepció hide again by the well, even though that meant being in the company of the two dead soldiers. The girl did not protest: she headed down there and fixed her attention on the walls of the well to avoid looking at the bodies. It was better to keep the bishop bound for now. The superintendent had his own gun, but he grabbed one of the soldier's rifles and filled his pockets with bullets from both of the dead men. He walked back up the stairs, ready to hold out until the end. He suddenly felt like weeping; it wasn't easy to hold back the tears.

Gil Portela and Antoni Ordaz approached Manuel Escorza.

"What now?"

"Go and get him," replied Escorza. "Have all the men go. How many can he kill? Three—four? He won't be able to take them all out. He's done for."

"What about the nuns?" asked Aureli Fernández, distressed.

"Later," said Manuel Escorza. "Besides, that is a more— how shall I put it?—personal matter. Isn't it, little sister?"

The mother abbess said nothing. With her hands on the railing, she contemplated the massacre with petrified eyes. The militia moved about in the courtyard, one of them flicking his cigarette ashes on Brother Plana's body. She continued to pray.

She was the first to see him coming. Then Escorza did, and the rest.

"What the hell is this?" asked Antoni Ordaz, a look of horror on his face.

From the door to the cellar, Superintendent Muñoz also spotted Brother Darder—he had no trouble recognizing him—riding into the cloister mounted on Hadaly. The great black horse, shiny and powerful, and its tattered, filthy horseman cut an enigmatic image that seemed spawned by a madman's dream. The horse advanced slowly toward the cloister arcade with a majestic gait. Everyone watched in a stupor, some with mouths agape, as though faced with the apparition of a ghost or an angel. From atop his saddle, Brother Darder observed the scattered bodies of his massacred brothers. He did so calmly, with a touch of apathy even, as if contemplating a diorama. A certain affliction came over him on spotting the body of the indefatigable Brother Lacunza, and a modicum of pleasure when he saw that of Brother Plana, that rat.

"He's the one who killed Burntface!" cried Gil Portela.

Brother Darder said nothing. He and Hadaly circled the scene of the massacre, entered the courtyard from the side, and slowly approached the corner where Escorza, Ordaz, Fernández, and Portela had gathered. Brother Darder stopped in front of the men and looked at them attentively, a severe expression on his face. The horse's coat glistened in the sunlight. Not knowing what to do, the soldiers regrouped on the far side of the courtyard. The mother abbess stopped praying and appeared as dumbfounded as the rest.

"That was one hell of an entrance, *hermano*—I grant

you that," Manuel Escorza said at last, trying to maintain control of the situation. "May I ask where you are headed on that imposing steed of yours?"

Brother Darder smiled. "To hell," he replied. "I've come to take you with me."

It all happened very fast. Hadaly rose on his hind legs and let his forelegs come down on Manuel Escorza, who lost his footing and collapsed to the ground, sending his large boots and his crutches into the air.

"You bastard!" shouted Escorza, breathless.

Ordaz, Fernández, and Portela made as if to help him, but before they could get close the animal turned on its legs and delivered a brutal, precise kick to Manuel Escorza's head, crushing his skull. His face was reduced to a bloody pulp.

Gil Portela was the first to react: "Kill him! Shoot, for God's sake!"

As the soldiers scrambled to load their rifles, Gil Portela lifted his weapon and shot Brother Darder; he groaned as the bullet hit him in stomach. With that, Hadaly seemed to suddenly go mad, rearing and neighing with formidable force. A well-delivered kick to Antoni Ordaz's chest killed him on the spot. Aureli Fernández, who had been standing beside him, started running without looking where he was going and a few steps later tripped on the bodies of the dead Marists.

The militia reloaded their weapons and discharged them on horse and horseman. Gil Portela emptied his gun on Brother Darder, who felt the bullets that pierced his flesh as a blessing that brought him closer to rest.

If God so deems it . . .

The men continued to shoot, wounding Brother Darder in the chest, side, back, and legs. *Stigmata*—he still had time to think. Finally, a bullet drove through his ear and put an end to his pain. But not that of Hadaly, who also had five or six bullets in his body, and yet continued to put up a ferocious fight—more ferocious with each new wound he received. With Brother Darder's body still mounted on his back, the horse neighed profusely and foamed at the mouth, as he delivered kicks right and left. One kick left two soldiers dead on the ground, another badly wounded two others. Some reloaded their rifles and continued to shoot at the horse; others began to flee in all directions.

Gil Portela had used up all his ammunition and decided it was time to get out of there. He would make his way to the street and take one of the cars, and he would not stop until he was across the border. To hell with everything, he said to himself. He turned to the mother abbess, who appeared mesmerized by the whole spectacle, shoved her, and made as if to run off.

"Not so fast, Gil," he heard someone say.

He had time to catch a glimpse of Superintendent Muñoz's face before he heard a shot and everything went black.

The militiamen who had survived Hadaly's attack ran

toward the main door out of the convent. The horse was breathing laboriously as it lay in the middle of the court-yard beside Brother Darder's body. It was dying—if creatures such as Hadaly ever died. Did monsters die?

Only the mother abbess and Aureli Fernández were left standing. Fernández was plowing through the bodies of the Marists as though he had gone mad. The superin-tendent approached him and aimed his weapon at him.

"Don't," said the mother abbess. "Please. You're not like them. You are not a criminal."

Yes I am, he thought, but he lowered his gun and took a deep breath. He still felt like weeping, and he was unspeakably exhausted, but he knew he had to hold up. He looked at the Mother Abbess.

"Are you all right?" he asked.

She nodded. She glanced at her brother, sprawled on the ground, his head smashed. The sight made her feel better.

"And Sister Concepció?" the mother abbess asked anxiously.

"Unharmed, I believe," the officer responded. The mother abbess breathed a sigh of relief. "I'll go and fetch her and Bishop Perugorría. You can let the sisters out of the chapel now. It's time to get out of here."

The superintendent descended the steps once more. He untied the bishop and then approached the novice.

"Come," he said. "Don't be afraid."

She smiled and let the officer pick her up; he felt a

sharp pain in his back as he climbed the stairs with the girl in his arms. At the top, he lowered her to the ground and together they walked toward the cloister. The twenty-seven Capuchin nuns were there, weeping and gesturing wildly at the sight of the carnage. The mother abbess ran toward Sister Concepció and embraced her with a tenderness that seemed almost indecent amid such horror. Perhaps the novice had found a mother in the end, the superintendent thought, and the idea comforted him.

"You seem to have succeeded," said a familiar voice behind him.

He was not surprised by the arrival of Doctor Pellicer, accompanied by Judge Carbonissa.

"I'm not at all sure about that," responded the police officer. "But thank you anyway."

"No need for that. Poor Brother Darder came to me looking like a dead man. We only helped him to fulfill his last wishes."

The superintendent approached Hadaly. The horse made a deathly rattle, and Muñoz saw a light going out in the animal's eyes.

"I'm sorry," he said.

"No matter," said the judge. "It's the cycle of nature. Life, death, followed once more by life. It has always been this way."

"Even for vampires?" joked the superintendent.

At that moment, Bishop Perugorría walked by. He

seemed engrossed in thought and appeared not to see the superintendent; he was holding a notebook and a fountain pen in one hand. The nuns observed him anxiously as he contemplated the cadaver-strewn courtyard as though it were a sunset over the sea.

The superintendent, the doctor and the judge followed him with their eyes. The bishop approached the arcade, opened his notebook and scribbled something with his fountain pen.

He wrote:

ABOUT THE AUTHOR

Sebastià Alzamora i Martín was born in Mallorca in 1972 and graduated from the Universitat de les Illes Balears with a degree in Catalan philology. He first rose to prominence as a poet with a collection called *Rafel*, which he published in 1994. Since that time, he has written three other volumes of poetry and five novels. He has been awarded numerous prizes for both his fiction and his poetry, including the prestigious Sant Jordi Prize for *Blood Crime*. He is the editorial director of the Catalan magazine *Cultura* as well as a regular columnist for various newspapers, including *Avui* and *Ara*. He lives in Barcelona.

ABOUT THE TRANSLATORS

Martha Tennent & Maruxa Relaño are a mother-daughter team of English-language translators, working primarily from Catalan and Spanish. Martha Tennent has received a fellowship from the National Endowment for the Arts for her translation of *The Selected Stories of Mercè Rodoreda*. Maruxa Relaño was a translation editor for *The Wall Street Journal* and has written about immigration, local politics, and the Latino community for several US publications, including the *New York Daily News*, *New York Magazine*, and *Newsday*. They currently live in Barcelona.